THE SEER ABLAZE

By Quinn Elmsworth

The Seer Ablaze (The Viridian Curse #1)
Copyright © 2025 China Dennington (otherwise known as Quinn Elmsworth) and Double Eagle Media

First edition.

ISBN-13: 978-0-9907274-7-7

Cover Design by Miblart
Library of Congress Control Number: 2025919610

Printed in Atlanta, Georgia in the United States of America

To my sapphic lover.

Tamquam Alter Idem

‘

Chapter One

Isolde

23 Years After the Viridian Phoenix's Rebirth

P erhaps Isolde should have paid more attention to the birds. They scattered from the trees with harrowing screeches, their flight shockingly violent. The sound of armored footsteps clattering on the road below, although frightening to the birds, did not scare her. Then again, Isolde had never been particularly attuned to nature or its omens.

While fear left her alone, a clawing desperation at the thought of the lies the people would try to wring from her took hold. Isolde walked purposefully to the second-story window, only to see the prince's soldiers bounding up the marble steps of her grandparents' manor. *Not yet.* The girl closed her eyes against the sight, grasping the richly-colored curtains so tightly that her fingernails tore at the threads.

The peals of the death bells tolling for the king met her ears in a relentless rhythm. She still possessed no answer to the perilous question of who should sit on the throne, despite her angry pleas to the Salamanders to grant her true foresight. As if they had ever honored her requests before.

Isolde didn't have to be a real seer to know what the soldiers, on their way to persuade her of the prince's worthiness to claim the crown, thought her answer *should* be. They wondered if perhaps they could persuade her to lie and say she'd seen the prince as king in a vision. But if lies about the future must be spewed, then — at long last — they would be her own lies. They would no longer be the false prophecies her grandparents had stuffed into her mouth since she was a child.

With a deep breath, she opened her eyes. For now, Isolde needed an escape from the pious forces that would petition for her support as the great seer of Viridian. She needed time to think without their incessant voices ringing in her ears, asking her what she knew about the future when, in truth, she knew no more than them. With all the strength she could muster, she sent a silent scream out into the void, meant to summon Ryth to her side. Even assuming the creature heard the call, there was no guarantee she would show up.

Isolde surveyed the large, yet simply furnished, bedroom. Something in her wished to never see the place again. Echoes of her grandmother's sharp whispers and a hungry stomach clung to the walls. But permanently forsaking it was only a dream, for now at least.

If she tried to leave through the front door, the soldiers would surely stop her. Her eyes landed on the only means of escape — the window. It rested deep in the dusty stone walls of her room and refused to open, which left only one option. The window must be sacrificed to her cause.

Ryth appeared outside the glass, hovering blue-green in the twilight like an offshoot of the sunset itself above the glowing green meadows. Never had Isolde been so happy to see the

Viridian Phoenix. Her lips tightened, however, at the indifferent amusement playing around the phoenix's eerily-large eyes.

A cacophony of shouting voices grew closer. She snatched up a lantern and matches from a table. The young woman braced herself for the noise her escape would make, as it would certainly be loud, and she had no intention of being stopped by her manipulative grandparents or the incoming soldiers. Taking the heavy oak chair from her desk, she hurled it at the window with all the force she could muster. It shattered on impact, sending shards of glistening glass flying out in every direction.

Without hesitation, the seer climbed through the window and onto the phoenix's fiery back. They flew away from the cold manor, leaving the confused soldiers and her grandparents behind.

As they rose through the clouds outside the city of Viridian, Isolde stayed silent, ignoring even the crimson gashes she'd obtained by pulling herself through the broken window. Ryth could feel her emotions, and she could feel the phoenix's. Neither the creature nor the false seer wished to speak.

Instead, she watched the steam rising from the golden-red phoenixes bathing in the River Camlann as part of their solemn evening rituals. She could imagine the priestesses in their scarlet robes down below, dousing the water with richly-scented oils and drawing runes in the mud on the sodden riverbank to honor the Salamanders.

Isolde felt grateful Ryth had shown up at all. It spoke to their bond. Perhaps they weren't friends —Isolde doubted they would ever be — but they were partners. If one died, so did the other, which meant they both had an interest in preserving their mutual life.

Grey mist swirled around them. Isolde breathed in the damp air wafting up from the ocean as they glided through the darkening sky, the smell of salt bringing her comfort and reminding her of life. Sharpness. Clarity. Pain.

Her thoughts shifted to the prince and the high king's brother, who would presumably both try to claim the throne. A deep fear swept through her. The phoenix had warned her of something boiling under the surface just last night.

~

As Ryth and Isolde had soared through the air together the evening before the king's death, the phoenix hadn't bothered speaking. Instead, the pair simply enjoyed each other's rare company. Two souls, equally as stubborn, yet always bound together. Even though Ryth possessed a unique identity, as the only blue-green phoenix and one who had worked with the Creator to draw the world into being, Isolde felt no special awe in her presence. Frustration and anger, yes, but not awe.

The seer reached out and gently brushed the feathers on the creature's head. Each extended at least as long as her white forearm and nearly as wide. They were incredibly soft, and despite herself, Isolde smiled. Her smile quickly faded, however, when they began to descend through the wispy mist and she saw where they were going.

White cliffs overlooked a wide beach. She occasionally indulged in the pastime of watching the waves from this vantage point. From here they seemed far away and almost calm. The distance hid the violence that lurked beneath the water, expressing itself every time a wave hit the surface. The phoenix landed in the mossy grass that blanketed the area between Viridian to the north and the ends of the cliffs in the south. The green carpet spread in either direction as far as the eye could see, refusing to burn despite the phoenix's flames due to an ancient deal between the grasses of Viridian and the Fire Folk. At least, that's why according to 'The Sacred Tales.'"

They stood there together for a second. simply admiring the view and possibly hoping to preserve the peace through silence. Neither had many friends, and company proved as valuable as any gold to both of them. The sun sank lower until, finally, only Ryth's blue and green flames lit the dark. Isolde's lilac dress, chosen by her grandmother to signify her connection to the divine, seemed too gentle of a color in the phoenix's harsh lighting. Even the ocean seemed to have disappeared, swallowed by the void of the night. There was nothing left to look at, and so the conversation began.

"I came to wish you good luck," the phoenix finally said, her voice almost disinterested.

"And why would I need luck?"

"That I cannot tell you. I only hope that you will listen to wise voices in the coming days," the phoenix said.

"Wise voices such as yours?" Isolde scoffed, shaking her head in disbelief. A wave of nausea washed over her. "Why do you act like you care? Your hypocrisy utterly confounds me."

"Be combative if you want, child, but my words stand and you'd do well to listen."

Isolde considered that. "And your vague good wishes were so urgent, why?"

"You'll know soon enough."

Isolde fixed her eyes on those of the phoenix. "My question is not unreasonable. Why do you act like you care? If you gave me real prophecies, my grandparents wouldn't be exploiting my sacred bond with you and making me give false fortunes."

"It is my duty to care," the creature replied in a tone dripping with sarcasm.

"A duty established by whom?"

The phoenix looked away before answering. "The Creator, of course."

"Duty is not love. Condescension is not caring. Do what you will, but don't pretend you care."

"I don't care what you think of me, Isolde. I am only here to fulfill my duty and to warn you of what I see."

"And yet will you tell me what exactly you see?" Isolde challenged.

"Of course not," the phoenix replied tiredly.

"Will we ever leave this argument behind us?"

"Not as long as you keep asking me what I know," the creature replied. "You want me to take all the pain that I have seen and distill it into wisdom for you? How very human."

Isolde tried to bite back a bitter smile. "You will wish me luck, but not tell me what I am to face? How cruel, Ryth. How very cruel. Even for you."

To her astonishment, that remark silenced the phoenix. The creature turned away and looked out into the darkness. What she saw there, Isolde didn't know.

"I warned you. Don't say I didn't warn you," said the phoenix. Then she vanished into the night.

The very next morning, the death bells rang out. The way the sadness in Princess Turia's eyes had contrasted with the repressed joy in Prince Edrune's expression during the announcement of the king's death earlier in the day haunted Isolde. While standing by her brother on the dais in the Great Hall of the palace, the princess' neck had jerked to the side in a complicated rhythm while her hand danced through the air in a different pattern. Her ailment seemed to grow worse when stress heightened.

Despite her hectic movements, Isolde saw Turia's sharp eyes and guessed that she had a better idea of the dynamics actually going on in that room than anyone else. Though she'd rarely spoken to the princess, their few encounters had been unusual. Never once did Turia ask for a prediction. She didn't seem remotely interested in knowing what her future held. Rather, they had engaged in normal, if short, intelligent exchanges. The kind that Isolde yearned for more than anything, though she would never admit that to anyone.

After the death announcement, members of the court had immediately bombarded the seer with frantic requests, yearning to uncover the future with their desperate hands before the corpse was even cold. They wanted to know who should rule. Who was *destined* to rule. What a horrendously big lie if she said anything.

The prince seemed bent on asserting a right to the crown, despite the fact that it was not his to claim. The king's younger brother, who served as the prince of the Kydis province, stood next in line. By law, the throne passed to him, but the king's sons had been known to challenge their uncles for the crown before, feeling some misguided right to do so. After fleeing to her home, she'd locked herself in her room, away from everyone and the lies they demanded from her.

Chapter Two

Isolde

23 Years After the Viridian Phoenix's Rebirth

Isolde could still hear the death bells tolling for the king, even perched on Ryth's back, flying far outside the city as they fled the prince's soldiers. She was no closer to choosing which candidate for the throne to throw her support behind. If she chose no one, it would certainly appear suspicious. She would lose power in the new court. Freedom from her grandparents seemed so deliciously possible, almost close enough to touch, but still just out of her reach. It might be forever gone if she failed this test of her false powers of prophecy as the Viridian seer.

Yet, for now, her words held power. Perhaps even enough to sway the outcome. The precarious nature of her position had never been clearer. If she chose the wrong side...All of her precious plans, gone, like sand washed away by the tide. A gloating sensation fell from the creature's mind into hers.

She sent back a sharp rebuke, which Ryth answered by executing a pointed drop that left her trembling and hanging on to the creature's neck for dear life. Anger flared within her, and she let it pour out so it would hit the phoenix with its full force. A sigh drifted to her ears on the wind.

The sun fell below the horizon as they arrived at their destination. Isolde dismounted and immediately turned her back on Ryth.

"Won't you even speak to me?" she asked.

"Not now," Isolde answered, refusing to turn around.

"Fine then."

The phoenix left, but she couldn't bring herself to watch Ryth go. Lighting a lantern, she set it down near one of the many silver-leaved trees on the border of the wood that pressed against the very edge of the cliffs overlooking the sea. She sank down against one of the trees and closed her eyes. The Silver Wood served as a sacred place. If examined closely, marks could be seen carved into the faces of the trees. They had been made by the many acolytes and pilgrims who had passed through the area, even though it was not nearly as popular a sacred site as the Temple of Zeuldian.

Especially in recent months, as news of a plague spreading through the neighboring Griffin Kingdom of Valsan reached the priestesses' ears through the tales of desperate pilgrims. Many hoped to bring the fabled healing ashes of phoenixes back to their suffering loved ones, but that was sadly impossible.

Most phoenixes died twice, but only ashes from phoenixes who could not be reborn were offered to supplicants and those were in low supply. The other ashes, from phoenixes hovering in the blue-green spirit world as they waited to be reborn, couldn't be scattered or the phoenix wouldn't be able to find its way to life in the physical realm once more when its time came. With fierce devotion, the priestesses protected the vulnerable ashes from thieving hands.

With a wince, Isolde pulled a few hairs from her head and laid them before her as a makeshift offering. Taking a match, she set them alight. Ideally, she would have something more meaningful and robust as a sacrifice, but anything that could burn would do in a pinch. Sending prayers to both the Salamanders in their domain of the rich earth and the Sylph in their domain of the wind-lifted sky, she buried her fingers in the dirt. She prayed for guidance and a life filled with her own choices. A breeze swept through her loose hair, which made her wonder if perhaps the Sylph heard her, in addition to just the earth-based Salamanders, who were the patron gods of the Fire Folk. Its cool embrace only reminded her of everything she stood to lose.

After she had exhausted the ears of the Soulless with her requests, she sat back and stared up at the strange reflection of the lantern's light in the silver leaves. It flashed and flowed like liquid fire against the stars. Maybe the answer would come to her if she waited long enough.

Isolde pulled her cloak tighter around her. In her haste, she hadn't thought about the cold that would come with nightfall. Her thoughts rolled on like the ocean she couldn't see in the darkness. She lost track of time. The hours crawled by and all she could do was watch them pass. If the phoenix would not grant her wisdom, perhaps the Soulless would. The immortal gods who had long ago lost their emotional souls might not care much about human affairs, but who knew when or why they might grant a sliver of their favor? That faint hope grew even fainter as the night progressed though. It seemed doubtful that they were willing to provide any answers.

A sudden sound broke her concentration on the stars above. She stared out into the darkness but could only make out a vague shape moving toward her. Withdrawing a sword from its sheath at her side, she rose, prepared for anything. As the figure came closer to the light, she saw a slight form with blonde hair spilling from the hood of her cloak.

"Who goes there?" she challenged, brandishing her sword.

"No one of consequence," a smooth voice replied. Her head jerked to the side suddenly, and recognition washed over Isolde.

She lowered her sword. "Now, I wouldn't exactly say that."

"Then you know very little." Turia threw back her hood.

Isolde accepted the insult graciously and motioned for the princess to take a seat on the ground.

"Why did you come here, Princess?"

"As I'm sure you know, you were summoned to the palace. After hearing what direction you were headed, I took it upon myself to find you and present my cause."

"And did you have an easy time of that?" Isolde asked wryly.

"If your purpose was to get away from people, picking a well-known pilgrimage site was perhaps not the best idea."

"You're the only one who has shown up so far," she replied with a shrug.

The princess stilled for a moment, then gave a sharp nod of satisfaction. Her uncle hadn't found the seer to present his case yet. She would have the first word on the matter.

"Then I have a request to make of you," Turia said.

Isolde looked away, tired of this same old game. "Of course you do."

"I want to know what you see first, though."

The seer laughed. "Make your request. It will not change what I see."

"Don't choose my uncle and don't choose my brother. Neither will rule this country well once they hold the throne of the high king."

Isolde was taken aback. "Who would you have me throw my support behind then?"

"I don't know."

The seer shook her head in disbelief. "Your brother doesn't know you're here, does he?"

"Not yet," Turia said.

"And, why, pray tell, are you disowning your own kin? Personal ambition, perhaps?"

Turia's eyes widened, and she shook her head swiftly. "Never. I have no desire to be the high queen." She looked down at her hands for a moment before looking back up at Isolde. "My…" she hesitated for a moment. "My brother has a temper. On its own that wouldn't disqualify him, but he also has no desire to listen to those around him. He acts rashly. I am terrified of how that personal flaw might play out in a wider way. With the fate of the kingdom at stake, I feel I must speak up, even if it incurs his wrath. Mark my words. If he becomes high king, we will go to war. I'm not willing to give up the peace that has held since the beginning of my grandfather's reign. I...I fear that your vision might confirm he is to be king."

Although the princess kept glancing away nervously, Isolde stared relentlessly into her face, trying to decipher what she saw there.

"And why not your uncle?"

"Do you even have to ask?" Turia said disdainfully. Penbrook of Kydis's reputation of being a warlord through and through was not lost on Isolde. As a lesser prince who had yearned for his brother's throne for years, his dream seemed to finally be coming true. Rumor had it he'd considered taking it by force but never had an army large enough to do so. It didn't help that his wary brother kept siphoning off his soldiers, in particular, for building projects throughout the kingdom. He'd never even had a fair shot at taking the throne. While Penbrook may have been an envious man, he wasn't stupid.

"He's a pig. A brutal pig who will also bring us war. This country deserves peace. It is a rare treasure and should not be easily relinquished," Turia said with conviction.

"Why should I say what I see at all?"

"If you do see that either of them is supposed to be king, please don't say anything. People will believe your words, as they should, of course." Turia paused, nervously rubbing her arm as she fixed the seer with an earnest stare. "Please. They speak of war. Even now, my brother is amassing his troops and I'm quite sure my uncle does the same. Blood will flow through the streets before the week is out. But your words, they can change that. People will believe you. Even the soldiers won't follow their leaders if they think they are defying the Soulless. Your words are divinely-blessed, and I pray you use that power to save lives today."

Isolde leaned back on her hands, considering Turia for a moment. "Who would you have me choose then? Assuming, of course, that I don't already know who will succeed. What if I see that your brother is destined to rule the kingdom? Are you asking me to lie, Princess?" she challenged.

"I...I don't know." Turia looked down at her hands again and kept her eyes fixed there.

"If I have no reason to lie..." Isolde proceeded.

The princess's head whipped up. "You would consider...bending the truth then? To save us? Would that change the course of your vision?"

"No," the seer stated. "I will not lie."

Turia's face fell, but she nodded in resignation. Her eyes held a quiet admiration. She herself had not wanted to ask, as she wasn't sure if the request would be insulting to the Soulless.

Isolde weighed the words about to come out of her mouth for a moment. They were heavy. But they didn't taste like sand. This would be her own lie and no one else's. In one ironclad moment, her decision was made. Isolde said, "I don't have to lie. They are not destined to rule. But you are."

Turia blinked. "Why would you say that?"

"I simply tell the truth. Your instincts are good. Neither your brother nor your uncle are fit to rule, but I have seen your blessed fate. You will be high queen, and you will be granted a long reign."

"You...you saw this in a vision?" Turia sputtered.

Isolde nodded. "All you must do is accept your destiny."

"Is that all? My brother will be furious, not to mention my uncle..."

The seer's voice cut like steel. "They must abide by fate, as must all others." Isolde's heart tripped as the lie spread through her veins like poison, but she kept her face impassive and her hands still.

Turia darted up, turning frantically in the darkness, perhaps not quite sure what she was looking for. Her eyes took on a wild light as the seer's words settled. "Impossible," she spit.

"Inescapable," the seer replied.

"I don't want the throne. I've never wanted it. You and your visions can go to the abyss." With that, Turia turned and stormed away, leaving Isolde sitting on the ground wondering what exactly she had just set in motion.

Chapter Three

Isolde

8 Years After the Viridian Phoenix's Rebirth

The weighted gambler's coin rolled across the padded table in the smoky pub. Isolde followed its predictable path until it fell on the side that would give her grandfather the win with a soft thump. A restrained smile crossed his lips as the other people gathered let out a collective groan. When he cheated, he did it carefully, so as not to arouse suspicion.

As he scooped his winnings off the table, he eyed Isolde in the corner.

She sat calmly by herself, notably the only child in the establishment. What she lacked in height, she made up for with restraint and politeness. Her hands rested folded in her lap. Besides, she was used to sitting in the pub for hours upon hours, night after night as Ireld of House Merlin grew ever-riskier with his gambling. He stayed stone-cold sober though, the shrewdness in his eyes something Isolde hoped to one day emulate.

The Soulless knew they needed the money, even if it was earned through less-than-scrupulous means. The fishing yield had been particularly low that season and just keeping food on the table was a struggle. Isolde noted her grandparents' resentful eyes when they served her dinner. Even if they tried to hide it, she already knew she was a burden.

The child observed everything from her vantage point. She saw the way men ignored the women around them, raising their voices to drown out reason and opinions not their own. She watched old women hide cards, cheating to win what they wanted, but still making missteps in the process so they lost anyway. She noticed the gleam of addiction taking root in previously reasonable eyes as every night went on.

Her grandfather paused, an idea lighting in his eyes as he looked at her. Lowering his voice conspiratorially, forcing those around him to lean in, he said. "My little Isolde told me I would win twice in a row if I played tonight and she's said other things that…make me wonder."

"Wonder?" A sturdy man asked.

"You know how she's Bonded to the Viridian Phoenix? They say the creature, unlike the red phoenixes, has the gift of foresight. I believe Isolde might be able to see the future like her Bonded."

All eyes turned to the previously-ignored little girl in the corner, drunken eyes glazed with awe and fear.

Chapter Four

Isolde

12 Years After the Viridian Phoenix's Rebirth

The steady, divine eyes issued a challenge to the child. *What do you think you know?*

Such profound eyes. Perhaps the phoenix could offer the very thing Isolde desired. Fire rippled over the large creature's feathers in secretive shades of blue and green. She looked like the Silunir Sea would if it caught fire. The world faded away, irrelevant in the presence of such a fearsome thing. Its wings beat in a terrible rhythm, which commanded the air as much as danced with it, allowing the phoenix to stay afloat above the waist-high golden grasses of the Pramath Plains beyond Viridian.

Isolde walked forward at a resolute pace, keeping her eyes fixed stubbornly upon those of the creature and holding her hand outstretched in greeting. She had never been one to look away. The phoenix took its time to speak, and, indeed, its voice didn't sound until the girl had halted in front of it.

Although she should have felt the heat from the flames, she felt nothing but the breeze from the whooshing wings. Pushing her black hair back from her face, as she always did when lost in thought, she wondered what this creature had endured. Fury and betrayal lay buried in those irises. They rested deep beneath a carefully constructed facade of pensive wisdom.

Even if she wished to, she could not speak first. To do so would be an insult of the deepest kind to the sacred creature, almost as bad as when Grandmother had doused her favorite dress in seawater so she could no longer wear it. Except for on The Day of Emergence, anything touched by the sea must be considered desecrated and unusable. She had spoken the wrong words. Or so her grandparents claimed.

Her arm grew tired as she waited impatiently for her bonded phoenix to speak its first words to her. But she already knew what they would be, for the words were written in the creature's eyes.

"What do you think you know?" came a voice wispy as that of an old woman, yet with a thread of steel running through it. The creature's beak didn't move. The girl knew no one could hear it besides her. It was as if a thought had been spoken out loud, drifting only between the two of them.

"Nothing."

"That's what you've been taught to say. Answer me honestly. As your lifeforce is tied to mine, answer me honestly, child."

"I know that people will always want love and in the end it will always hurt them. Same thing with power and with wealth," she replied.

"Do you think living in a good present is worth it if it's destined to end in pain?"

"No," she said simply.

"Hmm. What else?"

"People never understand what they truly desire until it is stolen from them."

"Intriguing observations from one so young."

"I never wanted to learn such things," the girl said bitterly, pulling at a loose thread on the sleeve of her purple dress.

"Hmm. We rarely do. Knowledge is a monster which consumes all happiness," the phoenix replied sagely.

The creature's eyes widened when the girl contradicted her.

"No. Knowledge gives us control."

"I see you think you know better than I?"

The child lifted her chin in defiance. "Perhaps I do. You are only a child yourself..."

"Oh, I know you're smarter than that. I am not like the red phoenixes, flaring into life as a new soul, energetic and excited to explore what this realm has to offer. I know better as the only phoenix who will be reborn twice. You forget this is already my second life," the creature replied, her voice dripping with bitterness.

"Yes, I am very well acquainted with your past, thank you. Nonetheless, you are new to the mortal realm." The girl's frown deepened at the mocking amusement in the wrinkles of the creature's face. "It is unwise to assume you know everything."

"Not if I am all-knowing. Unwise, hm? Wise? Is that what they say I am? I always wondered."

"They say you can see the future. Is it true?" she asked hopefully. Perhaps her Bonded could help her out of her current situation. If she knew the future...

"Maybe. But I won't tell you any of it."

The girl's mouth dropped open. "If you don't, what can I do? My grandparents...they..." she glanced back at the couple standing stiffly by the arched Northern Gate. "They already have me telling people the prophecies you supposedly gave me. They said you were able to speak to me even before our introduction because of your unique nature. I have to say what they want or they'll punish me. If you don't tell me the future, how can I combat that?"

The phoenix threw back her head and laughed. It was a harsh, grating sound the child wished she could unhear.

"Of course. If there is a profit to be made, humans will make it. I will not change my mind."

Angry tears welled up in the child's eyes. "Then why are you even bonded to me? Your existence has been a curse since my birth. I hoped you would at least bring some relief when we finally met."

"You were mistaken. Now, what is your name?"

"You know my name," the girl said through clenched teeth.

"Proper introductions warrant speaking names aloud. Mine is Ryth. If you would be so kind as to give me yours?"

"Isolde," she spit.

Ryth tilted her head to the girl and then began her ascent into the sky.

"When will I see you again?" she called.

The voice floated to her on the breeze, which was picking up its pace as storm clouds swept in from the sea. "Whenever you wish. I will be here but never to offer you comfort. That I can't do, child."

Isolde stood there for a moment after her phoenix companion left, thumb rubbing her palm and eyes squeezed tight against tears. She wondered, as she had so many times before, why her fate was tied to that of the primordial phoenix. She who rose from the sea had finally been given a mortal soul, but the girl couldn't fathom for what purpose. Some said it was a punishment, though the official tales said it was a boon for everyone involved.

Turning away, she glanced reluctantly at her waiting grandparents. Regardless of what the creature actually said, Isolde would be forced to be Ryth's representative to the Viridians. Even as young as she was, she understood the years of punishments she stood to face every time she disobeyed them. Her words might as well be that of the ancient being. No one would know the difference. It was a dangerous game, but one she would have to play until she could make a bid for independence. If people began to notice a trend of false prophecies issuing from her tongue...

The phoenix's words echoed in her mind. With them, her hope of divine help had been stolen. A new defiance entered her heart. In that moment, she made a promise to herself.

Chapter Five

Isolde

23 Years After the Viridian Phoenix's Rebirth

I solde spent the rest of the night shivering under the trees while she mulled over her decision and its consequences. She prayed for hours as the dew collected on the grass. If she was to retain her credibility and any power she might have in this cruel world, Turia had to become queen.

When the princess arrived at the sacred place with her strange request, she took it as a sign. While her intuition was not as reliable as a true seer's vision, it was not to be dismissed. Turia seemed to be a good woman, and she would be a reliable ruler. Whether she wanted the crown did not matter. The seer had asked for guidance, and the Soulless had sent her the princess. She might as well have seen it in a vision.

Something about Turia fascinated her and it always had, ever since the first time they'd encountered each other.

Chapter Six

Isolde

15 Years After the Viridian Phoenix's Rebirth

On the night Isolde first met the princess, she sat gazing forlornly into the fire in her large room. Although all of her possessions had now been tucked away in drawers and her own heavy quilt spread across the bed, it didn't feel like home. She doubted it ever would. As usual, Ryth had refused to give her any advice that would help her dissuade her grandparents from moving from the apartment in town to this stone monstrosity of a manor. The phoenix never proved to be much help. In the three years since their Introduction, she had learned nothing except that bitterness only feeds bitterness.

At times, the girl avoided the creature for months on end. Eventually though, she would always feel Ryth nearby and, with a sigh, go to meet her companion so they could have the same old arguments about wisdom and human nature. The creature refused to give her any real prophecies, which meant she had to keep spewing the false prophecies stuffed into her mouth by her grandparents. So much for her link with the one-and-only Viridian Phoenix.

A gentle tap sounded on the doorframe. Isolde didn't respond, but her grandmother entered anyway, sinking into the chair beside her.

"How are you doing, my darling?"

The girl met her gaze. "Not well. My head hurts."

"I'm sorry to hear that. Especially on such a momentous day."

"I don't want to go."

Her grandmother's tight smile grew even tighter. "Well, sadly you must. Remember how much is at stake. Your introduction at court may well determine the rest of your life."

"So I've been told," Isolde retorted darkly.

Her grandmother continued. "It is crucial that you keep in mind what you must say and to whom."

"I remember it all," she stated tiredly. "We've been through it a million times."

"Be sure you do. All of us should leave the palace with titles at the end of the night." Her grandmother's voice softened. "This is for you, dear one. You will thank us one day."

With that, she rose from her chair and swept from the room.

Isolde tried to swallow the knot in her throat, but it only made the sensation worse. Tipping her head back, she stared at the ceiling for a moment before pushing against the velvet arm of her chair with her fist, just barely keeping herself from hitting it. The walls felt like they were closing in on her. An intense wave of nausea and claustrophobia rolled over the girl as she imagined standing in the throne room of a palace with everyone staring at her.

Even now, she could see strangers whispering. She could see her grandmother with a vise grip on her arm, listening to her words like a hawk and waiting for any deviation. But she had no choice but to go and speak her grandparents' words as though they were her own. As though they came directly from the Viridian Phoenix, who was the first of the fiery creatures to be created. No other phoenix glowed that vibrant shade of blue and no other phoenix could claim the divinity of having helped create the world. It hadn't been a stretch for her grandparents to spread the rumor that, as Ryth's Bonded, she'd been gifted with the same foresight that the Viridian Phoenix possessed according to legend.

The thought of just leaving floated through her mind. A ridiculous daydream. Isolde had no friends, no place to go, and no skills to support herself. She was merely biding her time, because, one day, she would leave this all behind. She would escape her grandparents' clutches, and they would be shamed. Isolde had made that promise to herself when she first met her phoenix companion at the age of twelve, and she intended to keep it. Someday, after her first death, she and Ryth would be reborn into a new life, but until then, she had to live this life through. Ryth would live three lives instead of the typical two for phoenixes due to her unique position.

Focusing on her breathing, Isolde took a moment to collect herself before rising and facing the flowing purple dress draped over the door of the ornate wardrobe. Oh, how she hated purple.

When she descended the inordinately long staircase to meet her grandparents in the foyer, it was with a great deal of reluctance and more than a hint of resentment.

"You look like a proper seer," her grandmother stated. "Purple is just the right color for your first impression in court, you know. It will remind people that you possess a direct link to the divine and must be respected."

Isolde couldn't help but notice that her grandmother's translucent arm scarf glimmered the same purple as her own.

Her grandfather only nodded, being a man of few words, but Isolde knew better than to believe his quiet act. While her Grandmother Nerys did the speaking, Ireld made the decisions. She tempered her expression.

Pasting a smile onto her face, she replied with a simple, "Indeed."

Soon they were off. The manor sat only slightly to the north of Viridian outside the city walls, but the carriage ride felt like an eternity. Isolde kept her eyes fixed on the floorboards as her grandmother droned on about what she needed to say. She would have much preferred they take the trip on the backs of their phoenix companions. It was so much more convenient and comfortable. Her grandmother, however, found that mode of transport "much too common." She was eager to show off their newly acquired carriage, hoping that it would make their entry into the upper echelons of society more explosive. As if they weren't already the talk of the high king's court.

Isolde didn't bother looking out the window as they entered the city and rattled over the sandy road that wove through the spacious city. Everything from the sharp smell of the sea breeze to the sounds of the street musicians tuning their instruments felt painfully familiar. She'd grown up in a cluster of dwellings near the outdoor fish markets of the southern part of the city. Her grandparents saw her connection with Ryth as a godsend — as their escape.

While they made a decent living as merchants in Fishfirst, it was not a desirable job, and they were rejected from the more elite circles of merchants in the seaside city due to their connection with the sacred yet unclean sea. It had taken time to make the right connections. It had taken patience to put the legend of the first Viridian Phoenix to use and convince the people around them that Isolde had the gift of prophecy. A gift unseen in generations. Today was the culmination of all their years of work.

Isolde bit the inside of her cheek. If she succeeded, their position in court would be solidified. She risked a glance up at her grandmother and allowed a bitter smile to grace her features. They somehow failed to realize what they were creating. Eventually it would come back to bite them. She would make sure of it. *It is not yet my time*, she reminded herself, returning her gaze to the floorboards. They passed through a residential district and then through the tall structures of the Fabricfirst clothing markets with their painted archways. As they drew nearer to the castle, the din picked up significantly.

The girl finally looked out her window and was greeted by the familiar sight of the steps leading up to the gray stone castle. The open square before it looked packed. People darted every which way carrying all manner of goods and trying not to get crushed in the chaos that was numerous carriages attempting to unload their occupants for the events of the evening. The sun sank behind the mighty turrets. It seemed to Isolde that the dusky twilight lent the mayhem an almost Otherrealmly quality.

Her grandmother yanked on her wrist, pulling her out of the carriage. Her grandfather stepped out behind her and, before she knew it, they were ascending the stairs with a milieu of other finely-dressed court denizens. They were swept inside. Wide, arched hallways extended before her, but she barely had time to look around.

She caught glimpses of fine drawings hung on the stone walls, of ceilings painted with meticulous seashell designs, and of painstakingly-intricate patterns in the marble beneath their feet. A vivid tapestry of the ancient High Queen Maeve hoisting the legendary lost sword of Caliburnus high above her head as she shouted some message lost to time grabbed her attention in particular. Yet none of it truly awed her. It was a palace, after all, and so she had expected it to be luxurious. No, something altogether different caught her off-guard. As they entered the Great Throne Room, it became even more apparent.

Lonely, desperate people surrounded her. They chattered on in groups. They flirted. But they were very much alone. She could see the nervous light in their eyes, and suddenly she wanted to run. It was much too late for that though and she had never had the choice in the first place. Whispers began to tread on her heels. People snuck furtive glances at her as news of her arrival spread from those who had come to her before seeking prophecies about their fortunes. She tried to swallow the lump in her throat and hold her head high despite the tight grip of her grandmother's fingers on her arm. The matriarch's eyes darted through the room as she searched for those who would be of the most use.

The only person who didn't seem lonely was one of the few people who was actually alone. More than anything, Isolde wished she could take shelter near one of the large plants stationed throughout the room, just like that girl was doing. She looked like she was in her own world as she stood there, tall and willowy with her hand resting gently on the bark of the tree next to her. Isolde herself was just as tall, but had a much studier, curvier frame. Loose, blonde ringlets framed the princess's pale white face, which had a constellation of freckles scattered across it.

She reminded Isolde of a nymph, utterly connected with nature in a way beyond human understanding. They locked eyes. She'd been caught staring. Unable to help herself, she waved, wishing for some scrap of attention from such a lovely person. An embarrassed blush rose to her cheeks, but the girl granted her a soft smile in return. Isolde's attention was soon stolen from the girl when the high king entered the room.

Silence fell as every member of the court strained to see him above the crowd as delicately as they possibly could. At first she could only decipher where he was in the room by the motion caused by people clearing the way for him.

She caught her first true glimpse of him as he ascended the stairs to the dais and took his place on the silver throne without a moment's hesitation. He wore only a thin circlet, a curious choice for the high king of Morya, but perhaps one that spoke to his power as well. He didn't need to display his wealth to command respect, Isolde realized. There sat a man who understood what her grandparents did not. Envy sparked in her stomach. His control over his own life was never in question. Dark hair curled around the circlet and transitioned into a full beard. There was something in his semblance, around the nose and perhaps the expression in his eyes, that reminded Isolde of the girl who had been standing by the tree.

She looked back toward that spot, but the girl was no longer there. She was, however, standing on the dais when Isolde looked back. With a start, the seer realized the girl in question was, in fact, Princess Turia.

A steward stepped forward and announced the royal family, as was proper. The princess stood to the left of the throne, eyes fixed on the ground. She looked much less at ease than earlier. Another figure stood to the right of the throne—a boy a few years her senior. The prince's hair matched the color of his father's, but his eyes were not nearly as kind. Isolde couldn't help but wonder what had been the cause of his dour expression. The steward turned and offered the high king his goblet. With a gracious tilt of his head, the king took the first sip of his wine and the festivities began.

Conversation picked up once more. The buzz irritated Isolde. She much preferred the quiet to the growing number of people eager to engage her in conversation.

"Will my fishermen make good catches this season?"

"Will my daughter ever have a child?"

"Will my uncle recover from his illness?"

The endless flood of questions made her want to scream, but she kept that inclination to herself. Instead she did her best to answer vaguely while demurely hinting that any favor shown to her was smiled upon by the Soulless. A number of coins were already pooling in her pocket. With every grateful smile given as small tokens were pressed into her palm, she had to hide her wince. She was all too aware of her grandmother's grip on her arm as she talked with each noble. Most were genuinely respectful as they asked for her help. She tried to ignore the earnest looks in their eyes, the relief as they thanked her for seeing their future, but she never looked away. Every lie tasted like sand, but she looked into the eyes of the people she was lying to so she could remember that feeling when she finally escaped her grandparents.

Somewhere off to her left the dance floor had opened up earlier in the evening. Music rang out from that corner of the room, a pleasant distraction from the suffocating press of people surrounding her. Because she was straining her neck, trying to see what was happening in that direction, she missed the sudden silence that fell around her. For a brief instant, she forgot where she was and simply admired the sweep of dresses and magnetism of the energetic steps as partners weaved around each other in intricate patterns.

She had always wished she could dance, but there was no one to practice with or teach her as people tended to keep their distance from the seer. It didn't help that her grandparents carefully managed her time and where she went. Perhaps her grandmother would let her learn now that they were to frequent court. Maybe she would finally have a friend in whoever taught her. She pushed her loose hair out of her face with a sigh. Even if it wasn't realistic, she could dream that she would someday have the company of someone besides her acerbic phoenix companion or her frustrating family.

The tight squeezing of her arm pulled her attention back to where she stood and she soon saw the reason for the silence. The high king stood before her. The princess stood shyly behind him, her eyes fixed on the ground and her hand moving in endless small swirling gestures. The prince was nowhere to be seen. To Isolde's surprise and discomfort, the king sank into a polite bow.

"I've been eager to meet you for many years, Seer," he stated, his voice quiet, but weighty.

She bowed herself. "I expect so, your highness."

At first, the king paused. Then he let out a surprised laugh that shook his shoulders. What would have been insolence from anyone else would be accepted from her. Isolde took note of that fact. She could feel her grandmother's eyes drilling into the side of her head, but she refused to meet her gaze. No one could make her look where she did not desire to, especially when she held the attention of the high king himself. For a fleeting moment, she had unassailable control of her path and the feeling swept through her in an intoxicating wave. The wiser side of her reminded her to bide her time. So, she did. But she held onto that moment for years like it was a raft and she was floating in the midst of a great sea. Once the king had stopped laughing, he sobered quickly.

"Tell me what it is like to be Bonded to She Who Rose From the Sea," he asked.

Trying was the first word that came to mind, but she didn't say that. After a moment she replied, "Equal parts calming and frightening."

"How so?"

The girl chose her words carefully. "The breadth of our sight spans generations. We see the same mistakes made, oaths broken, and cycles repeated. There is a terrifying order in the convoluted chaos of time. But there can be comfort within this idea as well. We are connected to those before us in ways most of us cannot even begin to fathom. Contradiction exists. Even if it feels like it shouldn't, this great contradiction exists. So, our choice is either to embrace it or defy it to bitter ends and, I will not lie, embracing it requires a strength of will that few possess. This knowledge is Ryth's greatest treasure. We speak of it often." The lies rolled off her tongue like water, and she wasn't sure if she would ever be able to stop the flow.

"The wisdom of your words is to be admired. I certainly hope that this visit to court will not be your last. Please know that your counsel will always be welcome within these halls."

"That is much appreciated, your highness." Having spoken her own words, Isolde's throat tightened with distaste at what she had to say next. If she didn't spew the words her grandmother told her to, then there would be consequences later. Maybe just a slap on the wrist, but more likely several days without food or time locked in her room.

"I do have one request."

"Anything."

She held her head high. "I will best be able to serve you if my grandparents and myself are in possession of official titles and the benefits that come with those titles."

At first, the high king seemed taken aback. Such requests were seldom made and it was even rarer for them to be granted. Titles came with farmland and a responsibility to provide knights for the high king's army. Truth be told, sometimes knights from different provinces fought each other on orders from their respective princes. Morya's small provinces spread out to the north of the Silunir Sea, through the plains and forests, all the way to the base of the snowy Telifae Mountains. Each was given sufficient independence to operate as needed under its own prince, but the high king in Viridian—the founding province—ruled all.

Isolde waited patiently for his response, her gaze unwavering. He looked away as though he was considering her words, but Isolde knew he didn't want to risk the wrath of the Soulless for refusing the seer her request. Everyone knew he was a religious man. A pang of regret hit her stomach. It would cost him. He would have to anger some of his nobles to create new titles for them and angering nobles was always a dangerous game to play. But that was his problem.

"So it shall be," he stated in clipped tones.

With a nod, he turned and was gone as quickly as he had come. His daughter wavered. Isolde caught her eye for a moment, but the princess looked away and hurried after him. Her grandmother's hand squeezed her arm gently in approval. The hours passed in a blur after that.

Curious, Isolde watched the movements of the princess through the night. She had her stories of Princess Turia's strange ailment, an inability to stop moving or, sometimes, even to stop speaking. Although whispered about in circles beyond the palace walls, inside was a safe haven for the princess, for her father was fiercely protective. The only time he had even mentioned it at court, he had named it a blessing from the Soulless. Rumor said that, although her attendance at court events was fickle, her father had never tried to hide her.

Isolde didn't even try to remember the names of all the people she met that night as it was a pointless endeavor. Her grandmother guided her around, never leaving her side even once while her grandfather floated about the room talking with as many lords as possible. The high priestess of The Salamander Priesthood—a wrinkled wisp of a woman—bowed before her. The event lasted well into the night. When they finally left, Isolde found herself grateful that her grandparents were too tired to chastise her for any of the multitude of mistakes she knew they would find in her conduct that evening. She knew that they would be forgotten by morning in light of her success. The king would be sending an administrator to meet with her grandfather and discuss the details of their new titles within the week.

While she hated the crush of people in court, at least time passed faster there than it usually did for her. Walking down the steps of the palace, Isolde looked at the ground and she reminded the Salamanders of the promise she'd long ago made to one day escape her grandparents' schemes.

Chapter Seven

Isolde

23 Years After the Viridian Phoenix's Rebirth

When Isolde finally moved from the place where she knelt, her joints ached from staying in one position for so long. After a moment of searching for her phoenix companion with her mind, she located and called out to Ryth. The creature soon appeared. As she spiraled into a landing she asked, "What happened last night?"

Isolde laughed as she climbed onto the phoenix's back. "You think I'd tell you?"

Taking off, Ryth said, "I cannot help you if you don't tell me what is going on."

"I thought you were all-knowing," Isolde mocked.

The creature didn't reply, veering sharply to the right to throw the seer around and mark her displeasure.

"I'd like to go to the palace," she said after a long pause.

"In those mud-stained clothes?"

Isolde shrugged. "Let them see the signs of piety. It makes no difference to me."

When they began to spiral downward, she saw that they were still outside the city walls, but she didn't say a word even as her jaw tightened. The creature clearly wished to pay her back for her harsh words. With a cold thank you, she slipped off Ryth's back and made her way to the palace.

A manic energy coursed through the streets. It made itself known in harried whispers and more lively discussions by those who were perhaps less discerning of the precarious nature of the situation. She kept her head down and the cloak of her hood up, hoping not to be stopped along the way. Her wish was somehow granted, though she knew her luck wouldn't last once she passed within the walls of the great palace. Even so, she could try. In contrast to the hubbub out in the city, the palace stood eerily silent, as though it was holding its breath and waiting to learn its fate.

Few people talked. At least in the outer halls. The nobles keenly knew what they had to lose if they professed support for one party and the other ended up in power. Isolde possessed a single goal. She had to find Turia and she desperately needed to convince her of her words. Isolde licked her dry lips. No doubt it was a heavy lie, but the more she thought about it, the more she believed it was the only way. If what Turia said was true, the kingdom was at a turning point. As if she could outpace the twinge of guilt in her heart, Isolde quickened her steps.

If the tension in the hallways felt palpable, the sense of unease in the throne room was deafening. Penbrook's soldiers loitered together in small groups, the palace guards stood at attention with a brightness in their eyes Isolde had never before witnessed, and the prince sat on his father's throne surrounded by his attendants. She eyed him. A bold statement to be made at a fraught moment. But no matter. He would soon be irrelevant. She scanned the room for her query, until her gaze fell upon Turia, quietly twitching in the shadow of one of the large plants. With quiet steps, she skirted around the room in the shadows, keeping her head down to avoid recognition. Despite her best efforts, a nobleman did spot her, but she waved him off until she had made her way to Turia. It wouldn't be long until she was swarmed with questions now someone knew she was present. The girl refused to meet her gaze, instead pressing herself into the pillar as though it could absorb her.

"May I have a word, your highness?" Isolde asked, trying to catch the princesses' brilliant green eyes.

After a heavy pause, the girl replied, "I am occupied at the moment."

Isolde took a step closer. "Occupied though you may be, fate will not wait for you. You might as well be prepared when it comes about."

That caught her attention and the girl finally looked up with great reluctance.

"Ah, so you do care about fate's reckoning?" Isolde said, smiling wryly.

"Only fools don't," the princess replied, turning away almost dismissively while motioning for the seer to follow. They strolled silently through deserted side passages of the palace into the endless maze of hawthorn trees that made up the palace gardens. Few people frequented the area at that time of day, so they were left alone, hidden from view by the trees.

"I see you refuse to leave me alone," Turia stated quietly, paying an undue amount of attention to a leaf she'd plucked from a bush lining the pathway.

"Would you want me to leave you alone when the fate of your people is at stake?"

"I don't take well to hyperbole."

Isolde seized her wrist, forcing the princess to look her in the eye. "I assure you, I don't speak of this lightly."

Turia glanced away, shaking her wrist free and continuing her walk.

"What has you so convinced that I am the only correct answer? The kingdom's only hope? That seems at best unlikely and at worst utterly ridiculous."

"Be careful not to insult the Soulless, Princess," Isolde said coldly.

Turia bowed her head in apology. "Forgive me, Seer. This is just all...overwhelming."

"Understandable." Pity and regret pulsed through Isolde's heart as she remembered that it had been less than two days since this young woman had lost her father.

"Will you answer my question?"

"I have seen it. You will rule. It will be easier if you accept this now, you know. I only speak in your best interest."

"I'm sure," Turia muttered quietly as her head jerked to one side.

"Let me prove it to you."

Silence hung in the air for a moment. Isolde carefully kept her breathing steady and her attention fixed on the princess.

"Let me prove it."

Some relief lighted in Turia's eyes. Proof. Isolde understood it was a comforting word. A lie. But a comforting one nonetheless.

The princess stopped, raising her eyes to the face of the other woman and taking her hands. "Can you tell me one thing?"

"You are free to ask."

"Will I have to kill to take the throne?" the girl whispered, tears shining in her eyes.

Chills raced down Isolde's spine. A warning from some other force. But she said the words anyway. "If I could see that, this would be much easier."

Turia winced at the coldness of the words and turned away once more, Isolde suspected, to hide her tears. The seer seized the princess's spindly hand. "I swear you will have the proof you need, Princess. But first you must commit to your destiny. Believe me, it will be easier than if you try to fight it."

Turia's eyes traveled from their joined hands to Isolde's eyes. There was something in the intensity of her stare that caught the seer off guard, making her question her assessment of the sheltered royal. "Will you swear fealty to me?"

Isolde's lips thinned. "I am only bound to serve the interests of the Soulless."

"My father never needed your loyalty, but I do if events are to play out how you say. If your words are true I need someone I can trust to the very end if need be." This time it was Turia keeping hold of her hand with a firm grip.

"Oaths are not to be taken lightly."

"Hence why I ask," Turia replied, a hint of tension in her annoyed tone.

Isolde held her silence until the princess dropped her hand sharply, realizing she wouldn't be able to wring loyalty from the lips of the great seer.

"I expected more courage from such a gifted individual."

Isolde scoffed. "It's not a matter of courage. Do not question the will of the Soulless, Princess."

"What now, then?" Turia asked tiredly. No trace of her prior bravado remained in her voice. She plucked a rose from nearby, twirling it, only to wince when one of the thorns caught her finger.

Chapter Eight

Isolde

23 Years After the Viridian Phoenix's Rebirth

The sea whispered tales Isolde couldn't possibly understand. Its faint voice drifted to her as she sat under a silver tree in the grove for a second night, still using it as a hiding spot, her hands buried in the dirt, trying desperately to sense the will of the Salamanders. Or even their inclinations concerning the kingdom. Anything.

Instead she felt their boredom. Their need for the dripping amber glow of fire. Their collective desire for nightfall so they could display their shining tails in their full glory as they held congress with the ever-fiery stars and regrew limbs lost in the pleasures of the day.

Withdrawing her hands and wiping them roughly on her cloak, Isolde sent down a hasty prayer. Perhaps the priestesses at the temple would be able to sense the shift in the mutterings of the Soulless. They were more attuned to reading the signs and the energy than her. People overestimated how much the Soulless cared about human affairs anyhow and maybe that was why she was so comfortable asserting herself as a mouthpiece for the divine. A rustling disrupted the silence alerting her to Turia's presence behind her, but she didn't turn around. Instead she took the moment to compose her features.

"I brought what you asked for, though I can't fathom why you would need such objects. These are not items to be trifled with," said the princess. A coarse bag clinked as it hit the ground. Sending out one more useless prayer, Isolde faced her.

"Don't worry your pretty head too much, Princess. The goblets will be returned to the royal treasury in due time. I must have freedom. And this is how I can procure it."

"Freedom from what? Cryptic as ever."

"Ah, how well you know me already," Isolde teased.

Turia eyed her with suspicion, not even bothering to smile at the seer's gaiety.

"Would you care to explain your reasoning again?"

"Not particularly. But I'm sensing you won't let this go."

"How perceptive," Turia drawled.

"My grandparents possess traitorous hearts. I have seen it. They will try to throw their support behind your uncle and try to force me to do the same."

"So, you wish to frame them for robbery to render them harmless. Why not just expose their actual treachery?"

"There's no time and I have no proof besides what lives in my mind, Princess. So it has to be done now. Don't doubt its justice, even if the accusations are technically false," Isolde said, her voice tight.

"They must not treat you well. You're so ready and willing to betray your very own family."

This statement made Isolde freeze, the soft sympathy of Turia's voice making her want to die. The feeling of being perceived and evaluated was wholly unfamiliar. Most people asked her to perform that service for them and, thankfully, didn't see her beyond her gift. She guarded her air of mystique with a keen ferocity. It kept her safe. It ensured her survival.

"There's no need for you to worry about my loyalty to you, Princess. I have already agreed to help your cause. Believe me, there is not a drop of fickleness in my blood," she replied.

"I did not suggest there was," Turia replied mildly. After a moment she continued, "My uncle's troops are massing quickly and the tension at court is already thick as honey. I fear we must act quickly if what you say is true."

Isolde clicked her tongue at the princess and turned her face away to stare at the sea. "Still doubting, I see," she said.

"It's the feasibility and the wisdom of it I'm having trouble with. I don't have the support for this, Seer. No one is even thinking of me as an option."

"Which is why you're perfect. It's why you're chosen. No one will suspect you."

"Because I'm not suited to the role? Too quiet and unambitious? Plagued by a strange ailment?" Turia asked.

Isolde turned back to face her. "No, because you're too kind, Princess," she said gently.

"But I don't think you understand. I don't like it when people look at me. I don't speak well. I never wanted to lead anyone, even if I felt like I should want to do so. Uncertain. Insecure. Overall, I'm much happier away from people, who are—for the most part—boring and stupid or both things at once."

"Are you done?"

"I'm not charismatic or charming and I've never really wanted to be," the princess continued.

"Well, I'd have to disagree with you there," Isolde said wryly, smiling at the earnest quirk of Turia's mouth.

"So, how can I even try to secure this position without any of those skills and no support from anyone. You do realize that I'm as likely to die a gruesome death as become queen if I try to assert my right?"

"You won't. I promise you. Trust the Soulless and trust me, Princess. All you have to do now is fortify yourself for the chaos of the days to come. Think of people who are worthy of your trust, people who are skilled, and people who are noble. Don't speak with them yet, but be ready to as soon as you are declared queen so you can gather them about you like a shield. Prepare yourself. The Soulless will declare you queen, so be ready to accept their calling in the next several days," Isolde stated.

"And you?"

"I will do the bidding of the Soulless."

"Which is?" Turia asked.

"That's not for you to worry about," Isolde said.

"I don't like uncertainty, Seer."

"Well, I fear you may have to learn to live with it for the time being," Isolde replied, rising from the ground and brushing the dirt off her cloak.

Closing her eyes she called out to Ryth and received her reluctant reply, as usual. The phoenix grew from a burning light in the distant fog to something akin to a specter judging by the look on Turia's face. She had never been that close to the Viridian

Phoenix before. To the one who helped create it all. Her eyes widening, she sank to the ground in a deep curtsy, even as Isolde climbed carelessly onto the creature's back. Without another word, Ryth rose into the sky leaving the princess alone on the cliffside.

It was just after dawn when they arrived back at the manor and Isolde slipped off Ryth's back. This time she did take the time to compose herself before she shadowed the door of her grandparent's home. As expected, a flurry of people greeted her as soon as she stepped inside. The talking died down as the prince's representatives caught sight of her. They must have stayed there the entirety of the previous two nights, awaiting her return. But she fixed her gaze on her grandparents. Her grandmother's back grew rigid. Standing calmly in the wave of silence, Isolde spoke.

"I have been granted a prophecy regarding the future of the kingdom and I must not be disturbed."

With that, she moved to the stairway and the room burst into motion again, several people trying to talk to her at once as she tried to navigate through them. Isolde's grandmother stood and darted toward her, seizing her elbow, which she promptly shook off with a glare. "Silence! Unless you wish to anger the Soulless," she bellowed, which only thinned the crowd somewhat, but it was enough for her to finally slip upstairs and out of sight. All that was important was that people knew she'd been given a prophecy. That news would certainly make it back to court faster than fishermen wash their hands. And she needed that. They would wait for her word and when the time came they would hopefully be more willing to abide by it.

Despite the ruckus below she collapsed onto her bed and slept, her dreams as heavy as the nights she inhabited.

Chapter Nine

Isolde

21 Years After the Viridian Phoenix's Rebirth

Isolde trudged through the streets, focused on her next magical project. Being an alchemir required Isolde to respect both factions of the Soulless. The Fire Folk typically paid greater homage to the Salamander gods who lived beneath the ground in fiery glory, constantly regenerating just like the phoenixes. The Griffin Lords, on the other hand, honored the Sylph gods who traversed the air.

Each faction of the Soulless granted requests within reason when the offerings pleased them, although they had long ago sworn a treaty between themselves not to directly interfere in wars. Those were up to mortals to win or lose. After all, their lack of souls drastically diminished their ability to feel any emotions strongly. A strange feeling careened through her consciousness, and she picked up her pace knowing it meant Ryth hovered nearby. She felt no desire to speak with the creature.

Isolde ducked through the open doorway of her destination. It took her no time at all to sweep her hair back with a tie, shed her shimmering purple arm wrap, and tie one of the large aprons hanging on a row of hooks near the door over her purple dress. Hay crunched beneath her feet as she proceeded into the building.

"Back so soon?" A pleasant voice called from farther into the dark interior of the building.

"I don't see how that's any of your business," she replied tartly, gathering a variety of tools from the side tables lining the walls of the forging alcove as the blacksmith made his way into the room.

"You are using my forge and requiring me to leave while you do so. I'm placing my entire life in your hands."

"And I'm paying you well for it, if I recall correctly, Fenrir. Now where did that pair of silver tongs go?" she asked as she looked around.

Fenrir held out the tongs to her with an irritated sigh. "I will never understand alchemirs. Why won't you just let me teach you? You would improve so much more quickly and you would waste less material."

She shot the blacksmith a glare for the last comment. "I don't waste. I melt it down again when I make a mistake."

"It still means I can't use it."

"Like I said, that is what I'm paying for. I don't want to have this argument again," she stated tiredly as she pulled on a thick pair of leather gloves. She glanced at him sideways. "You really aren't scared of my connection with Ryth, are you?

Fenrir shrugged and crossed his arms. "I'm a practical man. I don't have time to fear the great seer. My future will happen whether I know it or not."

"Well, alchemirs are practical too."

"I don't see how. If I just taught you…"

"You taught me the basic tenets of your craft and that is all
that's allowed by the alchemir creed. I must learn the rest on my
own or I won't be able to properly harvest magic. Yes, it will take
longer. But the magic can be used in a number of powerful ways
once I know what I'm doing."

The blacksmith rolled his eyes. "Yes, you've tried to
explain this all before. What I don't understand is what you would
need that kind of magic for. I do just fine with the amount of
magic I can harvest. My swords are the finest in Viridian, if I do say
so myself."

Isolde slid a cauldron from the counter and slammed it
down in the hearth with more force than necessary. "But you're
only just scratching the surface. The magic you access gives you
skill, but there is so much more power that can be accessed if one
has patience and that's my calling as an alchemir. It's not about
crafting a good sword for a standard soldier or forging a solid
horseshoe. It's about understanding the world in a deeper way. So,
if you please, leave me to learn in peace."

The blacksmith sighed before shaking his head and
walking away. "Whatever you say."

"That's right," she muttered to herself once he was gone.

Isolde stoked the coals and watched the satisfying red glow
spread through the forge. Setting down the poker, she took a
moment to bend down and buried her hands in the dirt.

"Guide my fingers, Salamanders. I humbly request your
protection and goodwill. As you heal, may I heal. As you rest in fire

without sustaining injury, may I rest in fire without sustaining injury. Let all things be weighed and tempered."

She rose and reached both hands into the air. "Be my instinct, Sylph. I humbly request your guidance and grace. As you flow, may I flow. As you strike, may I strike. Let all things be weighed and tempered."

With her invocation to both Soulless factions—as pointless as it was—complete, she was ready to begin. She felt the phoenix's presence and call from just outside, but she ignored it. Instead she focused on the feel of the metal in her hands. She gently swung its weight around for a moment before stilling her hand. Breathing deeply, she tuned into the Otherrealm, something everyone could do to some extent, but not usually in the way she did. The Blue Otherrealm hosted the souls of the dead as well as the in-between souls of phoenixes and humans who had yet to be reborn. It brimmed with the magic of creation, death, and the great cycle.

For most people the magic manifested as a better sense of focus, as an energy that flowed through them when engaging in their passions. Most people who worked with their hands in any way had this gift. Alchemirs, however, let themselves sink fully into the Otherrealm. They became one with it in order to shape and understand matter. The world came into focus around her. Not all had that ability, but it could often be achieved with time and dedication. Isolde came by it naturally.

Everything shone sharper and clearer, as though the whole world had previously had a veil draped over it. Emotions shifted. The past and the future disappeared. Suspended in time as though they had never existed. Souls floated about the Blue, mostly observing the world as they waited to be reborn. They hovered on the edges of the frame, never quite clear to her, but she knew they were there. All sense of Isolde as an individual expanded into something larger. She was space and strength and muscle. She was pure energy as she brought down the hammer and struck the metal on the anvil. Again and again she lowered the hammer.

Isolde pulled energy not her own from around her and channeled it into shaping the red hot metal into a dagger. Sparks flew, but her skin was impervious to the fire in this realm of pure energy and matter. What she came to understand when she existed there was that everything was the same. All things existed at once. Flowing together. Indistinguishable and unique. The great contradiction existed everywhere.

She pulled the tools into sharper focus until they were part of her. The only things she saw were the anvil, the tools, and the fire. They became her. She was deft and strong in her work. The dagger came into being exactly as she wanted. Through her energy. Through her skill. Through her soul into being.

Then came the sense of the phoenix's presence. She called to Isolde, reminding her that she waited outside the shop. It pierced a hole in her psyche. All the emotions came roaring back into her mind. For a split second she fazed out of the Otherrealm back into the mortal realm. She dropped the hammer in surprise, confusion flashing through her at the myriad of disorganized emotions coursing through her. Uncontrollable. Uncontainable. Uncertain. She fought, she couldn't breathe as she fazed between the two realms. In her panic, she realized what was happening and she screamed with frustration. Everything compressed. She couldn't breathe. Then it was over. Opening her eyes, Isolde realized she was lying on her back staring up at the ceiling. She pushed her first against the floor. Not again. Something always interrupted her focus. Any reminder of the world pulled her out of the physical realm and changed the nature of what she was doing. She harried a glance over at the anvil and hearth just feet away. A half-formed dagger lay on the ground by the dim coals, metal melted over it in ugly heaps. Her technique had to be exquisite in both the mortal realm and the Otherrealm for the magic to be imbued in the object and the object to exist at all. She hadn't been able to forge a magical object yet and she'd been trying for months.

Isolde grit her teeth together. That stupid phoenix. She couldn't have waited until she was finished? Although Isolde had dabbled in different alchemir pursuits, as was the creed, she had chosen blacksmithing as her primary interest. It attracted her in a way that nothing else did. Even strong metal could be broken. When melted down in a fire hot enough, it could be reformed. It became something new. With strength and skill, she could create items that the world had never seen before. She could fill them with power. She could use them to forge her own path.

This was hers. Isolde never chose to be linked to the Viridian Phoenix or to be called a seer. She didn't desire a life floating about court, comforting people by telling them how to forge their futures. But she did choose this. She chose to forge swords. Like the sea, the forge was hers alone. The phoenix didn't understand what she called an obsession. She didn't understand why Isolde needed more. In her infinite wisdom, she didn't understand the simple human desire to love something, not because someone else tells you to, but because you truly love it. Why be an alchemir? You already have power. Why do you want to be more enmeshed with the Otherrealm? What is the point of that? Isolde rose from the ground, wincing at a new bruise sustained on her arm.

Although the phoenix's call was growing more insistent in her mind, she ignored it and took the time to properly clean up the mess she'd made. The blacksmith deserved at least that much courtesy. He was right, more time and effort wasted. Someday though. Someday she would be able to block out her emotions long enough to forge a proper dagger and eventually she would forge a sword. Isolde removed her apron, hanging it neatly back on its hook and then used a cloth to wipe the sweat from her forehead. With a sigh, she surveyed the quiet space one last time before turning and emerging into the street lit by the twilight, the hesitant candles of passerby, and the fire of the phoenixes streaking through the sky.

Chapter Ten

Isolde

23 Years After the Viridian Phoenix's Rebirth

Isolde had done her fair share of questionable things and tonight was no exception. She felt no shame slipping the necklace into the dresser of her sleeping grandmother, whose snores covered her light footsteps. Isolde was not particularly graceful, but she could be eerily quiet when called upon.

An anonymous note would find its way to the head of the palace guard in the morning alerting them to the presence of items stolen from the treasury in the grand house of the seer on the edge of town. She anticipated the guards would be trepidatious to accuse her grandparents, but she would testify if need be. They wouldn't escape this time. It was her cleverness and her lies which had kept them afloat all this time. With her words they had risen and with her words they would fall. But she had more important matters to attend to.

Slipping quietly back to her room, she faced the long night before her with a kind of wary anticipation. She had woken only just before sunset, which turned out to be convenient for her purposes. When she called Ryth with her mind, the creature did not answer at first.

I know you're awake.

She waited.

I can feel you.

The moon glittered in the clear sky as she stared outside, the warm night breeze wafting over her carrying the scent of pomegranates. Still no reply.

You can't ignore me forever.

Says who?

Finally. A response.

I'll walk if I have to.

So walk.

For once can't you just make things easy? Isolde asked.

Perhaps you weren't meant for an easy life, Seer, the Phoenix replied, a hint of mockery tainting her tone.

Isolde whirled away from the window, muting her words until they were like babbling brooks in the back of her mind. Hauling her bag over her shoulder, she tiptoed through the manor until she was securely outside. The horse made some noise as she saddled it in the bronze moonlight, but she truly couldn't care less. Maybe it was better she was alone tonight anyway.

Town was almost silent, except for the occasional murmur of a loose tarp in the wind or the singing of someone up much too late. The forge was dark. Thankfully the blacksmith she rented the space from lived elsewhere, so she wouldn't disturb his slumber.

After leaving her horse in the adjoining stables, she made her way into the interior of the shop, which was only dimly lit by the strong moon outside the window. Silence coated the air. She started the fire in the forge, stoking it steadily until it blazed high with melting red heat. Isolde pulled on gloves, ignoring the bubbling in the back of her mind from the phoenix who was still trying to speak to her.

Isolde glanced at the ground warily, sending a prayer to the Salamanders for good luck and skill, though she doubted they would hear or respond. With that she began heating and pounding out the metal, the sound ringing through the air. It sent a flock of birds sleeping outside skittering up into the night air in a panic. Maybe they were smart to flee.

Isolde purged her mind of memories and matter, swallowing the acrid smell of coal like it was holy. Her libations were the effort in her blood pouring itself into the metal as she bridged the realms of the soul and the physical. The forge melted away on the edges of her vision, transforming as a blue pall was cast over the world. Isolde no longer moved in any way she could sense, she merely formed, pouring blood through her fingers. Seizing moonlight in her mind and channeling it into the weapon forming below her in the smoldering starlight of the Otherrealm.

Persuasion and destiny. The movements of the planets and stars aligned in the minds of those who perceived she who the sword would choose. An undeniable claim to the throne because the sword itself spoke as the mouthpiece of the stars.

It glittered an unearthly shade of red as the tip sharpened and the weapon elongated. Ryth knocked in the back of her mind, but Isolde ignored that call, blocking every thought that might interrupt her, knowing this would only work if she became fully entrenched in the soul realm. She used the anvil to sear the thoughts from her mind, leaving only blinding pain, which she also channeled into the sword until everything Isolde was violently drained away. Until she could not breathe.

Only then did she pull the thorn that Turia had scraped her hand on from the pocket of her cloak, hurling it into the void and pulling at the knowledge her dried blood held until it deconstructed itself. The essence of Turia's human bloodline swirled around Isolde in strands of ghostly red and gray. With her last breath, Isolde sent the blood into the sword marking it as belonging to Turia's Unbonded bloodline and the month of her birth according to the stars. It would answer to Turia only. Unable to breathe, Isolde collapsed, falling and falling through the Otherrealm until she hit the dirt floor of the forge. Life spun around her, images she couldn't understand and later wouldn't recall along with a warning signal deep within her chest. Isolde forgot the world then.

When she came to, the fire still burned, but it was much smaller than before. As she climbed stiffly to her feet, she noticed that the sky outside the open door was somewhat lighter, but thankfully it still wasn't dawn. Isolde waited for a moment, staring at the door, reluctant to turn around and see her handiwork. For the first time, she had succeeded in crafting an Otherrealm item as an alchemir. Something about it terrified her.

But she did look, shaking herself of that silly feeling and picking the sword up to examine it without any further hesitation. The blade gleamed silver, reflecting the light of the dying moon. It was marked for Turia alone and would claim her as queen, convincing others that she was destined to rule through the power of the starlight woven into the sword itself. Engraved river-like patterns ran over the surface of the blade, offset by small blue sapphires and diamonds set into the hilt. Isolde ran her fingers over them, feeling the heat of the Otherrealm radiating from the convincing facsimile.

Sliding the sword into a plain sheath, Isolde carried it herself, reveling in its power and the success of her efforts. She considered the sword in comparison to the drawing she had flung onto the desk. Convincing. She doubted anyone would be looking that closely anyways or would know how to identify the legendary sword of the old High Queen Maeve, the first queen to unite the fire provinces. Caliburnus had long been lost to time. Its "re-emergence" would hold weight.

Leaving the fire smoldering, she left the blacksmith's shop. The phoenix sat perched on the rooftop across from her, still as a stone statue. She immediately felt her displeasure. Isolde turned away and mounted her horse, starting down the street.

What have you done?

None of your concern.

I swear to you, child, you will regret this.

How ominous.

Isolde rolled her eyes, ignoring Ryth sweeping through the sky behind her.

She headed toward the palace as the city started to wake. The sky was lightening, but the morning fog still had a hold. It didn't take long to reach the center of the town. With heavy steps she ascended the stairs until she was almost at the top, then she took a seat and closed her eyes against the blue in the sky.

Chapter Eleven

Isolde

23 Years After the Viridian Phoenix's Rebirth

Isolde could sense the guards behind her. They were too anxious to disturb the seer, even though she sat on the palace steps as though she herself was guarding the entrance to the throne room. Shadows fled over the stairs as the sea wind blew the morning clouds through the sky. Passing merchants and early risers glanced at her curiously and she knew it would only be so long before the news spread. As she expected.

Her dress was too thin for the morning air, but she hadn't considered that in her excitement last night. The phoenix had settled on a rooftop across from her, her glare fixed intently on the lone girl. With a sigh Isolde ignored the creature, instead turning her attention to the sword in its simple sheath. With a firm hand she withdrew it and laid it across her knees, knowing it would catch the sunlight and leave a dazzling impression on those who passed.

"Most esteemed seer."

Ah, the first challenge of the day. She didn't bother turning around to face the masculine voice.

"Yes?"

The man descended a few steps until he was perched nervously in front of her. "Is there anything you need?"

"Why? Am I bothering you?" she asked curtly.

"Not yet. But you are blocking the entrance and the prince's procession will be arriving to take their place at court shortly."

"Let them arrive."

"Would it be possible for you to move? I don't wish to offend, oh seer, but the prince will not be in a waiting mood this morning. I fear he will not want to be interrupted."

"I'd be careful insulting royalty."

"Not-not my intention. Please forgive me, Seer."

The man scrambled back up the steps. Isolde could faintly hear him whispering to his companions. They would send another guard soon, whom she would also ignore. The morning procession to the court was a well-loved ritual. People were even now gathering, taking a break from their morning tasks to catch a glimpse of the strong and elegant lords and ladies of Viridian. Telling that the prince had taken it upon himself to lead it even so soon after his father's passing. The funeral had only been held last night. It was a Weeping Night filled with a magic few understood, Isolde included. She'd given no thought to it as she forged the sword and it didn't even cross her mind as she sat on the steps waiting for the sound of the King's Drums.

People muttered to each other about her as they amassed. Isolde knew this but stared straight ahead as if she didn't care. As if she wanted to be seen. Only a fool would truly wish to be seen. In that case, she was most certainly a fool. The procession rounded the corner before the stairs, bringing with it the drumming music and the shouts of the crowd.

The prince led the procession, not even glancing at the people surrounding him. His focus rested elsewhere, his hand on his sword and his formal crown glistening in the morning sunlight. Arturia followed behind him, looking at the people and waving, though her smile stretched thin. After a dozen courtiers came the uncle with his soldiers, by far looking the most regal out of the bunch. Everyone gave him a wide berth, perhaps because his eyes and his clean-shaven jaw declared that he was not a man to be trifled with.

Two soldiers approached and tried to convince Isolde to move as the procession mounted the steps, but she only had eyes for Turia. Her focus stayed on the princess until the young woman felt the stare and they locked eyes. It was like Isolde could see the princess's heart stop beating in that moment. The seer rose and held the sword up in the air. The courtier beside the prince murmured something in his ear, his eyes lighting with confusion as he saw the woman with the sword blocking his path.

"Good morning, Seer. You wish to join us, I take it?" the prince asked, some hint of danger in his voice. Her mouth quirked up in a smile.

"I'm afraid not."

He eyed the sword with trepidation.

She stood her ground for an uncomfortable length of time. Prince Edrune's jaw ticked and he started to move around her. While humiliating, best not to anger the people by having the seer torn from where she stood by his soldiers. He needed their support desperately. Isolde held out her arm to stop him.

"I have something to say which I believe you'll want to hear."

"Say what you have to say, Seer, but don't test me further," he spat.

"It is time," Isolde declared, raising her voice so she could be heard by the crowd. As her voice rang over the city square, the people quieted, straining to hear her words.

"The Soulless have granted me a mission and a boon. They saw turmoil as they looked through the ether and saw the future filtering through, stained with red and blue-green pain. As soon as the king died, I was overwhelmed by their voices, by the amplified version of the future they saw as it broke over me. It invaded my mind, clouding my present vision more and more as it is coming dangerously close to passing and that future is fighting to emerge into reality. So, the Soulless gave me guidance. A gift. One to pass on to the good people of Viridian so you may avoid that stained future and instead trade it for a silver future glimmering in the starlight.

They showed me the location of the sword of High Queen Maeve, supposedly lost at sea. I went down to the water and as I watched the tides push forward in their rhythm, I heard a voice whisper that the gift of the in-between was to be ours. In that moment, I saw the sword, stuck in the sand of the beach, delivered from the depths of the ocean by the Soulless on the sacred Day of Emergence, just waiting to be found. The future went silent, softening to a glowing silver in my mind."

The crowd was entranced by her story—she could see that easily enough—but the prince was frozen in front of her, the red rising in his cheeks. That sight gave her pleasure. She had to suppress her smile.

She switched the sword to one hand and held it higher above her head. "This is that sword. The lost sword of High Queen Maeve who first united the lands of the Fire Folk. The sword of the woman whose blood runs through the veins of the royal family. The sword of the first human to ride the phoenix without being reduced to ash. Legend has it and the Soulless decree that the sword will only respond to the true heir of the throne of Viridian. It will answer only to fate and not to human ambition or guile. It will choose our ruler and then we shall have peace." She stared the prince in the eyes with that last word, taunting him, begging him to dare disagree with her.

"There will be no power struggle, no bloodshed, and no war. The people of Viridian will have peace." Everyone in the royal retinue squirmed uncomfortably, appalled by her directness. Unsettled by the fact that she was saying out loud what everyone in the court had been thinking since the king died.

"Does anyone disagree with the decision of the Soulless? If so, speak now. Otherwise hold your tongues for eternity."

The prince stuttered. The uncle smiled cruelly. The princess looked into the distance.

"That's settled then. If you wish to claim the throne, step forward and Caliburnus will let its verdict fall."

Hatred shone in the prince's eyes as he stood before her, trembling in anger at this usurpation of power on the part of the seer. But what could he do to challenge her? She held the people in the palm of her hand.

He stepped forward. "I assert my right to rule this land as the lord of the Viridian Palace and son of the high king."

"The sword shall test you," she declared, handing it to him hilt-first. He snatched it from her, uncertainty clouding his gaze. He tested its weight, grew comfortable with its heft. A smile flickered across his lips. "It hasn't rejected me, Seer," he stated with amusement.

Placing her hand firmly on the hilt, she pulled the object away from him.

"Rejection comes in many forms, my lord." His smile grew, an ugly thing that clearly conveyed this wasn't over.

"Step away, now. I'm afraid it is not your time."

"This is treason," he whispered, the smile still holding itself together through some hellish miracle.

"Step away. Or do you wish the people to know you have rejected the Soulless?"

"You are far from a god, my lady," he spat, even as he stepped stiffly to the side with his retinue.

"I never claimed to be one," she whispered.

Having cleared the way, the prince stared daggers at his uncle whose eyes were too keen and bright for Isolde's liking.

He seized the sword from her without any warning. Closing his eyes, it seemed as though he felt a power flowing through him. For a split second Isolde feared that she had made some dreadful mistake. That through some twist of fortune or fate the sword would answer to him. But her handiwork did not betray her. The magic held and the sword rested lifeless in his iron hands. The crowd watched, helpless against this sacred ritual. Children stood on their tip toes to get a glimpse of Caliburnus. Old women squinted against the morning sun reflecting off the ocean below, trying to make out the shining object.

"Time to bow out, Lord Penbrook. I suggest you do so gracefully."

"Oh, this isn't the end, girl."

"I think you'll find it is," she said, pulling the sword from his grasp as a thrill ran through her at stealing something from this man. Turning away, he stalked up the stairs behind her, his soldiers following in his wake. Her fingers tightened on the sword as she realized what he intended.

"You may want to think again, uncle," the prince called out. This was a morning of threats and warnings. What a magnanimous way to begin the rule of a new queen.

The king's brother didn't even glance towards the young prince's voice.

"Halt. You are not to enter the palace."

"Try to stop me," Penbrook declared. And the prince's soldiers did indeed. Within moments the heavy morning was torn apart by pounding feet and violent shouts, by metal on metal. Isolde searched frantically for Turia's face in the chaos. The princess stood frozen, her personal guard with swords out and backs to her. When she caught Turia's eyes, they held only sorrow. Not a trace of fear. That realization caught Isolde off guard, especially given the way her own skin felt tight and she could hear her heart pounding in her head. Once again, she had underestimated the princess.

A man keeled over next to her, his body sliding down a few steps. The seer quickly averted her eyes from the blood covering the side of his head. She'd never much been one for the gory and grotesque. There was only one thing to do.

Isolde charged down the steps toward the princess, thin blue dress giving her an Otherrealmly appearance. The princess's guards held their ground, but she could already sense their fear of her in the uncertainty of their tightened jaws and their uneasy holds on their weapons.

"Step aside," she commanded.

They refused.

"Princess!" she demanded, the sword hilt heavy and sweaty in her hand.

Turia stared straight at her without a word, or rather through her.

"Princess, heed my voice."

No change.

"I believe this is your time," she said softly, shaving the edges off of her words. She stood as close as the guards dared let her without explicit permission from the bleak princess.

The shouts behind them grew louder as more soldiers joined the fray. The crowd had backed away. People were fleeing, seeking their relatively safe homes and hearths. Many would wait to hear the fate of the kingdom from other lips.

"Princess, I need you to listen to me."

"Who said I wasn't?" the girl replied, so quietly that Isolde almost didn't hear her.

With a nod of her head she ushered the guards aside and the seer stepped closer, the sword in her hands hanging between them like an oath or possibly an omen.

"It's time for you to take your place. I have seen it." Isolde spoke for the benefit of the guards and the tremulous gaggle of courtiers behind her, but her eyes glittered with genuine concern that the princess managed to detect.

Letting her eyes flutter closed, Turia said, "Then perhaps it is time to put you to the test." With slow, firm steps, she ascended toward the brawl spilling over the palace steps. She had to be in sight of the remaining people below as they ducked behind wells and dipped into shops.

Breathing a sigh of relief, Isolde's uncertainty about the princess's feelings soothed, the seer followed in her footsteps. A woman of honor. No wonder the Fire Folk had long ago chosen to grant humans the throne. There was an old story about humans and the phoenixes and an unspeakable act of bravery that nearly ended them both, but few could remember the details of that tale besides the oldest priestesses.

The princess faced the city and the sea, her cheeks reddening and her eyes downcast.

"What do they want from me?" she whispered.

Isolde's brow crinkled in confusion, the sword feeling much too heavy in her hands at that moment.

"The Soulless? What do they want from me?"

Isolde met her eyes, the sadness stretching thin between them.

"Only my life? Well, then, time to ask what's next I suppose." Turia held out her hand for the sword. It was trembling, her short nails looking painstakingly ordinary and coarse. Isolde bit her tongue, nearly unable to breathe for a moment. But only a moment. With a smile fixed upon her stubborn face, she passed the dark hilt to the girl who in that moment became a queen.

Nothing happened at first. Relief crept into Turia's eyes, but it was soon obliterated. People would later say that started as a low hum felt in the streets throughout Viridian soon dove into a raucous melody. Words and whispers danced through the air, indecipherable except for their supernatural nature. The air directly surrounding the queen was deathly still, but the wind had picked up further away. The vicious song tore through the fighting men, knocking them to their knees, where it thought they belonged. One by one, everyone fell or bowed their heads of their own accord.

The sight took Isolde's breath away and something inside her yearned to cling to that moment, to the rising sound, and to the future she had created in a single night. The sword reflected the morning light proudly as Turia hoisted it above her head, which was impressive for someone with as thin a frame as hers.

There would be no doubt. Slowly, Isolde sank to her knees on the step in front of the princess, maintaining eye contact as she did so. But the princess wasn't looking at her. Once more Isolde couldn't tell where the princess's attention lay, perhaps somewhere deep in her thoughts. Whatever the case, it didn't matter. Her calm presence in the eye of the storm caused by the sword only served to reinforce the Otherrealmliness of her claim. It was a breathtaking sight. The green of her dress reminded Isolde of the moss growing at the base of the tree where she had been holding her vigil less than a fortnight prior. A sign. Isolde averted her eyes.

Turia tucked the sword into her belt as people watched. All the sudden she grew flustered, panic starting to sprout in her eyes. But it was still contained. Isolde could only spot it because she was searching for it. The song quieted, until at last only muttering courtiers and townsfolk remained.

"I vow to give my life to you," Turia shouted, her voice cracking in the middle of the phrase. It was all she said before turning and hurrying up the steps.

Not a soul tried to stop her.

Chapter Twelve

Isolde

23 Years After the Viridian Phoenix's Rebirth

"You'll regret you ever said a word," Isolde threatened.

"It's so painfully easy to get on your nerves," said the prince from behind the rusty bars of the cell.

Isolde seemed to be frequenting the prisons these days. But what choice did she have? While she had her suspicions that the prince had played a role in his father's death, she had no proof. Nevertheless, it was worth trying to pry from him any information about his allies, who might attempt to target Turia.

The queen was too uneasy with such things. She chose to cloister herself away in the bowels of the palace, trying so hard to erase her existence even as the seer tried to remind the court why she held authority. Isolde couldn't be truly free and in control until she secured safety in the palace. That would only happen once Turia's power was properly solidified and the dangerous people lurking in the court had been rooted out.

Until then, she walked a thin line, appreciating her expanded autonomy but tensing every time she walked around a corner in a too-quiet hallway or heard a loud noise. Isolde found herself chafing against a newfound set of restraints. She comforted herself with the thought that this unease would only last until she did what it took to make the palace safe and all the Fire Folk provinces had properly sworn their allegiance to Turia.

It wasn't that the few months after the miracle of Caliburnus had been difficult per se. Isolde now possessed rooms in the palace, a lie she'd given her life to forge, and an ever-present desire to be near the queen. But tension threaded through her days, from morning until night, especially since the queen simply didn't wish to be seen by anyone. Turia needed to be rallying support and courting public opinion, not hiding away.

Isolde launched a weary expression at the prince and then turned away. She bit down on her simmering irritation. After all, the prince could insult his sister as much as he wanted, but he wasn't actually a danger to her. Turia wasn't in any danger at this moment, the seer reminded herself. Isolde flexed her fingers as she walked away, leaving the prison for the more picturesque setting of the upper rooms of the palace. The prince would rot locked away in the prisons, his crown removed, and his title stripped from him. And that was exactly how it should be after the words he had for sweet Turia who had really done nothing to him. Prison was Isolde's idea, after all.

Ignoring everyone she passed in the brilliant stone halls, Isolde made her way to the small door of Turia's chambers. The royal suite remained empty. No matter how hard she'd tried to convince Turia to make the move, she was always met with silence and a dismissive wave. Isolde understood why though. A guard stood posted outside the door. She nodded to him and he avoided her eyes. It would always be the same.

Isolde knocked, but only as a formality, before she pushed the door inward. Turia wouldn't have answered otherwise.

"Princess!" Isolde launched forward with horror, hand outstretched. But the queen, perched precariously on the sill of the open window, granted her a small smile.

"Don't worry, Seer. I haven't tried that for many years now."

The implications made Isolde's mouth go dry as Turia turned her head back to look out over her sea. The palace stood directly on the cliff and this cozy room had the best view of the ocean crashing onto the rocks below. It brimmed with life, colorful fabrics draped in haphazard ways over the walls. Much of the floor was lined with live plants, including, perhaps most surprisingly, inside the dead fireplace. But anyone who knew Queen Arturia of House Pendamon also knew that she didn't shy away from the cold. In fact, she rather pursued it sometimes, to the amusement of her father and derision of her brother. Back before time had carved her into a more quiet and cautious being, she'd always talked of fleeing to the snowy mountains of Argothian. There, she said, she would happily live out her days as a spinster in the frosty forest, coaxing things to life that shouldn't be able to survive there.

The night she'd first taken the throne, Turia had conveyed this memory to Isolde, tears in her voice and the fire burning too hot as they sat in Isolde's new chambers. Isolde had pushed unwelcome feelings down, her jaw tightening against uncertainty tinged with guilt. This had to be done. For everyone. Turia had to be queen.

Isolde didn't like to remember the horror in the queen's eyes that night as the seer suggested they execute her brother. Isolde didn't like to remember the harrowing sound of the girl's sobs as she buried her face in a pillow, unwilling to let her grief be fully on display. Isolde didn't like to remember the way she herself had gone out to the sea and pleaded with the Soulless to take her own life because their seer had committed a great sin.

Of course, the next morning, she'd woken clinging to a hollow feeling of victory and trying to poke and prod the embers back to glowing. It had to be done, she told herself. There was no changing it now. What the princess didn't know wouldn't hurt her. In fact, Isolde had likely guaranteed her a more stable existence. The princess was now officially queen and had been formally accepted as such by the people of Viridian along with about half of the provinces so far.

If her brother had taken up the crown, surely her position would have been uncertain as she grew older. Especially if she ever had children. Children who might one day try to lay claim to the throne. Isolde may have manufactured the situation, but surely the Soulless had merely given the seer the tools to help events play out as fate intended. And fate meant to protect Turia from a gruesome death. Isolde was convinced of this. For someone so focused on independence, Isolde sometimes felt herself a hypocrite. It was so easy to pawn off her questionable choices on fate, but perhaps it was true. She would take the perhaps.

Turia now sat on the windowsill, eyes closed as the sea breeze blew into the room, ruffling her hair.

"You still call me princess," Turia observed, her eyes remaining shut.

"My apologies," Isolde said, decidedly more composed than seconds before. She carefully took a seat by the fireplace, fixing Turia with her eyes.

"It's true, isn't it. I can't be called a queen. That's rather ridiculous."

"Please," Isolde said dismissively. "You don't have time for useless thoughts like that."

"I may not have much time at all if you're to be believed," Turia said wryly.

"You know what I mean."

"Then why still call me princess?"

"Force of habit, I suppose. You've been princess all these years."

"Well, then."

"We need to talk though, you know. About matters more important than my slips of the tongue."

"I don't see why. Life will go on with or without me and so will this kingdom. You know that. A monarch is a figurehead above all else. A useless figurine locked in a display case. Let people who are much older and wiser than me make the important decisions."

"That's dangerous thinking, Turia."

Her eyes snapped open, and she fixed Isolde with a tired stare. "You're wrong. I'm too tired for this, Isolde. Can't you see that?"

"I see that. But you're missing the bigger picture. Your people just lost their king of three decades. You have to go out there. You have to appear strong. You have to show the lords in your kingdom and those at our borders that you are not someone to be trifled with because if you don't..."

"Oh, then what, Seer? What will happen? I will be murdered in my sleep by my most trusted companions? I'll be overtaken and crushed by an angry mob? Some more worthy royal will steal my crown? Well, I don't want it. Whatever future you saw is a farce."

"Bold words. Now you need to go and show the court the same amount of stubbornness that you put into hating yourself."

"What makes you think you can speak to me like that?" Turia asked, her voice frigid.

For a teetering moment, Isolde wondered if she'd misstepped by causing this outburst from the typically mild Turia.

"I apologize," the seer said softly, leaving her chair and sinking to sit on the cold floor below the windowsill. "I know this is difficult."

"I'm not sure you really do." Turia wouldn't meet her eyes.

"And yes, you're right to some degree. I'm afraid for you. Because while the kingdom might run, it won't be running very smoothly or well if you're not a strong presence projecting security from the court. People are evil, Turia. They take what they want, and they don't look back. There are already those here at court who are poking around, searching for weakness so they have an excuse to bring news back to their lords that the high queen's throne may be within their grasp. We've only received emissaries bearing gift swords to demonstrate their loyalty from some of the provinces. We must secure the rest."

"I lost my entire family in one day, Isolde. I know the world is an evil place and that I, for some reason more than most, am someone people think they can take advantage of without consequences."

Isolde looked away uncomfortably at this. She was only protecting the princess and herself.

The seer played with a shiny green button that had been discarded on the floor.

"What can I say to convince you?"

"Nothing."

Isolde rose and left the room without another word. Her steps were quick and efficient through the halls, out of the palace, and through the streets. It had been days of the same fruitless conversation over and over again. Turia had only shown her face in court twice since her quickly-planned coronation, which was a vague, too-bright memory for Isolde. The queen should have been sitting on the throne, hearing grievances frequently, if not every day. Courtiers were talking and for once she didn't know how to efficiently squash the rumors they were spreading. Spreading rumors had usually been her business. She wasn't quite so sure what to do on the other side of that experience besides try to reassure people. It was like playing a game or fighting a war. Maybe they were the same thing.

"The princess must be deathly sick. I've heard a doctor's been seen entering her chambers everyday," Lord Candille would murmur.

Overhearing, the seer would reply back. "The *queen* is of stout health. The doctor is merely an old friend. She's always had a keen interest in the science of the body and they quite enjoy having an intellectual conversation about the newest developments in the field."

"Oh did you hear that the prince still lives in his rooms and is secretly gathering his army even as we speak. I'm rather surprised the princess hasn't done anything to slow his efforts. Perhaps she doesn't have the stomach for it. We'll be at war before you know it."

At which point Isolde would step out from behind a pillar and say, "The prince? Oh, I assure you he isn't doing very well. He's in the prisons and I heard the princess actually ordered that he undergo interrogation because he wouldn't give out information about remnants of his supporters. I didn't have the stomach for it, but she knew what needed to be done."

These conversations were practically endless. Day in and day out Isolde listened and watched, weaving herself into conversations to defend the absent queen. She was painfully aware that she could only do that for so long before people truly became discontented and someone decided it was time for a new leader. If Isolde couldn't secure safety for herself and the queen, then her freedom from her grandparents meant very little. That possibility twisted around her chest, choking her hopes a little more with every day that passed. Two more provinces had sent their tokens of allegiance to the queen, but many more were biding their time, waiting to see how long the new high queen would last.

As she headed through the streets, she wondered what had become of Ryth. She could feel her disgruntled presence in the back of her mind every so often, but the phoenix had been noticeably absent. Pulling her woolen cloak tighter around her against the brisk air, a thought nagged at her. Had anyone else noticed the legendary phoenix's absence?

Not all believed in the Soulless. Some called it superstition or simply claimed all the old beings were dead. Some didn't believe in seers. Some didn't believe in her. But that wasn't the majority of the people of Viridian, so careful to not let their clothes touch the salt water and touching their cheeks to their shoulders whenever a thundering storm emerged on the horizon. Their trust and faith were a pillar of the city. Their broken faith—an even fiercer thing to behold. It was a dangerous game if anyone began contesting the strength of her connection with the phoenix or if anyone caught on to the signs of the phoenix's disapproval.

Isolde quickened her pace and rubbed her eyes as she crossed over into Steelfirst. Sleep hadn't been her friend the last few weeks. At the same time though, a frantic joy followed her steps, always on the edge of everything she did. For the first time in her life, her grandparents weren't charting her course and managing her tongue. Every word she said fell on her shoulders. She loved the weight of it. The weight of knowing the truths and lies and tales spilling from her mouth were all her own. She was able to taste all of the words, their bitterness and humor because she was no longer just a vessel from them, but their very source. There was a distinct euphoria in it, even if it was tempered by her need for safety and urgent desire to see Turia's reign properly established.

Isolde had asked Turia to banish her grandparents soon after she became queen. The seer had delivered the royal order to them herself as they knelt before her, forced to the ground by the royal guard. She read it to them in the dying light, savoring her words, brilliant with the force of the queen's decree behind them. Her grandmother was too proud to do anything but to stare at her with a hateful smile. Her grandfather, on the other hand, wore a look of noble betrayal. She swore she saw a tear glistening in his eye. Ironic. He was the one who would not allow her to eat until she spoke his words and who said no one would understand her. He'd told her once that no one would shed a tear if she happened to drown in the sea one night.

No. She would waste no more time thinking of them. The most difficult place to banish them from was her thoughts though. No matter how much she tried to forget them, they crept back in. They were with her when she wondered who really knew her. They were in her thoughts when her eyes absorbed the intonations and words of everyone around her. They were there when she woke in the middle of the night with tears on her cheeks and a screaming aloneness occupying her chest.

"Hey!" The voice broke her thoughts and she looked up, only just in time to see the horse barreling her way as she stepped out in front of it. She barely had time to move. Only a moment, really. She launched herself out of the way, but not quite enough. A flash of horse stench. A blur of brown hair. Tumbling onto the rough ground, searing pain burst through her ankle, caught underneath the horse's feet as they trampled onward. "Sorry about that!" The rider called as he kept going, urging his beast on faster, in a hurry to be somewhere that probably wouldn't miss him if he didn't show up at all. Someone cried out. Her breath came and went too quickly as she looked around, unable to process her surroundings for a moment. It had been devastatingly quick.

She lay there stunned, trying to catch her breath. A couple of strangers rushed over to her, taking a break from their busy days to see what a fool she was. The seer blinked, doing her best to ignore the blur of voices speaking at her. They couldn't see her like this. Weak and vulnerable and stupid. She shook her head at them as arms pulled her up and helped her move out of the road. Shaking her head again, she sat there for an indeterminable amount of time until she got used to the pain and the shock started to wear off.

Looking up, she realized that most of the people who had gathered to help had dispersed. Only one person sat beside her on the edge of the road now as people flowed around them. She blinked at them, realizing their eyes were far away and their hand rested on her ankle.

"What are you doing?" Isolde hissed, shoving the warm hand away. The memory of grandmother's hands carefully bandaging a scraped knee while chiding her for being so careless rushed through her mind. The person's deep brown face leaped back into full consciousness as they sat back on their knees, staring at her quizzically with an amused look in their gentle eyes. They appeared to be around her age.

"Fixing your ankle, I believe. If I'm not, by all means feel free to correct me. I mean, sometimes the process does backfire and I end up giving people donkey feet. I heal ankles a lot, you know. Practically my specialty. Why, just this morning some other poor girl tripped on a root in front of me, wouldn't you just know it and…"

She stared at them dead-eyed as they rambled on into some private joke she had neither the time nor energy to appreciate.

"Do you always talk this much?"

They just smiled a little as they brushed their tightly-curled black hair behind their ear, revealing a silver earring hanging down. The jewelry caught her attention, not only because it was antique and the style indicated they were nonbinary, but because the cut surface of the deep purple gem felt like it was brimming with reflections she couldn't quite make out.

They reached out again to return to healing her foot, which now only throbbed, even though it was still twisted at a sickly angle.

Isolde slapped their hand away.

"I can heal myself perfectly fine."

They raised their eyebrows as she grasped her own ankle and fell backward into the liminal space of the Otherrealm. She reached out desperately for the green healing light. Pictures of grass growing and seed sprouting fell through her consciousness. Isolde could almost touch them. They felt so frustratingly close as they passed through her. She should have been living them, experiencing their growth, feeling the way the moss reached for the sun, but instead all she felt was numbness. That was enough though. She let herself fall back into reality. She opened her eyes, a dull anger settling in her stomach as she examined her ankle. It obviously wasn't fully healed, even though it looked normal. It was, however, numb enough that she could climb to her feet. She fought the urge to wince.

"So, you're an alchemir also?" they asked.

She glanced dismissively at them. "Of course I am."

Most people had guessed that about the young seer, given her unique connection to Ryth.

"Does it feel better?" they asked quietly, their head tilted.

"What?"

"Your ankle. Is it alright? Can you get where you're going?"

She blinked at them. It irritated her that they were assuming she was incompetent when it came to healing. Of course, she was, but how could they know that?

They took a different tact. "What's your alchemir focus?"

This, on the other hand, wasn't something people knew. She hesitated. "I don't see why that matters."

She took a step and her foot almost lost purchase. The person darted forward, catching her arm to steady her.

"Can I walk you to where you're going?"

Isolde glanced at them.

"Please?"

"I suppose," she replied finally.

With a nod of approval from her, they slipped their arm around her back and she held onto their neck with one arm. Out of the corner of her eye, she caught their small smile.

"Which direction?" they asked.

Isolde collected herself and directed them back toward the palace. She'd been on her way to the forge, but clearly she needed to be somewhere alone with her alchemiric book so she could try to fix her ankle herself. The forge would be there later.

The pair walked in silence for a while. Isolde noticed that some people's stares lingered on her longer than usual. She ignored them. It had been that way all her life, but she hated people seeing her injured and helpless. This wouldn't do. She directed them down some side streets that were more isolated. It would take longer to get there, but it was worth it if less people saw her in this state.

Isolde tried to focus on the path ahead rather than the peculiar warmth of the arm around her. She wasn't used to having people so close, and it made her uneasy.

"Are you sure you don't want me to finish healing it? I know it can be difficult to continue the healing process once someone else has already begun. A lot of times the magic resists anyone who tries to wrap it up."

That was true, but it was also a minor factor. This person was clearly giving her a gracious way out. Isolde hesitated. They stood in an isolated back alley between a bookstore and some other shop full of useless knick-knacks. There weren't very many people milling about which put her more at ease with the idea of being seen unable to heal herself. A feeling stirred deep down that she'd tried to forget. Her natural tendency as an alchemir should have been toward healing and creation. Ryth, after all, was the patron of the healers, for some reason Isolde could barely fathom. Ryth represented creation and life. Seers themselves were tied to healing. But, then again, she was no seer.

Isolde sighed. "Alright, I suppose." She limped over to the wall and took a seat on a low bench. They knelt beside her and she took a moment to really look at them. Their movements were careful and cautious. Not hesitant, necessarily, but...grounding. As their fingers brushed her ankle, they closed their eyes. A breeze picked up, ruffling their hair as their face took on an Otherrealmly quality. Something about their face seemed familiar, like a memory she couldn't quite recall.

The wind clearly liked them. It was attracted by their act of healing and by the expression of power. Nature had never much liked her. Birds fled when she stomped through their forests. She was at odds with any sort of cat. Even the snakes knew to flee her presence. But no, the breeze itself liked this person. It played with their hair familiarly as they muttered words she couldn't make out.

She swallowed and averted her eyes, just feeling more at odds with the world. The person pulled their soft hand away. Rising, they took a seat beside her on the bench.

"Do you have a name?" she asked, curiosity finally getting the better of her.

"Tristan. How about you?"

She assessed them for a minute. "Isolde."

"I suspected that might be the case, though I've only ever seen you from a distance," they answered. "Couldn't be sure."

"I see."

The silence lasted for a few moments before they spoke again. "What is it like? Being everything you are?"

"Why do you want to know?" she snapped.

They smiled at her, their eyes dancing. "It must be difficult, but also wonderful, to have so much talent."

She wondered if they were poking fun at her. "If you must know, healing isn't my focus."

"I see," they replied. "What is then?

Tristan held her gaze, but she refused to look away. "Forging weapons."

They looked down. "That's something I've been wanting to learn how to do for a long time."

"You?" she asked, raising an eyebrow.

They smiled to themself. "Why not me?"

"I'm not sure. You don't seem like the particularly-good-with-weapons type to me."

"Perhaps you should rethink your assumptions about healers, Isolde."

Hearing them say her name gave her pause. It was too personal. Too familiar. But she wanted to hear them say it again. They didn't call her seer or sacred one. They didn't shy away from her gaze. There was also nothing aggressive about it though. Her name was a hateful word on the tongues of her grandparents. They'd always had some motive, some purpose for using it. But, coming from Tristan's mouth, it felt soft.

"Well, are you good with weapons?" she shot back.

"Ahem, there's definitely some room for growth there. But that's what I do. Never too old to start learning."

"I'm not sure about that. I don't think you can change a person's nature. Sometimes you are who you are and there's no altering it," said Isolde.

"That blocks off so many possibilities though, doesn't it? If someone can't grow to be better, why should they even try?"

"Exactly."

Their eyes widened. "You're very pessimistic for a seer."

She crossed her arms. "How many seers do you know, exactly?"

"Just the one."

"Well, you're lucky then."

Tristan winced, almost imperceptibly, but she caught it. "I don't know that'd I say that."

"When did you begin learning how to heal?" she asked.

"Oh, since the time I was a child. Never had anyone to mentor me though. Didn't personally know anyone else who was inclined toward alchemy."

"Better off that way anyway."

Their eyebrows wrinkled. "Why do you say that?"

She looked them up and down judgmentally. "You don't know?"

"Know what?"

"That you're a strange one."

Tristan chuckled good-naturedly. "Know what?"

"You lose power if anyone teaches you something beyond the basics. It's difficult to know where that line is, but if you learn it yourself through trial and error, your energy when going through a process is richer."

"Who says that?" they asked incredulously. "Sounds borderline ridiculous."

She rolled her eyes. "It's in the oldest alchemir text, "The Secrets" and it does make sense. You have to do it on your own for it to count."

"But wouldn't you learn faster if someone taught you?"

"Yes, but you're missing the point. The end result would be less power than might have been possible if you learned it on your own. Speed isn't everything, you know."

"Interesting."

"Anyway, I'm assuming that's for a primary focus. Surely it couldn't hurt a secondary skill, one that you'll never be the best at anyway."

"I guess that's true. In that case speed would probably be an asset."

Their eyes lit up. "What if you teach me forging and I teach you healing?"

She immediately shook her head. "I don't think so."

They were silent for a moment, pensive. "Alright," they finally responded.

"What, you're not going to make your argument?" she asked.

"Arguments have never really been my strong suit," they said quietly. Their voice was soft and musical as they said it, only adding to their point.

"Why doesn't that surprise me?"

They only smiled as they stood up. "Well, I think I need to make my way home. You're alright to walk now, yes?" But they already knew the answer. "Goodbye, Isolde. May I see you in another life."

Tristan turned and walked back down the alley, their hands in their pockets. She watched their back, realizing she didn't want them to go. This conversation was delightfully distracting and she needed more distraction in her life.

"I'm looking for an apprentice," she called out.

They turned around. "And I take it you're offering me the position?"

"On a trial basis. Obviously."

They dipped their head to her. "Of course. What would this entail?"

"I teach you to forge and you assist me with the tasks I don't have time for myself."

"Tasks of what sort?"

"You ask too many questions," she snapped.

"I take it I would also help you with healing?"

"Perhaps. Only if there's time."

"Oh, there's always time to practice healing, Isolde."

There it was again. Her name.

"Meet me at dawn in the palace courtyard tomorrow," the seer said.

"You're assuming I don't have any other obligations," they said wryly.

"What I'm assuming is you don't have any opportunities quite like this one."

"Well," they paused for a moment, rocking back and forth on their heels considering the offer, "I suppose."

Chapter Thirteen

Isolde

22 Years After the Viridian Phoenix's Rebirth

Isolde avoided Lady Lornton's eyes, which flickered with panic and confusion. The woman pulled her translucent blue arm wrapping closer about her.

"Please, tell me. Whatever it is, I wish to know," she pleaded. Her voice carried, even in the crowded court abuzz with other conversations.

"I would rather not…" Isolde's voice trailed off at the feeling of her grandmother's nails biting into her arm. One gaze at the matron's stiff smile reminded her of the words that had been whispered to her just moments ago and the meal she would be deprived of if she spoke incorrectly.

"You know how I prefer to be delicate about these kinds of matters." She leaned forward conspiratorially, casually slipping her arm away from the woman's hold. "The Viridian Phoenix, in her great wisdom, believes you should hold onto that parcel of land just beyond the Nadir that you've been considering selling. It bodes well for your future and shall be quite prosperous soon."

Isolde could practically hear her grandmother's hissing rage, even as she reveled in the flood of relief washing over Lady Lornton's features.

"Thank you, wise one."

"You must excuse us," her grandmother said crisply, reclaiming control of Isolde's arm as she pulled her away while nodding goodbye to the lady.

Isolde knew better than to resist. Several pairs of eyes followed their path out of the stone chamber, her grandmother being sure to smile dotingly and laugh at something Isolde certainly hadn't said.

"That is weeks worth of work down the drain," the matron snapped, hauling the girl through a network of high passages until they emerged into the misty sunlight.

"I already told you that I am finished doing this for you," she said, raising her voice just slightly higher than a whisper just to see the spark of fear in her grandmother's stately face.

"Lower your voice. You know better."

"I have no more to say to you," Isolde declared.

"You certainly do. Your debt does not just disappear because you decide you do not wish to pay it."

Isolde didn't grant her an answer. Her grandmother could mistake her silence for compliance if she so desired, but that assumption would be wrong.

Isolde yanked her arm away once more. "I will be home later."

"Walking away from your problems? How typical, Isolde. This conversation is not over. Your grandfather won't be pleased after hearing about your choice."

The matron twisted her hands together, one of the tall woman's few nervous mannerisms.

"Much love, grandmother," Isolde replied bitterly, already turning away.

~

The tall entryway was empty and all was quiet when she got home, but she knew that could not possibly last. Isolde began ascending the stairs to make her way to her room when a voice called out from a doorway to her right.

"I hear Lady Lornton is quite happy with her land beyond that Nadir and plans to hold onto it for some time."

Isolde turned and descended the stone steps again until she was facing her grandfather. He stood a good deal taller than her. His square jaw was set and his eyes flashed with an expression of anger that was all too familiar as he stepped closer to her threateningly. Her grandmother stood behind him, her lips pulled into a tight line.

"Lady Lornton is happy, as she should be." He tapped his finger on the doorframe. "But you told a lie. If I remember correctly, her land was cursed and needed to be sold immediately to avoid tragedy."

"Ryth never told me that, but grandmother certainly did. Aren't you done playing this game?"

He took a step forward, his heavy boots making the wood floor creak. "Our lives are not a game."

"You're right. The game is over because I am not playing anymore."

"Forget this foolishness, Isolde. You owe us at least this much."

She raised her chin. "For what."

"Don't make me say it." He looked pained.

She smiled. "It sounds so callous you cannot even speak the words."

"It is not callous, but it shouldn't need to be said, child. We took you in when your parents died. We cared for you and fed you and made sure you had every opportunity your parents would have provided. Your grandmother and I, we fulfilled our familial duty. Now you must fulfill yours."

"Must I?"

"Don't dig in your heels. It isn't becoming of someone of your status."

She laughed. "If you respected and believed in the sanctity of my connection, then you never would have dared to use the situation to your advantage. But you think you've created my influence at court with your tricks. You're gravely mistaken."

"You may be Bonded to that creature, but it has granted you no special abilities. We're not in any danger."

"You've simply capitalized on the legends of what would happen if the Viridian Phoenix ever returned?

"Exactly," he replied smugly.

"So arrogant." Isolde lowered her voice, forcing him to lean in to hear her. "I *can* see your future, grandfather. And you should be terrified."

She turned on her heel and ascended the steps, refusing to look back even as he shouted after her.

Chapter Fourteen

Isolde

23 Years After the Viridian Phoenix's Rebirth

Tristan squinted through the leaves of the tree spreading above them in the palace gardens. "I have to say, I didn't expect to be spending all day out here," they said.

Isolde looked up at them blankly from the book she was combing through.

Tristan sighed, pulling a needle through the hem of a brightly-colored piece of clothing they'd brought with them from home.

"I don't see the problem. Looks like you brought something to thoroughly occupy your time."

"But shouldn't we be exchanging information about forging and healing? Or at least be spending time at court? I'm frankly surprised you're not right in the middle of the action, Isolde."

"I'm not just reading. Anyway, all in good time, Tristan." She rewarded them for using her name by using theirs.

Tristan sighed, boredom written across their features, "Until then, I guess I'll just try to master the art of sewing."

"Seems like you've got that down on your own. Much better than I do anyway."

She was right, of course. Their fingers darted through the fabric expertly.

"What are you reading, then?"

"That's my business."

They bowed their head graciously and kept at their work as the sun rose higher overhead. Later, when she took them inside the palace and up to her chambers, they didn't seem much impressed. They watched the people passing with curiosity and stared at the high arched windows with gentle admiration, but never awe. Isolde saw this and smiled. She wondered if they were capable of feeling out of place.

Tristan was soft and unique in their own way—unusual in so many lights—and she couldn't see them fitting into the courtly mob or the lively merchants stalls at Fishfirst. Yet, at the same time, she thought they were alright with that. She got the impression they knew this about themself and it didn't bother them. Isolde quickened her pace and tried to refocus on something other than her new apprentice. How much could she truly teach them? They were the same age after all. But she did know she wanted to learn healing, and she was sure she could dig up tasks for them to do. One quickly learned that, in the palace, having a messenger you could trust tended to be useful.

Pulling open the door, she granted them entry to her room in all of its stark splendor. It was a simple chamber. Nothing hung on the walls. An understated blue carpet sat on the floor before the fireplace, but that was it. She liked it this way though. It reminded her that all things are temporary. That it could be gone in a moment. Better to be reminded of that than to let change sneak up on her because she got too comfortable. Maybe she could decorate once every province had pledged their loyalty to the queen.

Tristan leaned their head against the doorframe as they waited for her to say something. Instead, she started digging around in the single trunk at the end of the bed. Once she'd found what she was looking for, she placed it in their hands.

They took it carefully, running their finger over the blue and gold binding. "This is lovely."

Something in Isolde ached. She'd bought it the first time she'd stolen money from her grandparents. Two days without food had been her punishment.

"Now don't take too much time reading it and don't read it too carefully."

"What in the world are you talking about?"

"You're my apprentice, and I'm teaching you. Don't read it too carefully, like I said. It will diminish your power if you learn too much from the book rather than doing it yourself. Even so, there are some basic tenets that are useful for all alchemir skills."

"Thank you," they said.

Isolde just turned away. "I'll be back in a little while." With that, she headed down the hall and left them standing in her room, the book in their hands.

On her way to Turia's chambers, a messenger stopped her in the hallway and whispered something. Her face remained neutral, but her pace quickened.

Isolde knocked on the queen's door and then entered. Turia knelt on the ground beside a luscious plant, tending to its fronds.

"What can I do for you, Seer?" she asked.

"Your council is meeting within the hour, my queen. You need to be there to lead it."

"Why? I'm sure they're perfectly fine on their own." Turia's neck jerked to the side and she grimaced.

Isolde took another step toward her and waited in silence for her to look up. Finally, biting her lip, Turia stopped fussing over the plant and made eye contact.

"What's the matter?"

"There's news of a skirmish with the Griffin Guard in an outlying province."

"That's not all that uncommon. Tensions are always high on the border," Turia replied.

"True, but they're saying the skirmish left twelve dead and the Griffin Guard have pushed their perimeter past the outskirts where they are usually stationed and closer to the town."

Turia closed her eyes and sighed, rising. "You're sure the council can't handle this on their own?" she asked quietly, hopefully.

Isolde carefully placed her hand on Turia's shoulder, somehow surprised by the warmth emanating through the thin fabric of the queen's dress. Breathing seemed somehow harder when they were standing so close to one another. "No. They need to see you present and engaged. I can't overstate your importance, my queen."

What Isolde didn't say was that she feared threats from within the palace perhaps even more than the occasional border fight with the Griffin Guard.

The seer waited outside the queen's chambers while she prepared herself to be seen by the council. When she emerged, Isolde noticed how much she appreciated a fine piece of jewelry. A necklace of sapphires, that reminded the seer of Ryth, graced her neck. While Turia's style wasn't gaudy, it was somewhat extravagant, but all the better that when the queen did happen to be seen in public, she looked the part.

Isolde noted the fact that even the jewelry couldn't outshine the soft beauty of the queen's endless green eyes, framed by dark, delicate lashes. She breathed in the queen's typical scent, a mixture of warm honey and floral lavender. The gentle curve of her glossed lips drew Isolde's gaze, not for the first time. The seer swallowed, looking away from the queen at the blasphemous thought, eager to banish it from her mind.

They didn't speak as they moved down the corridor together, the queen in a shimmering layered skirt wearing her diadem and the seer wearing her simple dress with the sleeves pushed up. Let the focus be on the queen.

Isolde tried to figure out what was going on in the other woman's head, but it escaped her as the queen's face gave away nothing. Again, all for the better. The members of the High Queen's Council stood up from the round oak table in the middle of the room as she entered. They swept into bows, but she seemed far removed from the scene as she took her seat. Isolde remained standing to the right of the queen's chair. It was the first time the queen had appeared in public in weeks. The glances briefly exchanged between several council members didn't escape the seer's notice. They clearly hadn't been expecting the queen, which made her bristle.

The Minister of Correspondence read out the message from the soldiers stationed at the border recounting the incident and the casualties. Isolde couldn't even tell if Turia was listening to Lady Cador, but she did catch the fact that the queen's leg hadn't stopped bouncing beneath the table since the start of the meeting. Once they were finished, the table fell silent, everyone waiting uncomfortably for the young queen to say the first word.

"Have they taken any action other than moving their camp closer to the border? Have any extra soldiers amassed?" she finally asked in a quiet voice. Isolde wanted to tell her to speak up, but she bit her tongue. Some things the queen would have to learn on her own.

Sir Kaye, Minister of the Ranks, piped up. "Not yet, your majesty, though our soldiers are watching carefully. They'll report back at the first sign of any kind of additional movement. But it is worth noting there will be at least a three day delay between when that happens and when we hear about it here." His tone was somewhat condescending as he rattled on, explaining the logistics of conveying messages from the outskirts to Viridian itself. Isolde bit her tongue.

After he'd finished up his long-winded speech, Turia turned her eyes away from him, only saying, "Yes, I am quite aware of how travel and time work. Now, does anyone else have initial thoughts on intention. Do we know what sparked the fight?"

Isolde bit back her smile. The queen had surprised her once more. Her satisfaction at Turia's curt words faded though when she saw the offense boiling in the knight's eyes. That didn't bode well.

"We're not sure what caused it. I think the biggest question is our response," said Sir Gahera.

"Gahera, you're forgetting that intention is equally as important. Treating the symptoms only does so much if you don't know the root of the ailment. In fact, you risk prescribing the wrong treatment and making it worse," Sir Aeryt argued back, trying to make her fiery sister see reason. The two knights always approached matters from such different angles.

"Yes but not taking action can also make things worse."

"Perhaps one thing at a time," Turia interjected. "If not about this specific incident, do we have any other intelligence on the Griffin King's movements beyond our borders? Is he healthy?" she paused at that thought, then shook herself free. For a moment before she continued, it looked like she was fighting to not say something. "Is he being aggressive toward any other provinces? Is the … the plague I heard about consuming their resources?"

Most members of the council averted their eyes. Something about the topic felt uncomfortable since, so far at least, the Fire Folk had possessed the good fortune to not be affected by the Sleeping Illness. And, the few cases there had been within the borders had not proven…lasting. Humans and Bonded alike seemed able to avoid the brutal fever that eventually caused an eternal sleep during which the victim kept breathing, but never became conscious again. Only those Bonded to Griffins in Valsan were truly affected. The priestesses said it was the blessing of the

Salamanders. The commoners said it was the strength provided by the air of the sea and the plains. Isolde thought it was pure luck.

The Minister of the March responded to the queen's inquiry. Sir Bedivere was a man solidly along in years, but who still maintained some of the charm and handsomeness of his youth. Everyone knew he was on his second life as one Bonded with a phoenix, which afforded him some extra wisdom, at least according to public opinion. "Our scouts report that they've turned large cities into quarantine zones, but the spread of the Burning Illness has barely been slowed. More are dying every day and they say the royal court has been increasingly desperate, turning to false witches who promise relief and falling for unproven cures they are paying great sums to administer to their nobles. The king and his entourage are currently cloistered away in their mountain palace, my queen."

His voice held the respect Turia needed and Isolde silently thanked him. Several council members would surely follow his lead. "In my opinion though, the first skirmish was the result of some unfortunate personal disagreement rather than some kind of premeditated action and the camp has been moved as a response to it by the Griffin King."

"You don't believe it's part of some greater plan? Perhaps because of the ashes?" she asked him.

No one wanted to say it. Viridian had the key to the illness, in theory, of course. The ashes of phoenixes already born twice could be used for healing purposes, but they were only brought out in the most desperate of cases, not to mention they were limited in quantity and sacred to the Salamanders. Temples throughout the

Fire Folk provinces held the phoenix ashes, both from phoenixes waiting to be reborn and those who would not be born again. The Great Temple of Viridian, however, remained the largest site of ash preservation.

"That could always be a reason, of course. As you know, the enmity between us and Valsan runs deep and the blood of the past is not easily forgotten. That being said, it does seem to be an isolated incident, your majesty. I don't think the king will take any further action unless we give him reason to do so. He's likely fearing that we will make some kind of aggressive move ourselves."

"What does our intelligence network look like right now?"

Bedivere replied detailing surveillance along the border and the one inside source they had at the Griffin King's court.

"Do we know that our source within the court hasn't been compromised?" Turia asked, her eyes sharp. She was clearly still wondering if the information about the state of Valsan was accurate. Valsan and Viridian didn't even host each other's diplomats. Very little trade existed between them except through a single, heavily-soldiered outpost rife with tension and through illegal exchanges, mostly of stolen ashes.

"We last saw her only a week ago and she seemed to be in perfect health. Nothing seemed unusual," Kaye said.

Turia nodded, but Isolde could sense her anxiety.

"We need to strengthen our intelligence network in Valsan and move some of our troops closer to the border."

"That could prompt the king to make another move. We don't want to accidentally start a game of chess, my queen," said Bedivere.

"Well, the alternative is to do nothing, correct? That feels just as dangerous," the queen muttered under her breath. For a moment, Isolde worried that Turia's discomfort would become obvious, but the queen rallied and spoke again, louder this time. "It seems unwise to do nothing. There's also a chance that he's testing our responses and capabilities, especially since he knows a new queen sits on the throne. He asked a question and we must answer it. We are strong. We see him. We will not sit passively while he moves his pieces on the board."

Turia turned to Isolde. "Do you see any hint of what this decision will bring, Seer?"

"I see nothing one way or the other."

Turning back to the table, Turia asked, "Are there any objections?"

No one spoke. Bedivere tipped his head to her in deference. After several more minutes of discussing the details with the royal council, Turia rose and swept from the room as the council members stood.

Chapter Thirteen

Robin

9 Years After the Viridian Phoenix's Rebirth

The high priestess sat before the gaggle of young children, most of them girls destined for the priesthood. One child scratched at the elaborately swirled blue patterns on the tiles of the floor of the Great Temple in Viridian.

With her mop of brown hair and defiant green eyes, she looked something like a street urchin. She was paying no attention to one of the Tales being read from a crusty-looking scroll by the withering old woman.

"In the beginning, there was only sea and shadowed chaos. Waves turned and clawed at one another unable to find the surface because there was none. The Creator loved her work. She was content with letting the chaos take its course, with letting the currents flow as they would, but soon she found something lacking in her world. The Creator grew tired of the endless noise without a companion to love and mock it with her.

From the waves she crafted the first living being of this realm, but the being felt like it was drowning amongst the waves. This creature despised the water and its soul was simply too bright to exist there for long. So, the Creator, out of love for her new

106

companion, gathered the waves and scattered a new substance over their face called air.

The first bird delighted in this new substance. Once it emerged from the water, it took flight. Its soul burned away the water, and flames erupted from its wings in a burst of life and hope. The sea left only the color of the creature's fire as a marker of its birthplace.

The Creator discussed all manner of things with the first phoenix through those timeless, open days. They challenged each other to a race of creation. What wondrous things they discovered and built, endlessly delighting each other as the friendship between the two immortals grew. Together, they pulled the world into existence."

The girl started muttering something to the child next to her, a prim and proper girl with hands clasped neatly in her lap. The other child didn't respond, causing Robin to roll her eyes. The muttering, unfortunately, had captured the attention of the head priestess.

"Do I hear something?" she asked pointedly.

"Surely, no one would dare interrupt you," Robin said, earning her a smack from one of the lower priestesses standing a few feet away.

"We will have silence as you learn 'The Sacred Tales.' They are crucial for your confirmation into the priesthood. We will now turn to repetition."

The children rose to their feet, chanting the text as one. The only one whose mouth didn't move was the stubborn Robin. Long ago, she'd begun rebelling, at first hoping she would be sent home. When she finally accepted that there was no home to return to, she continued to play out act after act of defiance to the consternation of the priestesses raising her. Her parents, just like all others, had bargained with her. They had signed away her life to the priesthood when she was only five for the honor of that post and, of course, for the generous stipend that would help support them for the rest of their lives. Robin wouldn't see a coin of that money.

The priestess led the monotonous chant.

"Let us always be ruled by an Unbonded high ruler uniting the lords and princes of Morya. They rule to temper the pride of the phoenixes and their Bonded Fire Folk. Let all things be weighed and tempered."

"Let all things be weighed and tempered," the children called back.

"As it has been since the beginning, children of the Bonded are Bonded too. When this happens, a new phoenix bursts into creation, in a beautiful array of golden flame. Let the Bonded always be impervious to the flames of their phoenixes alone. Let the other flames sear them as is proper. Let their life forces be bound to each other to the end. If one dies, so the other dies. Let all things be weighed and tempered."

"Let all things be weighed and tempered," the children chanted.

"Let the ashes of phoenixes who have lived once be protected by our priesthood. Their souls hover in the Blue Veil in sacred slumber, until they awake once more and re-enter physical forms in the realm. Let all phoenixes be reborn to Unbonded parents as a gift. Let not their healing ashes be scattered to the winds. Let the Salamanders lead us in their continual fire. Let all things be weighed and tempered."

"Let all things be weighed and tempered," the children echoed.

Except for one who sent a different prayer to those she didn't believe existed. She thought of the princess as she said it.

"Let me be free and never tempered."

Chapter Fifteen

Isolde

23 Years After the Viridian Phoenix's Rebirth

I solde had to hurry to keep up with Turia's quick stride as she rushed back toward her room from the council meeting. Her head kept turning to the side as she walked, then her hand shot out in front of her repeatedly.

"You did well," Isolde stated.

Turia didn't respond.

"I have a suggestion."

"I have the feeling you'll make it whether or not I ask you to do so," said Turia.

"You're already dressed and prepared for court. It would be good for the other courtiers to see you alive and well."

"Is that what I am?"

"Truly. They need to see you. Even if it's only for a little while."

"I don't see the point."

Isolde took a deep breath to stop herself from saying something she'd regret. "Please, your majesty. There are still a handful of Fire Folk provinces who haven't yet formally pledged allegiance to you. I sent them all letters declaring your coronation but that only prompted action from a few. You're not understanding the dangerous balance you're striking by ruling without the full backing of the provinces."

They reached the queen's chambers, and Turia quickly shut the door behind them. "Why does everyone think I don't understand?" Turia whispered, staring Isolde down, pain in the creases of her wrinkled brow. "You think I don't know that at any time one of the lords or ladies could decide that they are a better candidate for the throne than I am? Well, I agree with them!"

"You don't mean that, my queen! You were the one who came to me, if you'll remember. You know how dangerous it is for the throne to be in contention."

"I regret that conversation, Seer. Who was I to think it was any of my business. Let the pieces fall where they may," Turia whispered fiercely, kneeling down by a small tree and running her fingers over the bark. It took Isolde a moment to realize that she'd turned away to try and hide the tears running down her face.

"Because you have the knowledge to make the decisions that need to be made. You learned from your father and you have a heart full of compassion, which every great ruler needs."

Turia glanced at her, her eyes bleak. "You have a lot to learn about history, Seer."

Isolde blinked. That stung somehow. History was what everyone expected her to know. She allegedly held the wisdom of the Creator and the weight of those memories after all. Turia was right though, she'd been glossing over the truth of history. Most of Viridian's most legendary kings and queens were brutal figures with very little room in their lives for words such as love or compassion.

"History is made to be reforged for the better. You care for your subjects and I think you'll find that, if you're talking about history, the longest reigning monarchs were in possession of the hearts of their people."

"Again, not always true," Turia said, shaking her head.

"Look at me. Very few things are always true. There are different ways to rule and I do believe that the less bloodshed the better. Surely, you can't argue with me about that."

"I can argue with you about anything, Seer," she replied with a subtle smile.

"So...what? You're just going to give up your throne and abandon it to some stranger after everything you've just gone through?"

"Perhaps because of everything I've just gone through. You want me to have so much compassion myself. Can't you find some of it in your own heart?"

"You'll end up dead, your majesty."

The queen froze.

"That's the truth. It's the reality of the situation. They'll kill you."

"You think I don't know my father was poisoned?" asked Turia.

Discomfort settled in Isolde's stomach. "Poisoned?" She had certainly suspected the role of foul play in the king's untimely demise, but hadn't been able to get much information from Turia, given the topic's sensitive nature.

"Surprised you didn't figure that out. I already have enemies at court and no way to know who they are. I could show up dead any day now. Maybe you should just let me die."

"Nonsense. Don't talk like that," Isolde said.

Turia remained silent, closing her eyes as her fingers fluttered over the leaves of the tree.

"If you die, who will take care of your plants?"

Turia didn't meet her eyes, but granted her a miserable smile.

"Oh, I'm sure any old fool would be able to water my marigolds and roses and ferns. Now my orchids might be a tad tricker. Maybe they do need me, after all. The palace gardener still can't figure out how I managed to grow the gardenias indoors."

The queen smiled at some private joke for a moment. Her head jerked suddenly and she sighed with frustration.

"How is your ailment?" Isolde asked.

Turia sat back on her heels, finally meeting the seer's eyes. "I would preside over court, but I...can't control myself today. Better that they not see their queen at all than to see her when she can't even manage her own movements."

"But people know that's something that happens to you. If anything, we can call it a sign that you're blessed. You've already been chosen by the Soulless and your authority accepted by your subjects."

"Blessed? I feel anything but blessed."

Isolde tugged at Turia's sleeve. "Just for an hour."

Turia got to her feet and, after taking a moment to steel herself, floated out the door with Isolde following her steps. The seer savored the success.

The mood shifted when the queen entered the room. People stopped milling about, and the musicians quickly transitioned from their former song to "The High's Queen's March." Arturia didn't make eye contact with anyone, instead heading straight for the throne and sinking gracefully into its hold. Her arms were tense beneath the opaque scarf which wove around them.

Within moments the whole room had sunk to a bow and the chatter had ceased. They waited for her, and Turia waited for something else. Finally, she rose and nodded her head toward them, acknowledging their respect and giving them permission to return to their business. In a low voice, she sang along to "The High Queen's March." Tradition dictated that the monarch sing along. If they didn't, it was said they would grow ill.

No one tried to speak to her, but Gahera looked like she wanted to try. Her eyes were full of curiosity and verve. Their brilliance against her liberally-freckled white face was hard to miss, even in the crowded room. It didn't hurt that the knight stood a few inches taller than nearly everyone else. She started to head for the queen, but her sister Aeryt—smaller in stature but not in ferocity—redirected her by the arm.

Perhaps, no, very probably, the lords and ladies weren't sure what to make of their queen or how to approach her.

Presiding over the throne turned out to be a terribly dull matter, especially in the waning heat of the afternoon when so many nobles were beginning to drift off to sleep. Isolde stood by the throne, refusing to take a seat and leave Turia. Since no one knew how to speak to the queen, Isolde did. They spoke in grave, hushed tones about the horrific brightness of Lord Ingold's tunic, which Turia seemed to think was rather fetching. Thankfully, the monotony was sharply interrupted by the rough opening of a door and a merry shout.

Isolde soon spotted the offender, a woman in hacked up priestess' garb charging right for the queen. She, at least, didn't seem shy. The woman made headway fast, turning the head of every person she passed, perhaps because it was not customary to run through the throne room. Isolde threw herself in front of the throne before this wild thing could reach the queen. The woman shot her an amused smirk as she came to a stop, waiting patiently for…something, hands clasped behind her back like a child. The lords and ladies took in her bedraggled state with thinly veiled shock and fear. But the woman's unabashed smile was a far cry from one of spite or malice, even if it was untenably mischievous.

"Robin!" Turia cried, darting around Isolde to throw her arms around the girl and ruffle her fine, short black hair. Isolde watched closely, an unexplainable pang rising in her as Turia brushed her thumb over this woman's fair hand in a manner that spoke of deep, abiding affection.

Isolde finally pulled herself together, clearing her throat as she stepped closer. Robin looked up, appraising her stiff countenance and dismissing the seer within the space of a breath.

"And who is this special guest who parades right into the throne room in such…interesting attire," Isolde asked carefully, politely even.

"Well…take a guess from my outfit," Robin said cheerfully.

Isolde stared at her and blinked. "I figured it was a costume."

"Unfortunately not. Oh, if only the girls back home could see me now. Would have made them even more heartsick than they already were." Then she had the audacity to wink. In that moment, Isolde hoped that the newly elevated high priestess would be sent back to whatever soulforsaken place she had come from.

"And you? The fabled seer, I take it?"

Isolde only bowed her head in acquiescence. Turia's eyes shifted between the two of them uneasily, but her smile soon recovered. The seer realized it was the first genuine smile she'd seen from the queen in quite some time.

Robin turned back to Turia and they talked as Turia sank back onto her throne. Robin regaled her with harrowing tales of the journey from the isolated temple she'd been stationed at and crude jokes, of which she had a seemingly endless supply. Isolde stood back, observing, trying to parse out the mystery of this woman who would be serving as the high priestess but flaunted her defiance by sewing her priestesses' garb into a pair of pants. They weren't even hemmed properly. The stitching was uneven and haphazard, much like the woman who'd likely done the job. Isolde looked away when Robin brushed a strand of hair out of Turia's face.

They only stayed for a few hours, but it was enough to assuage Isolde's worry at least a bit. Turia rose and took her leave, returning to her chambers alone. Normally, Isolde would have accompanied her, but eyeing the new high priestess as Turia embraced her, she realized that another matter needed her attention.

At least she'd convinced the queen to leave her chambers. If she'd done it once she could do it again and it was the first step to stabilizing the throne and Turia's claim to it. Which the queen didn't even seem to want. She quickened her stride to outpace the thought as she made her way to Robin who was schmoozing with a very pretty lady.

Turia might not care about dying, but Isolde did and, at this point, their fates were intertwined. She could, of course, always run away, but she felt an obligation to finish what she started. No need to throw away her reputation and power. She was free. That was all that mattered. Someday, she would forge her own path far away from this cursed city, but for now, agency was enough.

Isolde pictured the queen once more, perched on the throne, mouth pursed with some laugh she wouldn't let out. Robin was conveniently not there. But she was now in front of the seer. Isolde inserted herself into the conversation, interrupting some conspiratorial joke that had just sent the young woman into a fit of laughter.

"Excuse me. I'm afraid the high priestess and I have some pressing business, so I will have to steal her away for the moment."

Robin looked mildly disgruntled, but acquiesced to Isolde's hand guiding her arm away. She nodded to the young woman, then turned her attention fully to the seer.

"I assume there's no pressing business? You seem determined to ruin my fun, Seer."

"Quite the contrary. Take a walk with me in the gardens."

"Do I have a choice?"

"No."

"Fascinating."

Isolde ignored the comment. They walked in silence until they were outside and sunny warmth cascaded over their shoulders as the shadows of clouds darted over the hydrangeas.

"You certainly made an entrance today. Can we expect you to make the same kind of mockery out of your duties as high priestess?"

"Is that what this is about?" Robin asked flippantly.

"Did you think that kind of display wouldn't be addressed?"

Robin stopped and turned to face her. "Listen, Seer. Listen carefully. You aren't the first one to try to manage me and you won't be the last, but I chart my own course. Always have, always will. Surely that's something you can respect as one with such a unique…gift."

"What about your responsibility to the Soulless?"

"I'm not sure the Soulless even exist, but for Turia I will hold this office and do so as I see fit. Unless she comes to me herself and requests that I do things differently, I will act as I need to for everyone's sake."

Isolde's mind ran through calculation after calculation, trying to make sense of this woman, who had been trained as a priestess since she was a young child but didn't seem to care for that honor. She stepped closer and softened her tone.

"Regardless of your belief in or respect for such things, your recklessness could directly put Turia in danger. That's what I'm concerned about, not some superficial worry over a display of impiety. Not all here are on her side and she needs all the help she can to appear legitimate."

Robin crossed her arms. "If you do indeed have the gift of foresight, you should be able to see that that kind of thing won't work on me. I am on Turia's side, but that means doing what I see fit, not what you see fit. I've fought too hard to be my own compass and make my own decisions for someone to try to wheedle that treasure away from me." Robin considered Isolde. "I think that, perhaps, no one has checked you in a very long time, Seer. You should know those days are over."

"Are you threatening me?" Isolde asked, taken aback by the priestess' lack of timidity.

Robin smiled. "What do you think?"

~

The priestess wouldn't be an easy nut to crack as a spitfire with influence, and one who didn't believe in the thing that gave Isolde her power at that. Robin was a variable Isolde couldn't control. Isolde tiredly opened her heavy door, grateful for the prospect of rest only to stop dead in her tracks when she realized a young person lay sprawled on her rug in front of the fire. They rested on their back, the book held above them.

"You're still here?" she asked. She glanced out the window as the last of the orange sunset faded away into twilight.

"Did you not want me to be here?" they asked timidly, blowing a lock of hair out of their face as they sat up. Her eyes fell on the book again.

"Don't tell me you've been reading it this whole time!" she exclaimed, storming over and snatching it up off the ground.

"Not exactly." They nodded over to her bed, where a few of her dresses were laid out. Taking a closer look she realized they'd been... changed. A bit of lace here or an embroidered moon there. She ran her fingers over the work and then looked back at them, tilting her head. She didn't quite know what to say.

Tristan shrugged, standing up and pulling their sleeves over their hands. "My eyes needed a break and I saw the thread on your desk. Also, I ate some biscuits a maid brought up for you. Sorry about that."

They didn't sound sorry.

"Why didn't you leave?"

They raised their eyebrows. "Did you ask me to leave?"

Isolde didn't know how to respond. She had rather expected them to take the book and return to whatever place they called home. She just kept staring at Tristan, trying to understand why this person had stayed in her chambers embellishing her dresses and reading her book. Curious.

"How'd you know I'd like your additions to my clothes? Isn't that a bit of a risk?"

Their mouth curved up into a pleased expression as they looked at the floor. "So you do like them? This is what I do for my friends. You seem like a moon and lace kind of girl to me."

"Do I? Well, whatever the case, I believe it's time for you to go and get some rest."

Friend. Had anyone ever called her that before? A curious warmth prickled in Isolde's chest.

Tristan looped their leather bag over their shoulder and nodded their head toward her. "See you tomorrow, then?"

Isolde stood by her bed long after they left, running her fingers over the embroidery and marveling at it in the candlelight.

Chapter Sixteen

Isolde

22 Years After the Viridian Phoenix's Rebirth

“Oh, Lady Roshil, if you have a moment…” Isolde touched the woman's shoulder lightly, prompting her to turn around.

The woman pulled her arm wrap closer around her nervously, despite the fact that the throne room was warm from the afternoon sunlight streaming through the windows. Although the court was in session, there were only a few people strewn about the room, which proved to be a welcome relief for the ever-popular seer. She hated court with all her being. From the flowing finery to the presses of people, all with their own desires, it made her nauseous. Everything about it seemed superficial.

Isolde, however, was also well-aware of the fact that without court and the support of the high king, she had little power. Nothing like a real seer might have. It wasn't the first time that thought had occurred to her. It always brought with it a stifled rage aimed at her phoenix companion.

“You wanted to say something?” the woman prompted.

“My apologies. I was having a vision,” she said. It was a convenient excuse whenever she got distracted.

Lady Roshil lowered her eyes to the ground and murmured a thanksgiving to the Salamanders.

"What was I saying? Oh, yes. I wanted to tell you that I had a vision concerning your future."

Lady Roshil's hand fluttered nervously through her hair as she waited for Isolde's next words. She was a delicate lady of twenty-five given to fainting spells. Everything about her was refined. Even her hair, fastened in an updo rather than down, indicated a certain level of sophistication.

"You should expect good things. I believe the magnanimity of your title will soon be elevated, though I'm sorry to say I didn't see exactly how."

"Truly? Thank you, Seer. I am most grateful for you," Lady Roshil said, breathing a sigh of relief.

Isolde put her head in her hand and squeezed her eyes shut. "What? I don't understand."

Lady Roshil stood frozen, staring at her wide-eyed.

"Treason...someone close? It can't be," she murmured. She caught sight of a very anxious Lady Roshil and her expression transitioned to a smile once more. "Forgive me. These visions come at the most inconvenient of times."

After a gracious nod from Isolde, the lady hurried off to relate her good fortune to her friends. Crossing to the wall behind a column where no one could see her, Isolde leaned back and let her false smile fall for a moment. She ran her fingers over the rough surface of the stone blocks before leaning her head against them wearily. Last night she'd overheard Lord Trenson laying out his detailed plans for proposing to Lady Roshil. Most of her so-called predictions were simply based on relatively reliable gossip. His landholdings were much larger than those of Lady Roshil's father, so when she became Lady Trenson her status would be elevated. Most were much too coy to discuss status in such blunt terms, but Isolde took advantage of every boon that came with this curse. Not following all the ridiculous social protocol suited her. She dreamed of leaving this soulforsaken city behind. Perhaps someday that dream would drift into reality. She closed her eyes, the cool stone on her forehead soothing her nerves.

At least her grandparents didn't track her movements as closely as they had years prior during her introduction to the court. They had settled into their wealthy lifestyles quite easily. Her grandmother still dictated nearly all of her predictions and attended every large event with her, but on afternoons like this, she was free to do as she wished.

They had long ago threatened to discredit her if she ever dared go against them. Even they knew they couldn't lock her in her room forever. So, that left only one option if she was to keep the promise she had made to herself all those years ago. She had to discredit and humiliate them before they had the chance to do so to her. Isolde feared that, if given the chance, they would go further than even that and get rid of her entirely. Now that they were secure in their titles and well-established in the noble circles, what did they need her for? She possessed a good deal more knowledge about the crooked deals they'd made, both before and after their rise to court, than they would prefer.

Isolde saw the cruel glances her grandmother threw her way and the looks then shared with her grandfather. She was rather surprised she wasn't dead already. On days like this, she did what she could to lay the foundation for the day she freed herself of them, which she was becoming increasingly convinced needed to be as soon as possible. Lady Roshil would talk of Isolde's strange vision and mumblings about treason, then others would confirm what she was saying with accounts of their own.

Isolde decided that she had had enough politics for one day. She emerged from behind the pillar and strode directly toward the door, hoping not to be stopped by any well-wishers or people asking for predictions.

Chapter Seventeen
Isolde

23 Years After the Viridian Phoenix's Rebirth

"What in the world are you doing?" Isolde asked. Tristan turned back to her, almost dropping the heavy poker they'd been holding in the fire for the last few moments.

"I was going to stoke the fire, but then I got distracted by the flames, and then I was curious what would happen if I just left the poker in the fire. You know, I know next to nothing about forging, but I guess that's why I'm here. I do have a cousin who is an apprentice to a blacksmith, but from what she's told me..."

She shook her head, seizing the poker and using it herself. It was a bright day outside the blacksmith's shop. Almost too bright. Isolde often preferred the nighttime. It allowed her to sink into the Otherrealm more easily.

Isolde went about explaining the basics of the forging process to Tristan, who listened carefully, but was clearly rather confused. She made herself slow down, showing them one part at a time. She didn't mind slowing down so much though. It meant she got to revel in the joy of hammering out the metal.

"How long have you been doing this?" they asked.

"A few years," she replied.

"Why did you choose it?"

"I think it chose me, honestly."

"How?" they asked.

She paused, biting her lip. How could she explain? What did she want to explain? She observed their open posture and the gentleness in their eyes, but something in her just couldn't admit why. Maybe she didn't even know herself.

"Perhaps that's something you'll eventually discover," she answered wryly.

"I see."

"Back to business, apprentice. I think you'll lose respect if you learn too much about me."

"Oh, I doubt that," they replied.

"You'd be surprised."

"Now I *could* see being surprised. I am caught off guard much too often I'm afraid."

"Good thing you're not the one handling these weapons then," Isolde said, a smile creeping onto her lips as she turned away, lovingly testing the weight of a sword she'd recently managed to make.

"Probably so. Maybe you could teach me though?"

"Teach you what?"

"Sword fighting."

She raised an eyebrow at them. "Why would you want to learn that? Besides, who says I know much about sword fighting myself. As much as I'd love to claim expertise in every subject under the sun, that's simply not possible."

"Come on. The way you look at the swords hanging on the palace walls. The way you were holding that sword just now. I mean, you're usually wearing one. Your actions speak of familiarity with weapons."

"My next lesson. Familiarity doesn't equal skill."

"But certainly it denotes more skill than I have in that area."

"Probably," she admitted. "For now, let's just work on forging. I don't have all the time in the world, you know," she finished crossly.

Tristan didn't know what they were asking. She only ever practiced in front of Ryth. Like everything else in her life, she'd learned on her own and her style was somewhat unorthodox. She didn't know what it was like to face a real foe. Those whose faith supported her didn't need to see her actively wielding a sword. She feared what might happen if they saw the unmitigated anger in the eyes of their sacred seer. So she wore her sword around the palace but never drew it.

Part of her mystique was in her carefully cultivated detachment. That part of herself wasn't too difficult to maintain since most people didn't try to peek past it. Perhaps her anger would have a place in her world someday. For now she kept it caged, only letting it escape in harmless ways or in small, calculated actions.

Isolde eyed the fire. "Are you ready to try forging something?"

"I don't think I really understand..."

"Try anyway," she interrupted. "You're not going to know what you need to work on until you make a few mistakes."

"I'll take your word for it, Isolde."

"As you should," she replied. "Remember what I said. It's different from healing. You have to go toward pain rather than away from it. You're tapping into metal and sinew and the things that twist them together."

"Sounds somewhat sinister when you put it like that."

That irritated her. "Just do it," she snapped. "I will also."

With the materials ready, she reached out beyond herself. She could no longer feel her pulse, but she knew her heart beat somewhere far away. No need to reach for it now though. The Blue felt particularly cold and empty, so she breathed in the stars and called to the metal, letting it melt over her soul. It took a few moments, but eventually she became aware of another presence beside her. Tristan had managed to find their way, then. She couldn't see them because sight wasn't an accurate way to describe anything happening in the Otherrealm. Rather she sensed the vines stretching around their ankles and the feathers crowning their head.

Tristan was too full of life. Their pulse polluted the space, distracting her from the metal and the heat. She tried to separate herself from her frustration before it pulled her back to her world. Instead, she turned away from their soul, bursting with all things wild and growing. She plunged herself into silver, wrapping herself in its embrace. Isolde pulled the stars down to meet her. They couldn't refuse her call. Their hearts seared her heart beyond recognition until she was no longer the seer, she was no longer Isolde, and she was no longer a liar.

She didn't notice Tristan's presence had disappeared until she had finished shaping the broad weapon in her hand. After pouring herself into the black hilt, Isolde cut herself from the

Otherrealm. When the world came back into focus around her, she held the sword. A thrill ran through her. Ever since the night she'd created Caliburnus, the skill came easier to her. This one would be her own. Tristan was right. She had started carrying a sword since moving into the palace, but it was a clunky thing borrowed from the storehouse of the Phoenix Guard. This one was lighter and more elegant. She had a feeling it would serve her well.

A sound startled her, causing her to look up. Tristan stood staring at her, the confusion in their eyes amusing and the caution, also therein, angering. Their gaze was too pointed.

"Why are you looking at me like that?" she demanded.

"I'm just pleasantly surprised," they said, their features falling into an easy smile.

She snorted. "By what?" Isolde allowed her mouth to tilt upward also, but her eyes remained keen. She didn't know what to make of Tristan. "How did it go for you?" she asked.

They grimaced, an embarrassed flush crawling over their cheeks. They cleared their throat. "I wasn't able to stay there for very long. It was difficult to sense the heat, and I think you might have been taking all of it?"

Isolde rolled her eyes. "It's an inexhaustible resource. If you couldn't tap into it, it means you're approaching it the wrong way."

"Or maybe you're just too bright and I got distracted," they muttered under their breath.

"That's really not a good excuse," Isolde refuted.

Tristan looked startled. Maybe they hadn't meant for her to hear them. They looked up toward the ceiling, muttering something under their breath that she couldn't make out.

Chapter Eighteen

Isolde

23 Years After the Viridian Phoenix's Rebirth

The worst thing about living in the palace, in Isolde's humble opinion, was the constant sunlight. As daunting as the height of the ceiling and thickness of the walls were, the windows let in entirely too much brightness, somewhat lessening the intrinsically heavy aura of such a place. Every few feet was a carefully-placed window or an imperious skylight. It scared her somehow. So much was harshly illuminated, at least before the sun descended and the torches were lit. The shadows called to Isolde, wrapping her in the comforting familiarity of hiding, especially during her frequent late-night strolls.

But some things she would just have to suffer through if she wanted to keep hold of her position in court. A little sunlight was certainly better than ending up with her head on a platter because the nobility revolted. One thing was painstakingly clear. The queen was wilting without fresh air.

Isolde sat in Turia's chambers, noting the fatigued slope of her shoulders and the dark circles beneath her eyes. She clearly needed time outside, as well as more peaceful sleep.

Every few seconds, the queen quickly clenched her fist, executing a rhythm only known to her. Her eyes weren't on Isolde. They rarely were. Instead, the queen's eyes rested on an excessively large white and red blossom growing in an ornately decorated pot. It looked costly.

"Where did you get that pot?" Isolde asked, breaking the comfortable silence of the stuffy, warm afternoon.

"Leave it to you to look at the container and not the actual flower," Turia remarked. "It's beyond me. I mean, look at these gorgeous petals." Turia lovingly fingered one of them. Isolde could have sworn that the plant leaned into her touch. "This species of flower takes seven years to bloom and then you never know if it's going to bloom again. Some only bloom once in their lifetimes. Look at the way the red threads itself over the white in such intricate patterns. There will never be another flower exactly like this one and, by some chance of fate, you're here to witness the miracle."

Isolde examined the flower with new eyes, trying to see what the queen saw in it. She took a step closer. She saw the tear in the blossom, the green-brown leaf that was wilting on the stem, and the comparatively small size of one of the petals.

"It doesn't have the most pleasant smell," Isolde stated.

Turia laughed at that, shaking her head. "You wait seven years for a miracle flower to bloom and take care of it every single day, then we'll see what you have to say."

Isolde watched the way the miracle before her smiled, despite the pressure and pain and exhaustion. Just a singular moment of peace and happiness brought about by something others didn't always understand. Something in the seer craved the feeling that swept through her when the queen's lips tilted upwards. For all the queen had been through, she deserved to have that joy.

"You should treat yourself like you treat that flower," Isolde said quietly.

"I'm not nearly as lovely or unique, so what's the point?" Turia said lightly.

Isolde tilted her head, pursing her lips for a moment as she calculated. "But you smell better."

The queen broke into a laugh. "Barely, at this point."

"You need the same things as your plants. Water, food, and sunlight."

Turia scoffed. "Growing something is much more complicated than that, you know."

"No, I wouldn't know. But my point is, my queen, let's take care of just one of those right now. Sunlight. What do you say?"

Turia side-eyed her. "You want me to go out in public, don't you? I see. This really all comes down to me being seen by the people. As always."

It's not like that useful side-effect of going outside hadn't occurred to the seer, but something in her still felt taken back by the queen's accusatory tone.

"No, it's about making sure you remain happy and healthy. It can't be good for you sitting in these dusty chambers all day. Besides, you love being out in the sunlight, don't you?" On the rare occasions they were outside, Isolde had observed the brief moments Turia stole to tilt her face up towards the rays of the sun and bask in their glow.

"Yes, but I can't stand anyone's eyes on me today," the queen admitted, her hand shooting forward to tap the wall.

"Then wear a cloak and keep your head down. I'm not trying to convince you to be seen right now. I promise."

Isolde held her hand out to the queen to help her up from where she was kneeling on the ground. Turia always seemed to be sitting on the floor when in private, no matter how many chairs were present. After a moment of consideration, the queen reached out and placed her soft hand in the seer's.

~

Isolde glared at the sunbeams raining down on the sweltering street, already starting to feel sweat gathering where her brassiere met her skin. She glanced over at the queen, wondering how exactly she was managing to smile while also wearing a hooded cloak to avoid detection. It was a lighter cloak, meant for the autumn months, but it was still out of place. It served its purpose as an extra precaution against recognition.

Most had only seen the queen from a distance, which also helped. Isolde still drew stares from some, but no one would think her companion was, in fact, the queen. Not when she wore a simple pastel dress and walked without guards.

It had taken some convincing of Turia, but Isolde had the guards trailing them at a distance to allow them the freedom to venture out into the city. As close as it was, the queen rarely got the opportunity to see Viridian, and never while its chaos was in full swing and without a retinue.

As anxious as Turia was about the lack of guards, curiosity sparkled in her eyes as they moved down the busy street of

Fabricfirst. They stayed to the side of the road near the buildings as horses with carts trotted past. Turia peered into the shop windows with interest, drinking in the variety of flowy dresses and smart tunics on display. The queen tugged Isolde's hand, forcing her to stop so they could observe a woman spinning wool into yarn in front of a tiny shop full of inviting blankets and tapestries.

"Have you never seen someone spinning?" Isolde asked with surprise.

"No. My woolen wardrobe pieces are usually delivered right to the palace." To Isolde, it was so common that she hardly batted an eye at it. Her grandmother had owned a spinning wheel, back when her family was still struggling to get by. The item had been discarded as soon as they moved and the coffers were full. It wasn't unusual to see people sewing or darning holes on the street for some extra money. Of course, most street spinners didn't practice on days when room on the street was cleared for the royal procession.

The seer eyed the spinner's aged hands, deft and steady in their work. There was something beautiful about it, she decided. Perhaps it was the raw act of creation, deceptively simple, yet the foundation of so many warm and lovely things.

Turia stood still for a good ten minutes, just admiring the woman's skill, and Isolde waited patiently, unwilling to steal any moment of contentment the queen might claim. When they continued on, moving past Fabricfirst, Isolde found her wandering feet leading in a surprising direction. She had tread this path so many times before, but that was years ago.

The pair passed through Metalfirst. Rounding a corner, the seashore greeted them, along with the pungent smell of fish. The wooden docks of Fishfirst spread out, weathered and coated in vibrant green algae. Boats of all sizes bobbed in the water. Everyone moved quickly here, hustling along the dirt path in front of a row of run-down looking houses while shouting orders to each other.

"I've never seen anything like this," Turia muttered.

A wave of shame and something she couldn't name rose within her. She never should have brought the queen here. Because of how closely fishermen worked with the sea, their part of the city would never escape from the indignity of the association with uncleanliness. The old unfairness festered in her heart, but she had long ago accepted the fact of the shame.

Everyone understood that fishing jobs were necessary for food and trade and highly dangerous given the monstrous creatures lurking just beyond the bay, but that never stopped anyone from turning up their noses. No wonder her grandparents had been desperate to escape, especially after her parents had died an ignominious death at the hands of a kraken.

Everything in Fishfirst looked worse for the wear than she remembered. It appeared strikingly real and lived-in. In Isolde's memory, it had taken on golden and grey hues, somehow both a safe recollection of when things were simpler and the root of the disgrace that would forever permeate her being. No matter what, Fishfirst would always be woven through her veins. Even if she had purposely avoided it for years.

Here she stood exposed, her past flayed open in the salty air. The seagulls overhead knew her from when she would run along the docks trying to catch them as a child. The sailors knew little Isolde, who would stand in the shade, hoping they might give her a fish to take home. The boats knew the girl who played among the rocks, talking to imaginary versions of her parents, before she knew the burden of being gifted.

As a child, Isolde would watch the sailors coming home to their families, beaming at their children before pulling them into tight embraces that spoke of a kind of warmth independent of how much food sat on the table. She would tilt her head, trying to figure out what she needed to do to get her grandparents to offer her the same type of love these children were freely given. So she spoke little, followed the rules, and rarely complained, hoping that, one day, they would see her effort to be good and bestow love on her in return.

The queen glanced over at her. "Are you alright, Seer?" she asked quietly.

Isolde shook herself free of her reverie. Turning around, she said, "Let's go back to the palace."

Turia caught hold of her arm gently. Her touch burned, bringing a flush to Isolde's cheeks. The seer kept her face turned away from the queen's inquiring eyes. "Why leave? I want to see more. It's fascinating."

"Fishfirst? Fascinating? Are we seeing the same place?" Isolde asked.

"I'm fairly confident we are, yes," Turia said.

"It's unclean," Isolde remarked sharply. "You don't want to see more."

Turia reached up and turned Isolde's face toward her. "Let me decide what I want to see," the queen replied softly.

"Alright," the seer relented.

As they walked on, dodging messengers racing past and hand-driven carts of the day's seafood kicking up dust, Turia took in the sights with a level of awe that stirred something within Isolde. The seer walked stiffly, muscles tensing as the familiar smells wafted over her, almost managing to draw water from her eyes. She told herself it was just the sting of the salty air.

"If I remember correctly, didn't your family used to live in Fishfirst?" the queen asked carefully.

"We did," Isolde said. There was no denying it.

"Everyone here is so *alive*," said Turia.

"That's one word for it. Another is fighting to get by."

"We're all fighting in our own ways, I suppose."

"But some have more battles than others," Isolde said. "Most people in Fishfirst don't have the inherent social or financial capital you're used to just tossing about."

"That's true. Don't misunderstand me, Seer. I'm not discounting their struggles or saying they need those battles to be truly alive. Maybe awake is a better word. There's a vivacity and confidence in the air here. An opposition to complacency so rare amongst members of the court. They are actively using what's been given to them and facing the world. It feels brave."

Isolde glanced around at the chaos. *Brave*. "Perhaps you're right."

A street musician warbled an old sea shanty. Isolde hadn't heard it in years. A memory emerged from the recesses of her mind: her grandmother singing the tune in her reedy voice, pulling young Isolde into a dance. It stopped abruptly when her grandfather's shadow crossed the doorframe. Even that young, Isolde knew what fear looked like when it dimmed a person's face.

"I used to live there," Isolde said, pointing to a small building stuffed between two storefronts. It slipped from her mouth before she could stop it. Immediately, she wished she could reel the words back in.

"Oh?" Turia asked, her sharp eyes scouring the cracked plaster exterior. "Do you still own it?"

"Why?" Isolde asked suspiciously.

"Can we go inside?"

Isolde eyed the queen, forcing down her consternation. "In theory. But there's nothing in there besides dirt and dust."

"No harm in taking a look then," Turia said, a poorly-concealed curiosity to her tone.

Isolde sighed before marching to the door. She picked through the rocks against the wall until spotting one with a uniquely red surface. After a moment of trying, she found the latch and, with a click, the bottom of the rock popped open, allowing a bronze key to fall into her hand.

For some reason, her fingers trembled as she fit the key into the lock. The door creaked as Isolde pushed it open, sending up a flurry of dust that sent her into a coughing fit.

"See, I told you. Just a lot of dust."

Turia peered over her shoulder, then slid past her into the shadowed room. Dirt coated the windows, but a fair amount of sunlight still made its way into the space, illuminating the air in bright shafts. Light fell over pieces of furniture, covered in old sheets. Otherwise, the room sat bare.

Isolde's fingers trailed over notches in the doorframe that had marked her height over the years. Turia watched her, head tilted. The quietness of the room suddenly made it seem so utterly foreign to Isolde. It was *wrong*. This home existed like the one she'd known all those years ago. It was the same size and shape. The floor was still discolored where she'd spilled a bowl of tomato soup. The side windows, set high in the wall, still showed a view that was half-sky and half-brick. But the silence made it something entirely different. Somehow, this place didn't know the raised tones of her grandfather's angry voice ringing through the hallways or the warbling notes of her grandmother's clandestine singing. When they were gone, all that was left was Isolde simmering in her silence. Without their words and history, she was something different. Like this house, no longer a home.

If Turia noticed the tight pull of Isolde's lips, she said nothing. Instead, she floated through the space, peeking under sheets, running her fingers over the faded wood of the ancient piano sitting in the corner. Isolde never played it as a child since it was always out-of-tune.

"How long did you live here?" Turia asked.

"Until your father granted my family a title and lands. Then we moved to the estate," she recounted blankly.

"So, you ran through this very room as a child, hm? I'm sure these walls saw all of your joys and all of your sorrows. I love seeing one of the places that created you," the queen said.

"I didn't usually run when I was young," Isolde stated.

"What do you mean you didn't run?" the queen asked incredulously.

"Just that." Isolde looked at her feet, which had carried her quietly through life. "I always tried not to make a fuss. Running would certainly have done just that."

"I see," Turia replied perceptively. Without any warning, Turia fell to her knees on the ground.

"What's wrong, my queen?" Isolde asked hurriedly.

"Nothing at all, Seer. Come here. Take a look at this."

Isolde drew nearer to the corner of the room where the queen sat. She bent down, squinting into the shadows.

Turia gingerly stroked the leaves of a small plant pushing up through the floorboards. To Isolde, it looked somewhat sickly, but the queen marveled at it, turning toward Isolde with excitement sparkling in her eyes. "Isn't this beautiful?"

"I suppose so," Isolde murmured hesitantly.

"No, you're not understanding. This lovely little thing has survived in a place where it was never supposed to exist. It fought its way up between the wooden slats of the floor, laughing that the world thought it would perish when conditions weren't ideal for it to grow. But it grew, anyway, unfurling here in the shadows, despite having no one to see its loveliness or praise its tenacity."

"You see so much where others see nothing," Isolde remarked.

"Only sometimes. But there's one thing I'm certain of, Seer." Turia leaned in closer, making sure she'd caught Isolde's full attention. The scent of honey and lavender met the seer's senses. With cautious fingers, Turia placed her hand on Isolde's arm before looking back at the plant. "This living thing is a work of art."

Chapter Nineteen

Isolde

23 Years After the Viridian Phoenix's Rebirth

C oaxing the queen out of her chambers had gotten easier, which was a relief as Isolde's days were filled to the brim with conversations, research, and tea with curious nobles. The queen's paranoia did seem to be rubbing off on her, though. Every so often, when she was out and about on her walks or headed to the forge, she could have sworn she heard the consistent tread of someone following her. Isolde chalked it up to her imagination and frayed nerves.

More pressing issues, and people, clamored for her attention. The High Priestess, for example. The seer politely ignored Robin, who went about publicly courting every lady in Viridian, it seemed, despite the priestess's supposed vow of celibacy.

Robin wore the priestess robes tailored into pants and with the sleeves cut off, presumably so the ladies could see her strong arms. But despite that, she did perform her duties, for which Isolde was grateful. She presided over the weekly sacrifices and monthly blessings, saying every word correctly, if occasionally in a pointedly overdramatic, melancholic tone that made Isolde want to rip her own hair out. Unfortunately, Isolde also noticed that it always made Turia crack a smile.

Isolde and the queen would attend each blessing, standing before the altar in the Grand Temple with reverence. Isolde watched. Robin would never even look her in the eye, but Isolde knew her presence registered and she hoped that it carried some weight. That, perhaps, it reminded Robin that there was someone to keep her in check if she strayed too far.

Fortunately, she had years of experience navigating the choppy sea of Viridian's court. She understood its current and how to spot a brewing storm. The main difference was that she now navigated the waters on behalf of the queen. Every day, she visited Turia's chambers in the evening to tell her about the winds of the court. Often she suggested action and often the queen ignored her. Instead, she asked after Lady Ingold's petulant cat. She wondered about the state of the marigolds. She queried if the seer could tell if it was going to be an early winter?

Robin visited the queen as well. Sometimes Isolde would walk past Turia's door only to hear echoes of laughter from the queen and the priestess. Something always prickled in her at the sound.

Sometimes she eavesdropped shamelessly. Once she heard a conversation she wished she could forget.

"Do you ever think about when we were kids?" Robin asked.

"How could I not?" Turia replied softly.

"Sometimes, as terrible as they were, I miss those nights sneaking through your window."

"You always were a rascal."

"So I've been told," said Robin.

"No, but I do miss it. Why do you think I wanted you back in Viridian. I know you hate it, but I need you here, Robin."

"Cause I'm good at kissing?"

Turia snorted. "No, you scamp. You know why it didn't work out between us."

"Not the name-calling! I'm a respectable priestess now, you know," Robin said indignantly.

"Only because I say so."

"True, true. Thank everything you pulled me out of that backwards town. I wasn't going to survive there much longer."

"I need you," Turia repeated.

"And I've got you," Robin said.

Isolde walked away then.

~

Despite the queen's stubbornness, she showed up at court at least every few days. She was also often seen pacing around the gardens with the seer or even entertaining nobles for herself. Summer had passed and was slowly easing into the autumn months, but not quickly enough. In Isolde's opinion, the skies were too clear. Viridian never really held space for autumn anyway. It often slid into a misty cool winter soon after the summer heat grew softer.

Having visited the prince in the prisons once more, Isolde purposefully made the trek back up the dimly lit spiral of stairs. She'd been trying to figure out if he'd had any hand in feeding information to the Griffin King or even any knowledge about what happened to the king. While she'd tried to ask Turia, it was a sensitive topic. She doubted the princess knew any more than she did. Her intuition made her wonder if the prince himself had been the agent of his father's destruction. What an easy suspicion though. He was already locked away, which meant Turia was safe from his clutches. If it hadn't been him, then she was still at risk.

Isolde had done her best to quietly strengthen the palace guards, make sure the queen's food was properly taste tested, and every other security measure she could imagine. She'd spent hours writing and rewriting letters to the princes and princesses of the provinces who had yet to send their tokens of allegiance to the queen. Each word had to be perfect, balancing the vaguely threatening tone of power with delicate diplomacy. Several additional handcrafted swords had arrived at the palace since, declaring the loyalty of more provincial rulers to Turia. Every moment though, she wondered if it was enough.

Isolde closed her eyes as she walked, running her fingers over the gritty surface of the wall, made of rocks drawn from the ground hundreds of years ago. She whispered a prayer to the Salamanders to guide her steps. The rocks felt unusually warm under her touch, and she wondered if that was some kind of answer. Seconds later, she stumbled. Someone yelped. Caught off guard, she grabbed at the wall to steady her. When she looked up, she realized it was because she'd collided with the queen, on her way down the steps to the prison.

Turia recovered her balance much quicker than Isolde. The seer hadn't even heard her approaching, her footsteps were so light.

"Come to talk to your brother?" Isolde asked quietly.

Turia wouldn't meet her gaze.

Placing a hand on her arm, Isolde shook her head. "That won't do you any good."

"Have you seen that in a vision?"

Isolde paused uncertainly. Sometimes the lies didn't come as easily as she wished they would when she spoke with the queen. She sighed. "No, I haven't seen it, but my intuition tells me so."

"And do you value your intuition over mine?" the queen asked, finally making eye contact. This time Isolde looked away. The queen's eyes were much too sad for her liking. She couldn't tell if it was meant to be a joke. Turia's fingers tapped on the wall, tracing out some pattern known only to her.

"Have you been to visit him before?" the seer asked instead.

"Not yet."

It was inevitable then, from the sound of it.

"I'll come with you," said Isolde, turning to head back down the steps.

"Thank you," said the queen.

They descended downward until they reached the prince's prison cell. As far as prisoners went, he didn't look the worst. His eyes were still comfortable and his belly still full, even if his facial hair was starting to get the best of him.

"Back so soon, Seer?" he asked with a grating laugh. "If you want to see me more, maybe I should just move back upstairs. His smile faded when he saw Turia hesitantly perched behind Isolde. She shot him a warning look, not expecting him to respect it, but wishing he would.

"Ah, Ria. Finally decided to visit me and see your own handiwork, have you?"

"Caliburnus chose me," she said steadily. "It had to be this way."

"Why? I'm your brother, yet you've locked me up down here."

Turia sighed. "Always stating the obvious."

"Fair point, but you don't really think I would try to usurp your throne. Now that's just ridiculous."

Turia gazed off down the dark hallway lined with half-empty prison cells.

"Come on, Ria." Anger finally started to emerge in his voice along with something else. Pain maybe? Isolde couldn't quite tell, but she was surprised to see his cool exterior break. She took a step closer to Turia, glancing at her protectively. The queen's hands were shaking, but her voice was steady. "You forget I know you, Edrune."

He laughed at that. "I certainly thought you did."

"You were prepared to fight uncle for the throne, when it was his to claim. Why on earth would I be any different? You've never respected me and I didn't see you starting now, especially when you told Isolde as much during the ritual."

"Is that what she told you?" Edrune scoffed.

Turia drew back, surprised. She glanced at Isolde with uncertainty.

"How dare you suggest I'm lying?" the seer replied coldly.

"You'll believe her over your own kin?" Edrune exclaimed. "The only kin you have left, by the way."

Turia turned on her heel without a word and Isolde followed, only sparing the prince one more contemptuous glance.

"Are you planning on keeping me in here forever? I never thought you could be this cruel!" He shouted at his sister's back. Turia didn't stop until she reached her room. As soon as she got inside her movements became more intense, even as she remained quiet, sitting on her bed.

"He can't hurt you," Isolde said fiercely, watching her with concern.

"It's not about him hurting me, Isolde. I'm already hurt," she whispered, like she was trying to somehow contain her emotion. That skill, unlike Isolde, didn't come naturally to the queen.

Isolde sank down onto the bed beside her. "What is it about then?"

Turia just shook her head. "We need to go somewhere," she declared after a moment.

"Oh? This is taking an unusual turn," Isolde said.

"Don't get too excited, Seer. We're still not going anywhere people can see us." Turia stood up, seizing her hand and pulling her out of the room down the hallway. They made their way down the corridor to Isolde's stark chambers. The seer could see the judgment in the queen's eyes as she looked around at the bare space, but she ignored it as she scrambled to figure out the queen's intentions, a rising blush betraying a few errant thoughts.

"We're going riding on the Viridian Phoenix, if she will allow it of course."

Isolde eyed the queen with cautious surprise before sending out a mental call to Ryth with all the strength she could muster.

"She will allow it," Isolde stated. She hadn't received a reply from the phoenix yet, but the answer would be yes, even if Isolde had to cajole Ryth into it. She would gladly give the queen any shred of respite she could provide.

After undoing the latch on the wooden shutters, Isolde pushed them out, letting a cool breeze sweep into the room. At first, the phoenix ignored her. But that was to be expected. They hadn't spoken in weeks and Isolde imagined that bothered the creature, even if she didn't let on. She focused on channeling her intention. Finally, Ryth replied back, not fully able to hide her pleasure at the queen's desire to see the skies from her back.

Looking over her shoulder, she asked the queen, "Do you have your necklace?"

"Always," Turia replied, running her finger over the silver teardrop necklace at her throat.

"Are you sure you want to use it for this joyride? That vial is sacred."

Turia waved her hand dismissively. "Joy *is* sacred, Isolde. I can replenish it when we return."

"When was the last time you used phoenix blood?"

"I haven't properly used any since I was a child during the flight ceremony."

"So you haven't touched fire since you were a child."

"I haven't. You're such a bad influence, Seer, prompting me to use my sacred phoenix blood for something as frivolous as this ride," she said cheekily.

Shaking her head, the seer drew closer to the queen. She held out her fingers for the necklace and Turia handed it to her with care.

"Now, my queen," she said, opening the top of the necklace flask, "Ryth has agreed so it shall be."

Isolde poured a couple of drops of thick blood onto her fingers and then drew them in an arc over Turia's forehead. The queen winced, but only for a moment. She was the only human allowed to feel the sacred burn of the phoenix blood that would give her immunity to all fire, a gift not even the Bonded had since they were only immune to the flames of their own phoenixes.

The seer brushed a strand of Turia's hair away from her eyes. "There," she said, handing the vial back to her before grabbing her hand and pulling her to the window. With a great flourish of its hissing green-blue wings, the phoenix arrived.

"Are you ready?" Turia asked.

"I suppose. If it will make you happy," Isolde replied.

"Well, the aim is to make us both happy, Seer."

Isolde helped Turia onto Ryth's back—the phoenix blood protecting the queen along with anything she touched from disintegrating into ash—before slipping familiarly onto the creature's back herself.

The cliffside descended below them, dropping down into the churning waves which matched the color of the phoenix's fire. Turia's confidence evaporated. Her eyes remained wide as she held on for dear life and the phoenix climbed into the clouds. They headed away from the palace and out to sea. Isolde called out the phoenix with a feeling, asking them to be gentle, given Turia's newness to flying. The phoenix shot back a salty feeling conveying that she had already figured that out.

Isolde smiled as they swept through tendrils of mist, catching glimpses of the roiling sea every now and then. Her hair flew out behind her and she realized just how much it felt like coming home. This moment was exactly how life was supposed to be. Turia bent low over the phoenix's neck, anxiously holding on. Isolde laughed at her, but held onto her waist to make her feel more steady as the phoenix banked into a spiral.

Land emerged on the horizon and soon they were rushing over sand and fields of late-blooming flowers. They sailed over grassy knolls and small cottages along with things they couldn't quite make out from their height. All the while, the phoenix's fire sputtered around them, keeping them warm and secure on Ryth's back. It kept them steady, even as it fought off the world and grew into frantic tendrils whenever the wind blew harder. Turia turned her head and Isolde caught a glimpse of her wide smile.

Chapter Twenty

Isolde

23 Years After the Viridian Phoenix's Rebirth

"What elixir do you drink that gives you so much energy?" Tristan asked, collapsing in the soft grass of the meadow spreading out around them. They lay there panting while Isolde stood over them, sword drawn and satisfied smile barely suppressed.

"Surely you aren't giving up already?" she chided.

"Of course I am. Sometimes you've got to know when you're beaten," Tristan said.

"Hmm, that's not how I've lived my life," Isolde replied with slight disapproval.

"Oh, Seer. When will you learn that there are many, many ways to live? I, for one, long ago decided that I would always try my hardest to honor what I'd been given without sacrificing myself in the process. And that I would never again eat cheese. Disgusting stuff, really."

Isolde took a seat on the ground, gingerly balancing the sword over her knees. "And how's that going for you?"

"I have kept to my promise. Never touched cheese again! You know, I much prefer cake anyways!" they declared with a proud smile.

Isolde rolled her eyes and waited.

"Alright, alright. If I must be serious, I'll admit that I have a finely-constructed web of philosophies that I try to live my life by and yet I fail abysmally at most of my attempts to stay consistent with them," Tristan replied, carefully studying a blade of grass between their fingers.

"Then what's the use of fine philosophies? Morality is for those who can afford it."

Tristan winced. "Maybe you're right. My family can certainly afford it. I've spent my life trying to live up to all I've been given. I want to do right by them. It's my responsibility."

"Must be nice," Isolde replied simply, pinning them with her eyes.

"Now, I wouldn't quite describe it as nice. We all have our own self-made traps. Mine is my duty and attempts at morality. That's a trap I can't quite imagine you being caught in, Isolde," they said wryly. "So, what trap are you trying to claw your way out of?"

"Mine isn't self-made. It simply exists because of how the universe decided to set up the game of my life."

"Game? Is it at least a fun game? I wish you all the fun the Creator can offer. You know, I firmly believe that fun is a balm to our sorrows, but more specifically joy. Not happiness. Joy. I knew this boy once who was always ranting about stables and stable-care, even though I constantly reminded him that…"

Sensing Tristan was about to launch into one of their rants, Isolde interrupted. "It's the farthest thing from fun. The terrible reality of traps is that you are expected to get out of them yourself, even if you weren't the one to create them in the first place. A cruel lesson of the universe I've been blessed to learn."

"I have to disagree with you there, Isolde," Tristan said gently. "Sometimes getting out of a trap seems impossible because it is impossible...by yourself, at least. When I was a small child, I fell into a hole in the woods while playing with my older brother Hendrik. Oh, how we loved weaving through the trees, listening to the call of the...creatures flying overhead to see if we could name them. Let me tell you, I burst into tears. He told me to suck it up...which was not helpful. After a minute, he figured that out and reached down into that dark pit. He rested his hand on my head to soothe my sobs and told me something I'll never forget. 'Together, you bawling idiot. We'll get you out together.' And we did. That's why we need other people."

"That's a sweet story, but I don't need anyone else's help," she stated.

"Maybe that's why you have trouble with healing," Tristan mused.

"Explain."

"Healing requires asking the environment for help. It's a collaborative effort and you have to be open to accepting that help."

Isolde sat in silence for a couple of minutes, contemplating that statement. Taking a deep breath, she stood up and held her hand out to Tristan while she tried to tamp down a flood of envy at their easygoing gentleness.

"Let's get back to practicing, apprentice. You desperately need to learn how to fight."

Chapter Twenty-One

Robin

23 Years After the Viridian Phoenix's Rebirth

"At the end of the day, I'm just a girl," Robin said, casually leaning against the wall of one of the many arched stone hallways leading into the Hippodrome. People streamed past them, filling the seats of the large ovular structure of the racing grounds.

The lady looked away, obviously flustered. "More like a woman," she muttered.

Robin shrugged before lowering her voice and leaning in closer to the noble. "Only on very special occasions."

"Aren't you supposed to be with your lower priestesses," came the seer's abrasive voice.

Robin turned around to face Isolde, not bothering to hide her eye roll.

"If you must know, they kindly agreed to finish setting up the center seating without my extremely agile hands." At those words, she shot a flirtatious look at the noblewoman witnessing the exchange, mainly to see the seer's frown deepen in shocked disapproval at her brazenness.

Isolde collected herself, glancing behind them. Robin followed her eyes to the queen and her court slowly making their way towards the entrance to the interior ring.

"Well, I certainly hope they're finished given that the queen has arrived."

"Excellent," Robin replied. She tipped her head toward the noblewoman as a goodbye and made her way against the crowd to Turia's side.

"Turia!" she exclaimed, giving her a warm embrace. Robin could sense the seer steaming, but she ignored her. "Are you ready for the festivities?"

"No," Turia muttered, glancing around her far too often, the fear in her eyes apparent. Robin's heart stuttered with sympathy, wishing she could ease the queen's feelings even a smidgeon. She tossed her arm around Turia's shoulders jovially as they moved. The commoners cleared the way for the queen's court.

"Come now, you know the races will be a smashing success. They used to be your favorite event of the year."

"A lot has changed," the queen said solemnly.

"Everything, but the way you wear your hair. I still say you should dye it a vibrant purple as a marker of your status," she replied with equal solemnity.

The queen cracked a smile at that.

As soon as they emerged into the sunlight, they could hear the roar of the crowd. Bright red and orange phoenixes circled overhead with their riders, stretching their wings for the games. The queen's court made their way to the small podium at the center, decorated with bright orange and purple banners to represent the sacred and the royal. The queen's throne was a simple, yet beautifully carved chair with a cushion on it, raised on a dais. The wide dirt track lay between the royal podium and the ascending seats of the stadium.

Gahera seemed ready to come undone with her excitement, bouncing up and down on her toes like a child. Aeryt kept whispering to her to calm down in tones loud enough to be overheard by the others.

Turia took her seat.

~

Isolde watched the high priestess stand, her wide pants swaying in the slight wind. Oh, how she despised that woman. She tried to keep the distaste off her face. Everything she was seemed a risk to Turia's reputation.

The crowd quieted at the waving of the wide red banners, ready to listen to the announcing priestess.

"With the blessing of the Salamanders, I declare the Phoenix Races open and ready to begin. We thank those below for their…magnanimity in this joint venture," Robin shouted. The acoustics of the Hippodrome were designed for people in nearly every seat to be able to hear her once they stopped talking amongst themselves. Every word dripped with sarcasm. Even if she didn't fully believe it, she could at least pretend she did. If the seer could do it, so could the priestess. Isolde knew the soulless existed, but they were usually unwilling to offer assistance. That didn't stop her from asking, though. The priestess, however, didn't seem to think they existed at all, which was simply a foolish thought.

With a few more tongue-in-cheek words, the priestess signaled the beginning of the first race. Phoenixes took off overhead, diving and whirling in sharp circles, their riders miraculously staying seated through the power of the creature's flames surrounding them. The games were as much about showmanship as speed. Turia's eyes were trained on the skies, but Isolde's eyes were trained on her and the way her gentle pink lips parted in awe. The roar of the crowd grew as Hermod and her rider took the lead. Her hues were a particularly deep blood-red shade, making her easy to spot. She and her rider had already been reborn. Rumor was they'd been champions in their past life as well and they were favored by many. As Isolde knew, the people liked a good story.

Aeryt stepped forward to the announcer's spot, which would allow her voice to resonate throughout the stadium, and began singing the Racing Song. She'd been chosen to sing it for the past several years, given her extraordinarily powerful and beautiful voice. That fact was something Gahera was always proudly reminding people of, even though Aeryt would try to shush her out of a mildly false sense of humility.

The sound of the song completed the Racing ritual, allowing a wave of nostalgia to wash over the seer. Even though the races had always been a time of extra lies stuffed into her mouth by her grandparents, she'd still always loved the sound of that song ringing out through the crisp air as the phoenixes zipped through the sky, setting the twilight on fire.

Round and round they went, staying on course, but frequently changing altitude and nearly colliding in attempts to get ahead of each other. One phoenix, whose flames were almost light enough to be called gold, was closing in on Hermod, causing a wave of virulent boos from the spectators.

Isolde noticed that both of Turia's legs were bouncing, an attempt to keep her movements from coming out in more noticeable ways, it seemed. The effort was only half-successful since her neck still jerked to the side from time to time. The noise was overstimulating at this point, a wall of noise that the Racing Song wove in and out of.

It was so loud that shouts from the crowd about someone crossing the track were missed. Turia's guards, though they were meant to be watching, had their eyes fixed on the skies just like the other attendees. By the time they looked down, the man was already making his way among the seated nobles, who were scurrying out of the way of his drawn sword. But he only had eyes for the queen. The guards rushed toward him in a chaotic tumble, knocking many a perturbed courtier out of his way in the process. The song came to an abrupt end. Isolde bolted up, but it was too late.

He stood within throwing distance of the queen. The guards had yet to reach him as they tried to get closer to Turia. The queen looked down with confusion at the tumult. She froze from shock at the sight of the man wielding a sword. Anger burned in his eyes.

"Death to the so-called queen. She can't even control herself, so how can she be trusted to lead us?" The man shouted, though the seer guessed few would be able to hear his words. He charged and, before Isolde could move to help the queen, Robin threw herself between the two. Though she bore no weapon, the priestess covered Turia, pulling her to the ground and out of the way of the sword as it came down. Within seconds, three guards reached them, seizing the man and knocking the weapon from his hands.

"Turia. Turia, are you alright?" Robin asked, helping the queen upright once more. Turia looked around with unseeing eyes.

Isolde fell to her knees beside the queen, wanting to take her hand, but not daring to do so. "Are you hurt? Please, answer." Turia just shook her head.

The stadium descended into chaos. The race overhead halted and people shouted, growing louder over each other as the news of the assassination attempt spread.

~

After ushering Turia out of the Hippodrome and sending her back to the palace with her trembling guards circling her, Isolde caught Robin's eyes and gestured with her head that they should step aside.

"Yes, Seer," Robin asked, as they both watched Turia's receding form.

"I just wanted to say… thank you for saving the queen. Those few moments…it made a difference." She said the words grudgingly, but the woman had earned some modicum of respect from her, and Isolde had long ago learned that enemies should be kept close. Hence, the gratitude.

Her statement caught Robin's attention. "Oh, really? The great seer wishes to thank me. Unheard of."

"I could just walk away right now, you know," Isolde bit back.

"You have the freedom to do so," the priestess replied.

"Indeed." Isolde looked her up and down, letting a spiteful comment slip out despite her valiant attempt to make peace with the priestess. "You know, it wouldn't hurt you to wear the proper priestesses' garb and at least act like you believe the words you're saying. You undermine Turia whenever you preside over ceremonies like this in such a...flippant way."

The insinuation was cutting and clear. Robin fixed her with a knowing look as she crossed her arms. "Listen, Seer, we've both been through shit. I don't know what happened to you, but here's the difference between us. You learned to be restrained and how to chain others up while I learned how to be free no matter what. I'll be damned if you think you can take that away from me with a few choice words. What happened today wasn't my fault."

Robin stormed away after the queen.

Chapter Twenty-Two

Turia

23 Years After the Viridian Phoenix's Rebirth

Turia held her sobs in until she reached her chambers. This is exactly what she'd feared. The seer assured her that the man had been a lone actor. But the words haunted her.

Death to the so-called queen. She can't even control herself, so how can she be trusted to lead us?

Turia surveyed her plants, the warm and lively space she'd created for her life, and she decided to stay there, safe behind closed doors.

Chapter Twenty-Three

Isolde

23 Years After the Viridian Phoenix's Rebirth

"We can't just let them continue this madness," Turia stated. It had only been a fortnight since the Phoenix Races had gone awry and already there was another crisis at hand.

"It's still unclear whether the soldiers are under direct orders from the Griffin King or if these incidents are spontaneous," Kaye stated.

"Either way, they're an issue. What if Zeuldian is breached? Do they want the temple and ashes stored there? You did say several items went missing at the temple, Sir Kaye?" asked Gahera.

"Yes, but that might have been the handiwork of local thieves. And, whatever the case, they weren't able to make it to the ashes. It wasn't an outright raid."

"But someone did report seeing Griffin soldiers nearby that night?" Turia asked.

"Yes, but again, the evidence is thin," Kaye emphasized.

Robin grimaced. "If you wait for enough evidence to accumulate, we'll all be dead. As much as you all irritate me, I've grown rather attached to you."

Everyone ignored Robin 's comment, as they'd long ago learned to do.

Turia jumped in. "No need to fear, Sir Kaye. I will not make any rash decisions, but I do need all the information. There have been, what, three more skirmishes now? What do they want?" she mused quietly, more to herself than anyone.

"Zeuldian is a good guess, my queen," said Sir Aeryt. "These incidents are all within a day's distance from the city. As you know, it was a point of contention in your Great-grandfather's war with them. They don't have any ports quite as prosperous as Zeuldian. Besides that, the temple has the greatest quantity of holy ashes besides the Great Temple here in Viridian. The king knows we won't budge on giving up the ashes, so maybe he's decided to take them. You know how old men and their wars are."

Isolde just managed to hide her smirk.

"The people are anxious near the border. With fourteen more dead in these incidents and the robbery at the temple, they're feeling more unstable," noted Lady Cador.

Turia turned to Robin. "Perhaps it is time for us to go evaluate the situation ourselves and report back. It's possible there are weaknesses in our defenses that have been overlooked. You know the city best, High Priestess, and may be able to pick up on things others would miss so we'll send you to make an assessment. Separately, Lord Pellinore will take another two leagues of soldiers with you to supplement the lines. The Griffin King needs to see us taking precautions. Zeuldian—if that is their target—is not about to fall within my first year as queen. Is that understood?"

Her tone was quiet, but it left little room for argument.

Bedivere inclined his head. "I'll make preparations."

Robin paled but nodded.

"It's worth discussing whether we should send a diplomat with a message," Isolde stated.

Turia looked up at her. "Formally acknowledging the tension is a dangerous move. If we're the first ones to admit fear, that gives the Griffin Court the upper hand. We should only send a diplomat if the situation escalates further."

Sir Gahera nodded her agreement and the room fell quiet. The tension was palpable from the sweat on Lord Percival's brow to the tightness in Turia's jaw. Turia finally rose from her seat at the round table. "I look forward to hearing your report on the situation, Bedivere. I want to hear any and all information as soon as you are in possession of it."

"Understood, my queen."

Isolde followed her on her course out of the room, but lingered for a few seconds longer to assess the status of the council. Everything was lowered voices and concerned looks. The seer knew that news of growing tensions at the border would be the talk of the court before the day was out.

"It might be wise to host a dance tomorrow," Isolde stated.

The queen raised an eyebrow. "Why in the world would I want to do that?"

"Why would you want to host a ball? I was under the impression that that's what queens do for fun."

"And I thought you were starting to get to know me. Especially after the attempt." The queen looked down.

"This will be in the safety of the palace. Your guards have been reprimanded and some have been replaced with stronger candidates. You will be safe. I give my word."

"How can you do that?"

The seer sighed. "I can see that you will be safe if you choose to host a ball. Distract the court. It's not much, but it's better than nothing. Do what you can to provide entertainment so the nobles don't have as much time to gossip and get concerned. At the very least, it will provide a delay in public reaction that will give us more time to gather intel."

"Oh, Isolde. Nothing will stop the gossiping tongues of the nobility. Not even a ball."

"Perhaps not."

"But it's more than that? It's about demonstrating control?" Turia filled in.

Isolde didn't reply, but Turia had guessed correctly.

"It's always about control for you, isn't it?"

"More or less," Isolde joked, the words uncomfortably close to the truth.

Turia sighed and steeled herself. "Make the arrangements."

After a brief lesson in the forge with Tristan, the rest of the day was spent making preparations for the ball. It would be a small affair, but Isolde still wanted it to be extravagant. It had to be appropriate for the first dance since the queen's coronation. After all, it was a sign that court was returning to normal. Tristan quietly made suggestions about all of her decisions, which she vehemently rejected while informing them that they had poor taste.

It was an easy day, something like a dream, which put Isolde in a good mood. Choosing which garlands to use and what food should be served felt like some kind of playacting. For the day, she got to inhabit someone else's life. Even still, though, she listened to what the floral mistress told her assistant when she thought no one was paying attention. She saw Lady Delcort receive a letter from a messenger and hurry away from her friends while making her excuses. She heard every time whispers of war marred the air in her presence.

Even so, an extravagantly decorated pledge of loyalty had arrived, finally, from the queen's uncle, which made him less of an active threat in her mind. Perhaps the mutterings of war were actually pushing the provinces into the safety of Turia's arms. Now was not the time to be a lone province without the full backing of Morya's high queen. Several regions still held out though.

Isolde wished that she could visit the rulers who had yet to send tokens of allegiance herself, but she would instead have to keep sending diplomats and letters. Countless letters. She was often up late into the night, trying to pen the perfect turn of phrase that would be convincing enough. Every moment of Isolde's life in the palace was filled by her trying to keep Turia, and in turn herself, safely afloat on the tempestuous waters of politics. Once the queen's reign was fully established, she could step back into the shadows and bask in true freedom.

Tristan didn't seem to pick up on the uneasiness of the court or, if they did, they didn't let on to it. Instead, they placed a flower in her hair—which she promptly plucked out—and asked her about her favorite foods. They spent most of the next day the same way.

The room glowed, already alive with conversation and candlelight dancing across the ceiling when the queen arrived. Isolde walked behind her, taking in her handiwork smugly. It was a beautiful sight. Garlands of wisteria swathed the room. Ladies floated about in their most splendid jeweled circlets with their dresses flowing around them like goddesses. The flashes of color brought about the remembrance of her grandmother's eyes softening the first time Isolde had tried on one of the elegant, court-style dresses.

"You know, you would look just like your mother, if you were just the slightest bit prettier," she'd whispered dotingly. The red-hot compliment burned.

Suddenly, Isolde didn't want to be seen. This wasn't created for her. She could never be a true participant in this court, like these nobles spinning in ignorant circles, unaware of the things she knew about them. Something in her gave way to exhaustion as the queen sang her song and then the dancing began. It reminded Isolde of watching a play you desperately wish could be real.

After picking up a goblet of wine, she joined Aeryt, Gahera, and Robin as they chatted. Robin had apparently just said something that had Gahera in stitches. Aeryt smiled jovially too, but in a way far more reserved than her raucous sister. They all seemed like a scene from some painting. Isolde held her tongue as they talked, feeling a stilted sense of awkwardness that she rarely encountered. From what she could pick up, they'd all spent time together as children while Robin lived in the capital city, being prepared for the rites that would officially mark her as a member of the priesthood. Aeryt and Gahera, on the other hand, had been summoned to be Turia's ladies-in-waiting before they had reached their tenth birthdays since they were Unbonded young women deemed appropriate for the role.

"Lady Ingold never recovered. She jumps every time she sees a frog to this day," Gahera stated.

"What can I say, I did my job well," Robin said.

"You all were too much for the adults to handle, you know. It's a wonder you didn't get into more trouble," Aeryt said, excluding herself from the ways of the other childhood troublemakers.

The laughter died at that and Aeryt froze, realizing what she had said.

All eyes turned to Robin, who looked down briefly. She had been thoroughly punished by the priesthood for her so-called misdeeds. "Well, look at where we are now," she said, recovering her jolly demeanor after a moment. She raised her glass. "To troublemakers." Isolde joined the toast, but couldn't help but feel out of place.

Retreating to one of the pillars lining the room, she stood trying to dissect her feeling of unease. Could she never be part of the beauty?

"What an unearthly sight."

Isolde glanced over at Tristan, who stared out into the room with something in their eyes that escaped interpretation.

"I suppose it is," she replied cautiously. The white tunic they wore suited them. Her own burgundy dress was still fairly practical, but there was a small crescent moon embroidered on each sleeve.

"What are you thinking about?" they asked.

"Too many things at once."

"Ah, I see."

"I've never really liked these kinds of things," she confided finally, avoiding their eyes.

"Me neither," they replied. "I appreciate the music though. When the musicians aren't too drunk at least."

She cracked a smile.

"Where does your dislike for balls spring from?" they asked.

"Why do you want to know?" she challenged.

They chuckled. "People don't always have an ulterior motive for asking questions, Isolde."

"Don't they?" she pondered.

Isolde's eyes flitted to Turia, busy gracefully dancing with a noble. Her neck looked tense, but she wasn't twitching. Isolde swallowed. She knew how difficult it was for her.

"Are you going to stay for the entire ball?" they asked.

She looked over at them. "You don't have to if the affair is boring you, Tristan."

"Far from it. I was asking about you."

The seer nodded. "I don't despise it that much." She needed to stay for Turia.

"She'll be alright without you," they stated quietly.

Isolde looked at them sharply. "The queen doesn't need anyone to preside over a ball. Don't be ridiculous."

"I simply mean I know how loyal you are to her. You're dedicated. But you're also exhausted. You don't have to constantly stay in hostile environments."

She scoffed, her exterior cracking. "Where else would I be?'"

"You could come with me?" they said, looking down at their feet. Tristan couldn't hide their eyes, though, and they were sparkling.

"Alright," she said simply. "Lead the way, my liege."

They laughed at that, glancing at her with a kindness she saw in few people.

With one last look at Turia, Isolde followed Tristan through the archway into the hall. They walked in silence. Isolde rested her hand on the hilt of her new sword. It was a comforting feeling. Starlight shined in through the open windows as the music grew farther and farther away. The cool air gave her goosebumps as they wandered down the palace steps and out through the streets. It reminded her of when she'd first met them weeks ago. Few people were outdoors this time of night, so it was simply them and possibility.

"You going anywhere in particular?" she asked.

"Yes, in fact. You underestimate me."

"Oh, I estimate everyone accurately ."

"How do you do that?"

She tapped her temple. "Comes with being a seer."

"Especially the Viridian seer. That's a lot of memory you're drawing upon."

"It is," she replied soberly, years of her childhood sifting through her mind. "How did your family react when you chose to be an alchemir?" She had never told her grandparents she practiced.

"My mother was happy for me, but unsurprised. Our entire family is inclined toward it and I'm the youngest of my siblings. I do think she would have preferred I was gifted with some other skill though." They glanced her way. "Might be part of the reason I'd like to learn how to forge."

"But why? Healing is a perfectly useful art."

They grimaced. "She takes great pride in our family's image as strong and hearty. Where she comes from, healing is seen as a weaker skill. It isn't creation as much as repair."

"I'd argue it's still a creation in its own way. It's just foolish for that to be seen as weak."

"Not when your brother has cultivated alchemiric sword fighting, and your mother can turn any object into silver."

Isolde raised her eyebrows. "Now that's a rare skill."

They nodded. "She uses it sparingly. In her eyes, it's a gift that she must use appropriately."

"How noble."

"How stubborn," they corrected. "My brother swore he would refuse to use his talents if the family tried to force me to cultivate an alchemric skill besides healing. When Hendrick told me he'd issued that ultimatum to our parents, he claimed it was because I would clearly outshine him if I tried anything else, and his ego couldn't take it. I'll be forever grateful. It took some of the pressure off my shoulders and allowed me to explore what I love." Tristan smiled softly, lost in the memory.

"He sounds like a good brother," Isolde stated.

"Painfully annoying at times and mischievous to a fault, but always there when I need him. He never treated me as anything other than a sibling, even though my mother married his father after she'd already given birth to me. She was widowed young.

"Hendrick met me when I was still a young child. He's five years older than I am. I remember him looking down at me when we were first left to play with each other, tilting his head with that curious look of his. I'm sure I seemed terrified. I was a lonely child and other children often picked on me. After a moment, he took my hand and said, 'You're my sibling now. That means you'll always be safe with me, alright?'"

Isolde tried to imagine what her life might have been like if she had possessed a brother like that. "What a beautiful stroke of fate that you ended up as family," she murmured.

They meandered onward, the stars twinkling above.

"Are we going down to the sea?" Isolde guessed as they turned down the road that led to the wide beach.

"Do you still want to learn more about healing?" they asked cautiously.

"Perhaps."

"Then the sea is the place to go."

She seized their arm. "We have to be careful. It isn't the Day of Emergence."

"I know," they said softly, taking her hand and pulling her along.

The black sand winked up at them in the starlight. The waves churned heavily, drowning out any remaining noise from the city above. Farther away, she could see them crashing onto the rocks at the bottom of the cliffs, perpetually repeating their fury. It smelled like life.

They wandered along the beach in silence for a time. Tristan finally turned to her. "Are you ready?"

"It depends."

They laughed. It was beautiful and she desperately wanted to run away. They held out their hands. After a moment, she took them.

"Close your eyes and just listen. Feel your feet in the shifting sand."

"This is pointless," Isolde said, hands tense in the hold of the apprentice.

"It is if you don't try," they said, looking at her pointedly.

She glared at them. The audacity of throwing her own words back at her.

"Fine."

Isolde closed her eyes, but didn't let herself fall into the Otherrealm. Instead, the rhythm of the ocean seeped into her veins. She was surprised at how quickly it overpowered her thoughts. More than that though, the breeze drew her attention as it grew.

"What am I supposed to be feeling?"

"Something that can't be put into words," they replied.

She snorted. "If I didn't know better, I'd think you were trying to seduce me. It won't work, you know."

Isolde opened her eyes to see that they were already looking at her, something dark and amused in their expression as they wrinkled their nose.

"I'm not one for seducing people. Never have been, really. Kissing, not usually for me. Other things … well, not something I crave."

Isolde tilted her head, curiosity settling over her. "Is that so?"

They averted their eyes. "I don't know how to explain…"

"You don't owe me an explanation, but you can share if you feel like it."

"I am, after all, quite strange."

Isolde rolled her eyes. "You may be strange in other ways, but not wanting that form of connection isn't what makes you weird."

Tristan started pacing. "It's…complicated. I gravitate towards strong friendships, not romantic connections."

A part of Isolde breathed with relief, relaxing into the comfort of knowing Tristan didn't want anything from her besides companionship."

Isolde smiled. "Thank you for telling me."

Tristan glanced down at their feet. "Anyway, I may not seduce people, but, when I'm healing, I do mean to seduce the sea."

She clapped them on the back, turning toward the waves. "Good luck with that."

"None of it is luck. Healing is understanding how to use what already exists. Just like all alchemy, it's creation through transformation, but it's the kind that requires you to convince the most ancient of things to help you. Without them, you're lost." Their eyes were far away as they stared out over the ocean.

She crossed her arms. "I already know that," she snapped.

They sighed. "The wind and the sea want you to do more than just ask for their help. They are masters of transformation. You have to become part of them for a moment to bring them back to your craft."

"So, seduce them?"

"In a sense."

"What are your preferred methods of 'seducing' the sea, as you say?"

They smiled. "Maybe I have secrets also, Seer."

"I do doubt that," she answered, watching how at home they looked with the wind ruffling their hair.

"You want to try again?" they asked.

She paused. Isolde didn't want to try and fail in front of them. Her pride might not be able to withstand that kind of blow.

"Maybe it would help if we were in the waves."

"In the sea? What's the matter with you?"

"You know, no one's ever been able to figure that out," they said quietly, not meeting her eyes. Their smile fell though and the words felt too serious.

"Tristan, it's not the Day of Emergence."

"That much is true, but I don't believe the sea is meant to be kept from us just by words someone decided to scribble down one day."

Isolde breathed deeply, anger surging through her. "It's a sacred tenet. It's blasphemy to the phoenixes. They were given wings so they could escape it. We honor them."

"But you're not a phoenix. Your story is different."

Shame flashed through her as she tried to suppress memories of her grandmother desecrating her books and dresses in salt water, then splashing it over the young seer's hands. The woman had walked away, laughing. "That's for thinking you're sacred. See how the Soulless treat you now."

She hadn't told Ryth, but suspected the creature knew of her shame. Whatever the case, the phoenix had never said a word about it.

"Do you really believe it's that serious, Seer?" they asked, meeting her eyes.

"I do. It's blasphemy."

"Blasphemy to avoid the good and natural things in this world?" they asked. "Really? It never seems to hurt my alchemiric practice. I tend to think the Soulless don't truly care one way or the other. The ocean certainly chooses to help me."

Ryth had never said anything. Isolde eyed the rolling surface of the water. That old desire to wade into it and be lost at the hands of the ocean descended over her. Bitterness replaced fear as memories of her grandmother rolled through her mind once more.

Tristan took her hand again and took a step toward the ocean, seeing if she would come with them. The bitterness turned to anger. She let them pull her along, hoping the ocean would wash away her old fear.

The water soaked through the bottom of her dress, surprising her with its liveliness.

"It's not as cold as I was expecting."

They didn't say anything, but instead just waded deeper until the water was up to their chests. It was sharp and lovely. The salt in her nostrils swept away her thoughts. Thunder echoed in the distance. She caught a glimpse of lightning piercing the sky somewhere far away, but the waves pushed and pulled her, calling for her attention. She and Tristan kept each other steady, trying to keep their feet anchored in the shifting sand below.

"Maybe you should let yourself fall into the Otherrealm this time," Tristan suggested, their voice low. Its cadence reminded her of the ocean itself.

"I'll try," she murmured to herself.

They held their hands above the water and nodded to an angry-looking scratch running across the back of their hand. "Try to fix this. Just feel it. Don't think."

The water rushed around her while the wind quickened, bringing with it the smell of the distant rain. Suddenly, it became her whole world. Leaving her body behind, she drifted into the blue. She felt Tristan beside her, burning with renewed life, surrounded by impressions of spreading leaves and feathers surging in the wind around their soul.

The salt water pulsed through her soul or maybe she pulsed through the soul of the sea. She wrapped herself around the small injury, calling on the life held by the force of waves and currents constantly rearranging themselves to be in some other order. They flowed through her and she let them carry her rather than fighting to stay in one place. Her eyes flew open. She ran her finger over Tristan's hand where the scratch had been. It was gone, replaced by healthy soft new skin. With a smile, they threw their arms around her.

"That's the easiest it's ever been," she said in shock, embracing them back and savoring the feeling of their head pressed into her shoulder.

They pulled back, hands on her arms and said, "I'm glad." There was something subdued in their smile. It reminded the seer of the queen. The expression was strikingly similar. Isolde assessed them for a moment, once more unsure of what to make of them. Letting her hand sweep over the water for a moment, she kept them in her sights mischievously. They were far away but not for long.

Isolde splashed water toward their face. They broke from their reverie, sputtering and blinking at her before realizing what she had done. Then they went after her. Around and around, they pushed water towards each other, darting and diving in the midnight sea, until they were both soaked from head to toe.

"You look like a drowned phantom," Tristan called playfully, between getting hit in the face with volleys of water.

"You look like an eel," she said, grabbing their arms and wrestling to keep them from shoving more water at her. They didn't though. Their soft smile and seeing eyes glittered sacred in the moonlight.

Chapter Twenty-Four

Robin

23 Years After the Viridian Phoenix's Rebirth

R obin tossed and turned, tormented by the usual dreams. They screamed. Shamed her for what she couldn't help but be. They cast salt water over her hands and beat her saying she would always be an unclean thing. Unfortunately, the Priesthood was for life, which meant she had to live in its shadow or face death. She cried until she was laughing, simply unable to do anything else in the wake of her pain.

A mighty crash freed her. She scrambled up from the hostel pallet, wiping sweat from her brow. Robin blinked, hurriedly trying to get a sense of her surroundings just like all the other girls in the dormitory. They looked like phantoms fluttering about in their nightgowns. To the chagrin of many in her life, Robin wore only a simple shirt and trousers as her bedclothes.

Robin darted to the open window and was met with the sight of an explosion a few blocks over. She didn't have to look to know what they were targeting.

Girls crowded around the window, trying to catch sight of the thing. She turned to them. "Get out while you can!" she yelled, her voice somehow carrying authoritatively over the din. Soldiers wouldn't be far behind the explosions and these were all innocents.

Robin didn't leave until everyone was out. Instead, she snatched up her small bag of supplies and threw on her jacket, picking out her next moves.

Robin flew down the stairs to the dusty street below. A cool sea breeze wafted over her, offsetting the violence of shaking ground as another explosion hit. She knew that she should do exactly what she'd told the others to, but the high priestess couldn't help herself.

With a quiet swiftness, she swept through the shadows, heading toward the site of the explosions rocking the buildings near the port. Turning a corner, it came into view: the temple where she'd first been inducted into the priesthood. Its towers twisted upward in dizzying spirals that made her want to vomit for more reasons than one.

With purposeful steps, she made her way into the open courtyard and entered the main hall. She stood there for a moment, watching the torches flicker with their eerie, knowing kind of light. The emptiness filled her soul, and she cursed. Another bang shook the building, throwing her to the ground and sending pain through her face with a crack.

The temple itself wouldn't burn. It was expensive, after all, coated with fireproofing resin from the far north so phoenixes could parade inside its sacred walls. No, it wouldn't burn, but it could fall. The ornate, dark hall had ceded to the silence. Despite the pain, Robin rose, wiping the blood from her face. She turned in a circle, letting all the shame and fear and defiance of the memories wash over her heart.

For a moment, she was entirely at the mercy of the past. Slowly, the silver pain transformed into golden anger. Taking a deep breath, she put one foot in front of the other as a boom echoed through her bones. Satisfaction burned in her as she walked slowly down the hall, just daring it to cave in on her. She needed it to fall and it obliged her, just as she finally made her exit.

Chapter Twenty-Five

Isolde

23 Years After the Viridian Phoenix's Rebirth

The letter arrived at dusk, as the fire of phoenixes soaring through the sky reflected off the watercolor clouds. Isolde sat in her room, trying to warm her perpetually-cold hands in front of the dancing flames of the hearth. The welcome heat made her close her eyes in thanks. When the messenger knocked on her door, she expected a summons from the queen or perhaps news from the front, but the lilac color of the envelope quickly dislodged those expectations.

Isolde clenched it in angry fingers, begging her hands not to tremble while closing the door and setting her back against it as if that could protect her from the contents of the message. She recognized the stationary. Perhaps one of them had died. That made her stomach drop with a confused amalgamation of relief and horror.

After taking a deep breath, she tore open the letter. Unfolding the perfect, crisp parchment, she got stuck on the first two words: *Dearest Isolde.*

Something in her knew she'd never been her grandmother's dearest. That title belonged to her grandfather. Her grandmother had demonstrated that every single time she'd starved

Isolde at his behest, or told her a new lie he'd dreamt up to advance the Merlin family's status. Images flashed through Isolde's mind. A flower crown of red asclepias blooms, her favorite flower, even now, tucked gently into her hair by her grandmother's hands. A comforting hug when she was sick. A clandestine wink and smile as her grandmother snuck her an extra piece of candy. Oh, how Isolde had lived for those smiles when she was a little girl.

The competing shame at the severe frowns when she didn't behave "correctly" dug its way into her soul, becoming a constant companion that she somehow couldn't quite shake, even now. By the time she realized that maybe she didn't deserve the punishment and maybe they were exploiting her Bond, the damage was already done. Even as she'd tried to distance herself from all the sweet moments they'd shared as a family, they always stayed in the back of her mind, making her question herself. That is, until the next time her grandmother denied her dinner, and her resolve hardened yet again.

Another knock sounded at the door. Isolde hadn't even been able to get past the first two words. She folded the letter and stuck it in her pocket before answering. The messenger let her know the queen desired her presence.

With a deep breath, Isolde proceeded down the dark, torchlit halls until she reached the queen's chambers. Turia sat cross-legged on her rug, staring at the plant in the otherwise empty hearth with a tilted head.

"Do you think there's room for a pot of dahlias in there next to the orchids?"

Despite herself, that question pulled a small smile from Isolde. "Is that why you summoned me?"

Turia looked up at her. "I needed a second opinion." The queen paused, eyebrows drawing together in concern. "But now I also need to know why the stoic seer's eyes look sadder than usual."

Isolde was taken aback. She rather prided herself on being able to hide her emotions and the fact that Turia had picked up on her disquiet frustrated her. "You must be imagining things," she stated.

"Walnuts!" Turia shouted suddenly. Isolde ignored the outburst, knowing that was one of the common words she said when she didn't mean to because of her ailment.

After a moment of staring her down with those seemingly all-knowing eyes, Turia simply asked, "Am I imagining things?"

Isolde stood stiffly in front of the queen, her throat suddenly thickening with tears she hadn't realized she'd been holding in ever she recognized the stationary. Almost of their own accord, her fingers withdrew the letter from her pocket and handed it to Turia. The tears would spill if she tried to speak. With gentle motions, Turia took it and glanced over its contents.

"Have you read it?" she asked.

"No. Did one of them die?" Isolde asked, her voice cracking in the middle.

Turia sighed. An angry red rose on her cheeks. "I don't think you have to read this unless you want to do so."

"I always wonder whether her words, her hands, her looks will sting or not. Even now it seems."

Isolde fingered the soft petals of one of Turia's red roses.

"When I was younger, she remembered that my favorite color was red and would always make me garlands of red asclepias flowers for special occasions. But then she forgot. At some point, every garland and crown became purple to remind people of our status and ties to divinity. What a farce."

Isolde couldn't meet the queen's eyes. Something about Turia gaining a glimpse into her childhood through the message and her own admission eviscerated her. Her breaths came heavily as she tried not to cry.

"I think this letter is fire fodder. What do you think?" Turia asked gently.

Isolde nodded.

With deft fingers, Turia rose and dropped the letter into one of the sconces on the wall. They watched it disintegrate together.

Turia slid down to sit on the floor and patted the ground beside her. "Come sit down."

The seer complied. At the end of the day, it didn't matter what was in the letter. Probably some cloying attempt to re-enter her good graces. The nerve.

They sat together in silence for a moment. When Isolde continued hyperventilating, Turia sat up on her knees and faced the seer, brushing back the golden curls that had fallen into her eyes. With a careful slowness, like she was taming a skittish animal, she reached her hand out in front of Isolde.

"What...?" Isolde asked.

"May I?" the queen asked.

A crimson blush spread over the seer's cheeks as she nodded.

Turia pressed her hand firmly to Isolde's chest. Its pressure and warmth flowed through her, sweet and slow like honey. "Breathe with me, Seer."

Their eyes locked. In and out. Isolde couldn't look away as their breathing synced. In and out. In and out, with Turia's hand resting near her heart.

Chapter Twenty-Six

Isolde

23 Years After the Viridian Phoenix's Rebirth

"You're terrible at this."

"Thanks for the encouragement," Tristan shot back, retrieving their sword from the ground where it had fallen when Isolde knocked it out of their hand. She'd decided that she could use the practice. Every day that passed, rumors of war grew, rooting themselves throughout Viridian. It didn't hurt to be prepared, and Tristan wanted to learn more about sword fighting.

To be fair, she wasn't sure practicing with them would do her any good at all. They could barely block any of her lunges, but it was amusing to see the stunned look on their face every time she managed to disarm them. She dodged their swings easily enough as they practiced out in the tall grasses beyond the gardens. It was quiet out here. No one was there besides them and the occasional phoenix swooping overhead.

"It feels like you're not even trying," she taunted them.

They shook their head. "We can't all be as gifted as you, Isolde."

"I suppose you're right," she replied, disarming them for the third time in a matter of minutes.

"Then again, I am also using this second-rate sword I borrowed from the storehouse."

Isolde laughed. Her new sword felt good in her hands. Its black handle glittered in the cold sunlight and she couldn't help but take a moment to appreciate her handiwork.

She sobered when she spotted a messenger making his way across the fields to them. The break from prying eyes and endless charged conversations had been lovely while it lasted. Sheathing her sword, she walked toward him. All she had to do was examine his tense face to brace herself for bad news.

"What happened?" she asked.

"There's been an attack on Zeuldian."

Her brow tightened. "What do you mean an attack? A border skirmish?"

"No, an attack."

Isolde didn't wait for them to finish before quickening her pace back toward the palace, making them scramble to keep up.

"The Griffin Guard marched on it just before dawn yesterday. One of our legions was transferred from there to farther down the border. They attacked before the smaller legion meant to supplement their removal arrived. General Soder said that it seems like they were prepared to march on the city, so they must have known that change was taking place beforehand. The fighting is still going on, but the city center has fallen to them and they've established a perimeter around the city."

Isolde broke into a run with Tristan at her heels. Curse her lack of intuition. She should have stayed closer to Turia in these unstable times. She should have been there when the queen received the news. Images flashed through her mind of the queen frozen in disbelief as nobles heard the news and bombarded her with questions.

Zeuldian was an excellent target for a first attack. The trade running through the port city made it a significant loss. Isolde cursed under her breath as the palace came back into sight. Rushing through a side entrance, she headed straight for the queen's chambers. When she pushed open the door, she found council members scattered throughout the room. Turia stood against the wall, her face as cold as the stone as she listened to them throwing their opinions at each other. This time, everyone had made their way straight to the queen instead of convening in the council chambers. Robin stood solemnly before the lot of them, arms crossed and face smudged with dirt. She'd ridden straight through the night to make it back to Viridian.

"They destroyed most of the temple with explosives and flooded the city with soldiers. My guess is all the ashes stored there, including of phoenixes who haven't been reborn, are long gone. I was lucky to even get out. I don't see that we have a choice besides retaliation as they've made their intentions clear."

Silence hung heavy and thick in the room. The violation of something sacred. Those lives would never be recovered.

"It's simple. We send several legions out to recapture the town and push their army out of our lands."

"That's hardly a plan, Gahera," Aeryt retorted. "Besides, there's been no formal declaration of war, even if the cost we've paid is already too high." Her voice sounded tight with unshed tears, likely thinking of all those who would never be reborn again because their Bonded phoenix's ashes had been corrupted, scattered, and used.

"I'm no great lover of that temple, but that was a declaration of war if I ever saw one," Robin jumped in.

"This does feel like declaration enough," Turia interjected quietly. It didn't seem like anyone heard her. Isolde made her way to the queen, taking in her expression and trying to figure out what she was thinking.

"What do you see?" Turia whispered.

"Nothing yet."

"How helpful," the queen remarked.

"I'm afraid this decision may be left solely in your hands, my queen," Isolde replied. "The general said they knew when to attack."

"So I heard."

Neither of them said the rest of the thought. They both surveyed the room, well aware that someone in it had fed information to the enemy. Someone here was aiming for war. Isolde eyed Robin, who studied the queen with a kind of unabashed fondness that made the seer want to shake her.

"War is upon us," Turia said, speaking up. The rest of the room fell quiet. "It's clear that the Griffin King has his sights set on Zeuldian. We must consider our options carefully and see if this path can be diverted."

In that moment, Isolde's anger at Ryth threatened to brim over into her face. Why hadn't she warned her? Isolde knew why. When had Ryth ever helped her anyway? But surely, she could have the decency to tell Isolde war was on the horizon. Every silence from the phoenix was a betrayal.

The talk went on for hours and at the end, they were no closer to a decision about how to proceed with the exception of dispatching more soldiers to reinforce the moved border with orders to not engage. Isolde watched the muscles on Turia's neck tense as she tried to keep her movements under control. At last, the queen declared that she would consider the matter further in the privacy of her rooms. One by one, the council members left her there, some staying to try to talk with her further. Isolde kindly intercepted them, guiding them to the door while reassuring them that the queen would consider their recommendations. Soon all that was left was Turia, Isolde, Tristan, and Robin. The priestess had managed to evade Isolde's deft attempts at shooing her away.

"What do you think, Tristan?" the queen asked tiredly. "I'm sure that you, too, have an opinion."

"Not one worth your time," Tristan replied, inclining their head respectfully. Not for the first time, the seer noted a similarity in the faces of the two.

"I doubt that's true."

"What is true often depends on who you ask," said Tristan.

"I wish I could ask my father," the queen muttered. "His version of the truth was always so reassuring."

"Our parents often seem to have a certainty about them when we are children, but that perception tends to gradually fall apart as we get older and realize they are just as human as us," Tristan replied.

"Indeed. It used to be so easy to accept my father's version of the world as irrefutable truth. But now it's up to me," the queen said, running her fingers over one of her plants.

"It sounds like that certainty was comforting. He must have been a great man."

"I like to think he was," Turia replied.

Isolde stared out the window.

"We need to know who fed the Griffin Guard that information." She said, finally bringing the conversation back to the current matter and letting a warning infuse her words, hoping that the priestess would recognize the threat. Isolde didn't know if it was gold or freedom or a harem of women that had lured Robin to betray their queen, but she knew with a raw certainty that Robin was a fickle thing.

"It could be anyone," Turia said in a monotone voice while sinking onto her bed. "I need to rest."

Robin brushed her hand over the queen's shoulder. "No need to worry for now. After all, I'm here and I only ever speak the truth, so you must believe me."

"Is that how that works?" Turia asked dully.

"Have I ever steered you wrong?" Turia side-eyed her. "In recent memory at least?" Robin amended.

"Will you ever take anything seriously? War has come, Robin. It's at my doorstep and I've never been a fighter. I don't think you understand, it's not something I have within me. "

"Oh, believe me, I am taking this seriously. I *always* take you seriously," the woman replied.

Chapter Twenty-Seven
Isolde

23 Years After the Viridian Phoenix's Rebirth

I solde stood there watching the queen and Robin for a moment before finally nodding. She left without another word, her arms crossed and thoughts heated. Tristan followed her, but she waved them off, telling them to go to the throne room and listen to what the nobles were saying.

They nodded but observed her with concern for a moment before leaving. She immediately went to her chambers and furiously scribbled letter after letter to the remaining provinces who had not pledged allegiance to Turia.

Isolde's journey through the palace and out into the streets felt like a blur. Her mind flew elsewhere as she called for the phoenix, screaming for her presence. She soon understood that Ryth was going to make her journey out to where the creature was perched by the cliffs on foot. Her steps quickened with rage, but her eyes were open. She noticed the uneasiness on people's faces and the whispers as she passed them. Isolde pulled her green hood up over her head, hoping that she could avoid at least some of the scrutiny.

As she emerged into the square of Flowerfirst, fire met her eyes, bringing her to a halt. She drew a sharp breath. Orange flames wove through the large sconce in the middle of the space. They twisted upward, licking at the sky, hungry to send up an answer to the sun's fiery gaze. The people had lit it during the daytime. It was a prayer to the Salamanders.

Continuing on, she made her way through Fabricfirst, Fishfirst, and Steelfirst. It was the same in each square. Fire crawled upward in the normally dead sconces, lit as a way to beg favor of the Salamanders. The flames were a solemn statement of fear.

Isolde ignored the worried glances cast her way as she picked up her pace. Leaving the city, she finally reached the grasses stretching over to a cliff and there was Ryth, staring out into the distance. The creature didn't even look her way.

"The people have lit the beacons. They believe a war has started and they're pleading to the Soulless to help them!" she said through barred teeth, keeping her distance, not trusting herself to be too close to the creature while such a barrage of feelings flooded through her.

"What did you expect? It seems to me a war *has* started. It's a reasonable response."

"This isn't a war. It's a brief conflict. It will be over within months."

The phoenix didn't respond and the old bitterness welled up in her as she interpreted the silence. "You mean it won't be over soon," she spat.

"I didn't say that."

"You didn't have too. You're a terrible liar."

"My intention is never to twist the truth. I leave that to you humans," the phoenix replied, giving her head a shake in the cold breeze blowing in over the sea. It sent the blue-green flames skittering about into the misty afternoon. Isolde could barely even make out the waves below.

"Always claiming the moral high ground, aren't you?" Isolde taunted.

"Your anger doesn't bother me, child. We have been through this conversation so many times before. Wars come and wars go. They are none of my concern."

"They are mine though. One would think you would care enough about me to tell me when something this destructive is on the horizon."

"It wouldn't matter if I did."

It was the phoenix's old, self-satisfied answer and Isolde was tired of hearing it. The sound of the words burned her ears. She turned on her heel, trying to tamp down the borderline hatred stewing in her chest. She paused, not looking back to the creature.

"Can you at least tell me how long this is going to last?"

"No, Isolde. You've chosen your path."

"That could mean anything," she muttered impatiently. "If only you were some noble I could talk the truth out of."

The phoenix paused for a moment, head tilted as if making a decision. "I can see it all, child. And it is horrid. It always has been and always will be. I tried to change things myself once. I say all these things from experience."

"You mean because of your punishment?" Isolde asked. She had always assumed the texts were wrong, and it was a punishment. Ryth was nothing close to a benevolent artist, joyfully assisting the Creator in her sculpting. The tales said that the

Creator went missing at the same time that Ryth was given a mortal soul and sent to await life on the mortal plane.

"So you've guessed. How brilliant of you, Isolde," Ryth replied sarcastically. Isolde bit back a tart response. She'd asked before, in the early days, but had given up once it was clear Ryth had no desire to share.

"She was a beautiful, if cruel thing," the Phoenix started.

"The Creator, you mean?"

"I always called her Mabel, but yes."

Isolde almost chuckled at that but stopped at a harsh look from Ryth.

"What I felt for her was something you couldn't even begin to comprehend." Isolde wondered if maybe she was beginning to understand a feeling like that.

"It was...the most real thing I've ever experienced." Ryth gave her feathers a shake, settling into her spot on the ground.

"But I made a mistake. I can't..." The phoenix's speech stumbled, before hurrying on. "I loved her. She cast me out because she was going to destroy it all and move on. She had become bored and horrified at the same time. I challenged her decision. The pain had spiraled out of her control, you see. The pain of this world she'd created...she couldn't tolerate it, so she decided to start over, saying it had been this way with every world she'd ever made.

Before moving on to create another place, she stole the immortal souls of her court to leave them behind as a punishment for siding with me. They were left with little ability to feel or care. But for me...that would have been too easy. She allowed me to feel. Looked me in the eye and said, 'If you love these beings so much, I sentence you to pain. You will watch their cycles of destruction, again and again, with the knowledge that it will always end that way. Your only duty is to offer support and the warnings they will ignore.'

And so I have watched, from the Otherrealm and now here on the mortal plane. I've watched kingdom after kingdom burn. My love was right, and she left me behind because I pleaded for the likes of your kind. So you will surely forgive me if I am tired of such talk, child."

Isolde considered Ryth for a moment, arms crossed. There was something she'd left out of the story, she could sense it, but what did Isolde care? Let the creature have her secrets.

"I'm sorry for your pain."

Ryth snorted.

"I'm sorry for your pain, but I implore you to think that maybe your pain is not the only pain that matters. Who's to say if you told me more, if you warned me as the Creator bid you, the outcome could not be changed?"

"Have your ears fallen off? It always ends in tragedy. Always."

"But what if it doesn't have to?" Isolde yelled, finally losing her sense of composure.

"The pain of knowing how it ends would only ruin the time you have now. Besides, you will have another life after this one. A fresh start and the chance to see brighter days."

"But Turia won't. She's just an Unbonded human, so this is the only life she'll have."

"This queen seems like more than just an Unbonded human to you," Ryth observed.

Isolde turned, stalking away and pulling her cloak closer around her as she made her way toward the trees. She kept walking until some of her anger had dissipated. She'd approached the phoenix knowing she likely wouldn't get much information, but she felt obligated to try. There was so much knowledge just on the edge of her consciousness. She could feel the phoenix in her mind, but the creature refused, as always, to grant her any access to its visions. Only one thing had become clear through the conversation. Isolde's stomach dropped, and she cursed her lack of insight as she forced herself to head back through the city. This war was just beginning.

~

Once she'd made her way to the palace, the seer went straight to the throne room, hoping to find Tristan and see if they'd learned anything useful about the mood of the court. Instead, she found the queen perched on the throne, doing her best to disguise the tightness of her mouth and the terror in her eyes. The court was ablaze with noise. It was filled to the brim with people. Nobles who usually didn't spend time at court had broken their habit to seek out the queen and hear the latest news. Flashes of frightened eyes merged with bright headache-inducing colors to remind Isolde of how much she hated this place. Then, the people saw her, and it grew worse.

She had just managed to spot Tristan—talking with a woman in blue in the corner—when the noble mob caught wind of her presence. Her effort to keep her head down failed miserably, so she pushed her way through instead, making herself a path to the queen. Voices assaulted her ears, pleading and questions and insistence. She had no knowledge to give them beyond her own predictions. Hands brushed her sleeves. One would think they were animals rather than humans. *They're just afraid*, she told herself. But she had little patience for other people's fear. She kept her eyes fixed on Turia, tumbling and shoving her way through the masses. Someone pulled at her hand, and she jerked it away.

"Enough," she said, but no one heard her. For all their desire to see the future, they couldn't even hear her above their own inquiries. Finally, reaching the dais, she climbed the stairs in relief and made straight for Turia. Isolde only had eyes for the queen, sitting there like a statue caught frozen in the moment before it took action. Hand clutching the arms of the throne. Eyes unseeing as she stared over the crowd and out at the sea. Her breaths came quickly as she hyperventilated at the sight laid out before her.

While she desperately wanted to take Turia's hand and ask her if she was alright, she knew that wouldn't aid the queen in gaining control over the court, so instead she positioned herself beside the throne and looked out at the people. She met their eyes, staring them down fiercely in the stead of their queen. If it was possible, their calls grew even louder as they shouted at each other in confusion and tried to force their questions to her ears. Noise built upon noise. The Phoenix Guard stepped closer to the queen as the chaos erupted. She stayed frozen.

Isolde walked forward to the edge of the dais.

"I've received a vision! Calm yourselves and listen," she called. She shouted it out again and again until the people closest to the dais heard and the message began to spread. Like a wave, the noise fell to a buzz. A faint ringing sounded in her ears, perhaps the effect of so much hubbub or the impact of the intensity of her own thoughts.

Isolde held her hands out. "There is nothing to fear," she stated. "I have seen it. The Soulless have heard our prayers. They will bolster our efforts as long as we stay true in our loyalty to each other.

"I have seen it. It will not be without hardship. It is a test of your hearts, but it will not be in vain," she continued evenly. She had to sow some truth into this new lie.

"I have seen it. I have seen wreaths crowning us victorious as our fires burn stronger than ever. Walk in confidence and rest in this knowledge. May it provide you refuge through the times ahead. I have seen irises burning without falling apart. Remember these words and heed the blessing of the Soulless." Voices rose in confusion, but she continued, speaking louder than ever. "Let our fires burn."

The crowd erupted into frantic conversations once more. Isolde was finished trying to corral them. Only time would tell whether her words had made a substantial impact. Isolde hoped so, for the sake of the queen.

She peered back at Turia briefly only to see that the queen was finally looking at something besides the sea. For the first time, the fear in Arturia's eyes was directed toward Isolde.

Chapter Twenty-Eight

Isolde

23 Years After the Viridian Phoenix's Rebirth

Isolde watched from a window as people celebrated beneath her. Her eyes attempted to flutter shut, but she forced them to stay open. All day they'd been leaving small wrought-iron irises on the steps of the palace. They were gathering them carefully, wondering at their shape and the way the metal glowed from within without being hot to the touch.

The city had woken to a miracle. The strange irises were in every city square, resting beside the fires burning to the Soulless. The flowers were a promise. A vow. Fear lost footing as people smiled at the beauty of such small wonders and the fact that they had been given the privilege of seeing an omen firsthand. They now covered the steps, glowing through the morning mist with an unearthly light.

Isolde hadn't spoken to anyone for hours. Sinking down onto the window ledge, she leaned her head against the glass and fell asleep to the pulsing rhythm of the Otherrealmly flowers. She had seen an omen in her mind and summoned it to life with her hands. It was the deepest kind of magic. She just seemed to understand its cutting nature more than those around her. When she envisioned her own death, she saw herself bleeding dreams and omens so others could have a false sense of peace.

The blood followed her into her slumber. She stayed there in the window, high above the soothed world until the cold night pressing against the glass woke her. Someone was humming. Isolde glanced down and saw Tristan sitting against the wall. Their eyes were closed, and they sang some song she'd never heard, more to themself than to anyone else it seemed.

"How long have you been here?" she asked.

"I found you here after you didn't show up for your midday meal. The queen came looking for you in your chambers. I told her you were probably just off fighting monsters somewhere or devouring ancient secrets our brains wouldn't be able to comprehend. But I decided to interrupt your solitude anyway."

She scrambled up. "I'd hardly call you sitting against the wall and twiddling your thumbs interrupting me. Turia was searching for me?"

Isolde grabbed her cloak from the ledge, already in motion to go find the queen.

"The council is just at the same game they've been playing for hours."

"She's with the council?" Isolde exclaimed, her pulse thrumming. Of course Turia was. Damn her tired eyes. She'd slept the whole day away when the queen needed her.

"Slow down," Tristan said gently.

"Don't tell me you can't keep up," she shot back.

"What I'm saying is that they've been talking all day and they'll still be talking when you get there."

They were missing the point. People always did. "We're in a war. I have to be there, Tristan."

They put a hand on her shoulder. "Don't worry. I brought her messages every so often, so she could take a minute without everyone babbling in her ears."

Isolde reassessed them. Maybe they did understand. "I don't want her to be alone," she said quietly, admitting her vulnerability.

"I know," they replied.

Isolde swallowed, wanting to stuff the words back in her throat. It felt like too much information to be handing out. Oh, the ways that statement could be used against her. She thought of all the things she could do with that utterance, the schemes she could spin out and the stories she could build from seven words.

Isolde buried her uneasiness as she slipped into the council room, already making her observations. The way Aeryt leaned away from everyone else, her shoulders tense. Gahera's small glares in the direction of Kaye. Dark circles rested beneath the queen's eyes. Maybe neither of them had slept the previous night.

Turia waited impatiently for Aeryt to finish speaking before she looked up at Isolde hopelessly asking in a whisper, "Have you seen anything else, Seer?"

"I'm afraid I see fields of begonias, warning of unavoidable turmoil, and you rising, crowned in irises. Other than that, my visions are clouded," she said quietly.

The whole table heard her, but they held their silence.

"It's clear that the Griffin King has launched a war. There's no stopping it now," Robin stated.

"It might be time to build more weapons, maybe even test out the new Firefiend designed by the war alchemirs," Gahera states.

"The one that can burn through fireproof resin? That seems extreme when our typical weapons are doing just fine. I do think we're already taking the violence too far," Sir Kaye replied.

"We've been over this already," Aeryt said, her normally hearty level of patience wearing thin. "The question is how much of a response, where, and when. There is no longer a question of if we should. We have to mobilize our armies. It's time to call on the troops of the princes and princesses. We must assess our extra numbers while preparing the soldiers we do have to retake Zeuldian as our first move."

"Agreed. We have to recover the town quickly. Give these bastards an inch and they'll take a mile," replied Robin.

"You think there's no chance for diplomacy?" Lord Percival asked.

"Not when a king has war in his heart. He hasn't even made his intentions known with words. He hasn't demanded anything of us. He hasn't given us the chance to wage peace, instead just trying to seize our lands."

No one could argue with the queen on that point.

So it was. Letters were sent out to the princes and princesses of the Fire Folk provinces, calling on them to honor their loyalty to the high queen. They were sealed with hot wax and sent by phoenix with the hope they would be answered within the week. They spread maps across the round table, marking their soldiers and arguing with each other before finally settling on their strategy to retake Zeuldian. Some still disagreed on the details, but Turia made her wishes clear.

War. What a deceptive word. Isolde had made her peace with it, if one could do such a thing, but she could see it was just occurring to Turia that they were under attack. She sensed it in Turia's hands balling up fistfuls of her dress under the council table. Her eyes were distantly frantic, even as her mouth said the right words in her queenly, graceful tone. Her tone betrayed her and her emotions were splayed painfully across her face.

The seer watched the queen scurry away from the room, as she always did, fighting against her own body to get back to the anonymity of her chambers.

Isolde, as she always did, picked up her pace, tracing the queen's steps on the dark marble floor.

"Don't follow me," Turia stated quietly, not even turning around to meet the seer's eyes.

Isolde couldn't allow the despair in her voice to stand. She only quickened her pace until she was walking next to the queen.

"I'm afraid you can't stop me," Isolde said jauntily.

Turia stopped, turning to lock eyes with the seer. "Sometimes I fear your boldness."

An uncomfortable silence hung about them. "You shouldn't."

"Always so opinionated. But I guess I would be too if I was deemed sacred by the Soulless."

Isolde scoffed at that, for once letting her bitterness leak through her precise facade.

Turia kept walking. "Go play with your apprentice and leave me be tonight."

Isolde's eyebrows scrunched up, suddenly wary of the queen's perceptions.

"Do you take issue with my apprentice?"

"Don't be ridiculous. Companionship is such a marvelous and necessary evil."

"They've been wonderfully helpful to our cause, my queen. I wouldn't so quickly disparage building trust and loyalty with those around you." Isolde's voice was coated in ice.

Turia shook her head, her lips pursed with an emotion that was either disdain or pain. She opened her door only wide enough to allow her to slip into the room, before turning to face the seer, who still stood outside.

"You can't understand everything, Seer. I suggest you stop trying to do so."

Vague words were Isolde's game, and she wasn't sure she liked their look on the queen.

"Why are you so intent on being alone?" Isolde demanded.

"What are you, my nurse? I am not a child to be ordered about and held in suspicion."

Isolde took a different approach, making her voice softer and lowering her head in defeat.

"I'm sorry, my queen. I'm afraid humility sometimes escapes me."

Turia just stared at her disbelievingly through the crack in the door.

Isolde lowered her voice, so the guards down the hall wouldn't hear. "Talk of the war can wait. Are you…are you in pain? Is your own blessing painful?"

Turia avoided her eyes. "Irony suits you, Seer." She trailed away from the door fretfully, leaving it open. That was all the invitation Isolde needed to enter. She shut the door briskly behind her, only to turn around and find Turia already with her fingers steeped in dirt as she tended to one of her plants. The princess's neck jerked. She suddenly withdrew her fingers from the plants and then buried them back in the dirt once more. Her movements were explosive in a way they hadn't been in the hallway. Then they had been tensely contained.

"Does it hurt?" Isolde asked.

"Only sometimes."

"Is it worse after council meetings? You're always rushing back from them."

"Some days, I can keep it at bay." Turia ran a finger tenderly over a leaf before her fingers flew off into the air abruptly. "I can keep it caged. But it grows angry when I do that and makes itself more present later. It doesn't like being kept on a leash, which I guess I can understand."

Isolde opened her mouth to respond, but then thought better of it.

"Struck speechless, Seer?"

"Hardly," Isolde said. "Just considering what a burden that must be."

"Well, it can be pretty amusing to watch people's reactions."

"But?" the seer replied solemnly.

"You have to laugh at the world and your own misfortunes sometimes, Isolde. For all your wisdom, I'm getting the sense that might be something you need to learn."

Isolde crouched down beside her. "Is this you laughing at the world? Then I fear to see the day you're truly solemn."

She'd crossed the line once more. The queen sprang up. "How could you understand? " she simmered, moving to the window.

"I'm trying to understand."

"It's different than before. It's not something to laugh at anymore, now that I'm cursed to be queen."

"Most would call it a blessing to be queen. People die to be where you are."

"So you've said." The queen grimaced.

"I wish I could make you laugh."

Turia didn't look at her. "You do, on occasion. When you're being an uptight toad."

"What kind words for your seer."

"I save my kindest words for you," Turia said with a smile.

"I only wish you weren't being serious," Isolde replied.

"You're wishing a lot right now, aren't you, Seer? You don't strike me as someone who would be a proponent of wishing."

Isolde joined her by the window, leaning against the wall. She conceded the point with the tilt of her head. "I don't mean it in a half-committed, let-the-world-happen-to-you sense of the word. Wishing is like desire and for desire to mean anything you have to commit to doing what's in your power to show how badly you want it. Fate is forged, one way or another."

"Sometimes I think you're full of horse shit." The queen paused. "Do you think I'm only half-committed to my wishes?"

"I don't think you really want me to answer that."

Turia's jaw clenched. "I do have desires, you know. As much as you may think it, I'm not without ambition or grit."

"When did I ever say that?"

The queen turned away, stalking to her bed to hide the hot tears leaking from her eyes despite herself. "Every single day. And maybe you're right. No, I know you're right. My brother would have been better. Any of my uncles would have been better rulers, even Uncle Strawhead."

"I'm guessing that's not actually his name?" Isolde remarked wryly, trying to break the tension. It didn't work.

Turia just let out a strangled cry, curling into her bed as the last of the light died from the sky outside the window. The only thing to break the silence of the nighttime castle was the former princess's bitter sobs.

Isolde cautiously wandered over, unsure what to do with herself and the crying queen. "You can only feel sorry for yourself for so long. Eventually you have to pull your head out of the dirt. My queen, you have to recognize the truth and the truth is you are, without a doubt, the best option for the Fire Folk."

"Your…compassion…is…simply…stunning," Turia coughed out between sobs. The words sounded all gummed up and delicate.

The seer watched the girl turn her face away, hiding the tears in her pillow. Something fragile rose up in her chest as she watched, wanting to help, but holding herself back. She stood. She stopped herself from reaching out. Surely, the queen wanted to be alone and the seer was the last person she wanted to see her in this state. But as soon as the thought entered her mind, she knew it was a lie. And the glass wall between them broke.

Carefully, slowly, Isolde sank onto the bed and wrapped herself around her friend. As soon as she did, Turia's sobs intensified along with her movements, but Isolde held on, burying her face in the queen's hair. Finding the queen's hand, she entwined their fingers and let her thumb brush gently over the outside of Turia's own thumb. After a moment, the queen curled further into her and turned her hand to fully grasp Isolde's and pull it into her chest. They stayed like that as the darkness lengthened and the moon flew brightly through the sky, until the queen's breaths had grown steady and long.

Even though she was still awake, Isolde didn't move. She couldn't bring herself to pull away from Turia's warmth, even though she had planned to make an excursion to the grove to ask the Soulless for favor. One was most likely to catch their ear in the middle of the night when they were less concerned with their squabbles with each other and more focused on simply being in the world. Night was a quiet time for them but sleepless in its hold. As it turned out, Isolde was far from divine and far from sleepless. Darkness overtook her and the willowy queen, easing her into a sleep so complete that no dreams dared disturb her.

Chapter Twenty-Nine

The Spy

23 Years After the Viridian Phoenix's Rebirth

A figure scurried through the dark halls of the palace, light on their feet. They paused, pulling their hood closer over their head before easing open the door to the Palace Archives. A single candle burned at the desk of the head librarian, a surprisingly young woman with sweet eyes. She pushed her glasses up, leaning further over the text she was studying.

Thankfully, by the time she looked up at the sound, the door was already closed and all appeared normal. With a quiet ferocity, the intruder found the section they were looking for, produced a key they'd all-too-easily filched, and opened the box with the plans for the Firefiend inside.

It took them much longer than they would have preferred to carefully copy out the information in the thick folder into an empty notebook of their own. Even so, they had exited the Palace Archives before even two hours had passed. The librarian was none the wiser and neither were the queen and her seer sleeping in the chambers above.

Chapter Thirty

Isolde

23 Years After the Viridian Phoenix's Rebirth

Turia and Isolde woke to the hollow sounds of fists knocking on the queen's door just after dawn. Isolde self-consciously pulled her hand away from the sleeping queen's arm, where it still rested from the night before. The knocks registered again, this time causing Turia to stir. Neither of them had changed into nightclothes. Isolde tried to comb her fingers through her hair, but they kept snagging in the waves.

Without opening her eyes, Turia just mumbled, "Let them knock. No need to answer."

"I disagree."

"Of course you do. I don't want anyone here in my chambers. It isn't safe."

"Surely you don't think someone would have the audacity to attack you in your own chambers, especially while others are present?" Isolde asked.

"Certainty is a gift I haven't been granted."

"So you plan to avoid..." Isolde reconsidered her words, trying to sift through what might get through to the queen.

"For how long?"

Turia finally opened her eyes. They were dull and tired. "Until we understand what the hell is going on."

This answer stirred up Isolde's frustration.

"That could be a while. You know how important it is to let the court know you aren't afraid."

Turia didn't respond, closing her eyes again. Isolde's pulse quickened. The queen was afraid. Deathly afraid. And why shouldn't she be? There was no disputing a spy was at large. That wasn't even the most concerning part. Hadn't Isolde herself sensed someone watching her, tracing her steps on her nightly journeys to pray or forge? A sound where there shouldn't have been one. A scrape. A suddenly-ceasing footfall. There was something on the edge of her vision just beyond her sight. Until now, she had dismissed it as Turia's paranoia getting to her, but now she wasn't so sure.

Something in Isolde prickled at the idea that with all of her training and all that she noticed and all the pains she took to read other people, she could have missed something following her. That was part of the reason she'd not thought very hard about the possibility. If someone was following her, they were doing a godawful job of it. Even worse though was that her own pride had been a detriment to the queen. The very thing she was trying to avoid.

Isolde hesitated but decided it would be for the best. "Your highness, I may have the answer to your concerns."

"Oh?" she asked sarcastically, examining a newly-bloomed yellow flower.

"It might be beneficial to look into the high priestesses' movements."

"Robin? You want to spy on Robin?" Turia laughed. "Don't be ridiculous."

"I'm many things, but ridiculous isn't one of them."

"Why on earth would you think Robin is a threat?"

"Why wouldn't you? She openly defies authority, and gets away with it, I might add. She's brash. Has little regard for the wellbeing of others. And I don't think she could be penitent to save her life. That utter dismissal of your authority…it doesn't bode well. I don't think Robin is just a threat. I think she is *the* threat and one that's staring us right in the face."

"It's not my authority she's dismissing, Isolde. If you think that, you've sorely misjudged her. Robin defies the priesthood, the thing that has shamed her and kept her in chains since childhood. I still keep the faith, but after what happened to her, I almost didn't. People will always corrupt any formal organization in the end, even sacred ones. They had to drag her screaming to her confirmation. And they did it early because they found her kissing a girl." Turia didn't mention that the girl in question was herself. While the general population may have been fairly accepting, everyone understood that those who were holy must be held to higher standards.

"Surely she can understand that her flippant attitude puts you at risk."

"Not everything is about you or I, Seer. Certainly not about your political machinations."

Isolde paused at that, bristling. "Don't think she's not a snake just because she flirts with you like she does with every other woman in this soulforsaken palace."

Turia turned away then—tight anger written in the lines of her face—and Isolde knew the conversation was over.

~

Isolde made her way to Robin 's chambers, pounding on the door as soon as she got there. If Turia would not address the threat, she would.

"Goodness, just a moment." Robin cracked her door open, peeking out from behind it. "Oh, Seer. It's you."

Isolde got the distinct impression that the priestess wasn't fully clothed. If Isolde was someone less self-restrained, she would have sputtered right then. She glanced at the bright daylight streaming through the hall windows. Did the woman have no shame? She wasn't even pretending to be celibate, as the priesthood required.

"I need a moment of your time," she stated.

"As does every other girl at court," said Robin with a cheeky smile. She was too happy.

Isolde just grimaced in response.

"Should've known you don't swing that way. I suppose you're not going to leave until we talk?"

"For once in your life, you'd be correct."

"Have you considered that maybe it wouldn't be in your best interest to insult the high priestess?"

Isolde just smiled. They both knew who held more power.

With a dramatic sigh, Robin closed the door, chatting with someone inside and presumably pulling on her clothes.

When she opened the door again, black hair tousled and tunic untucked, she opened it wide enough for a blonde girl to leave. The lady quickly made her way down the hall, and Isolde didn't spare her another glance.

Isolde made her way inside the room. As soon as Robin shut the door she began.

"I know what you're doing."

"And what is that?" Robin asked tiredly.

"I'm not going to stand here and explain your own plans to you, but you will stop whatever you're doing immediately."

"You sound deranged."

"That may be, but I'm also right." Isolde stepped closer. "I see you, High Priestess."

"Do you?" Robin asked. She threw her hands up with a laugh. "I really have no idea what you're talking about."

Yes, Robin was lovable in a way Isolde would never be, but that didn't mean she didn't have the capacity for disloyalty or bloodshed or hatred. In fact, quite the opposite. And it left the seer trembling because of how much the queen loved and trusted her.

"Forgive me if I don't believe you."

"I think forgiveness is very much something you need. I see you, too, Seer."

Isolde didn't flinch. "If you continue, you'll end up with your head on a platter. I promise."

Robin paused for a second, taken aback by the violence of the outright threat.

"Turia would never get over it."

"I think you overestimate how much she cares for you."

Isolde could see from the expression on Robin's face that she'd hit home. She smiled with satisfaction.

After a moment Robin spoke. "Turia is something neither of us can ever be. We need her goodness and gentleness to temper our worst urges, certainly. Believe me when I say I would never cause her harm. I do many things in the name of my own pleasure, but she will always be the exception."

Isolde considered the way Robin's dark brown eyes sparkled as she fixed them steadily on the seer and the strength of her stance. It sent anger bubbling up in her. She could spot no lie, but that didn't mean there wasn't one. For the moment, though, she conceded with a nod of her head.

~

Turia would not leave her chambers. Not for meals. Not for council meetings. Not to visit court for just an hour. She even refused to see her beloved Robin.

Isolde fought with her. A heated conversation with a seemingly endless cycle of rounds. Isolde would make the same arguments. Damn good arguments in her opinion. Proposing survival. It was that simple. But Turia would retort, quietly, bitterly, and then proceed to not speak at all. When she was tired of the conversation and tired of Isolde, she just stared out the window and let the seer argue with the wall. Not just that though. She wouldn't see a soul except for the seer and while the seer understood, and maybe even felt somewhat honored by that trust, she knew that in and of itself was another foolish decision. The queen seemed bent on making near-suicidal choices.

It was not lost on Isolde how Lady Candille gave her a cautiously appraising look every time she passed them in the hallways or how Lord Trenson glared at her when she wasn't looking at evening meals. They thought she was controlling the queen. Maybe even had some unearthly hold over her. What other explanation was there for the queen abandoning her people while a war was beginning? All the while she continued praising the queen, trying to set the court's minds at ease with her soothing words. But there was only so much the seer could do.

She sat in at council meetings and listened as everyone provided updates on troops and weapons and attacks and casualties—all of which the seer communicated back to the queen. Isolde remained usually silent and watchful, trying to monitor what was really going on in the room. The exception to this was when she was conveying the queen's thoughts, always using the excuse that the queen had sustained an injury and, while healthy enough, was still being advised to rest by the physician.

The palace was silent. Ghostly almost. Brimming with the hushed voices of people who feared they might start a war if they spoke too loudly. What they didn't understand was that war was already upon them. Already an unusual number of young men and women were enlisting in the army. Enlisting was perhaps a generous word. The soldier's base commission had been raised by order of the council and for many families that kind of money could make a substantial difference. Besides, there was honor in defending one's home.

What wasn't quiet was the ghost trailing her footsteps.

Uneasiness crept into Isolde's stomach as she emerged from a small door in the northern wing. It let out onto a narrow cliffside path, one with very little preventing one from tumbling into the ocean below. With brisk steps, she pushed away her uneasiness. There was no point to it. A silly emotion without purpose.

The walk itself did, of course, have a purpose. Everything pointed toward a normal excursion for the seer. Normal pace. Normal path. Normal face. Not even looking back, but once she'd entered Fashionfirst, it didn't take too long for her to pick out consistently light footsteps among the few young people traipsing about in the temperate night. The intruder clearly didn't mean her any harm, at least not yet, given the goal seemed to be gathering intel. Her feet held steady as she headed to the forge. Tonight was her turn to get information. Her fist tightened, her steps slightly heavier with the anger flaring inside her.

She dipped inside the dark forge and began preparing her tools, taking her time and starting the fire. After digging around the shelves for a moment, she grunted with frustration and headed into one of the side rooms. As she cursed about not being able to find the proper tool, she carefully peered through the glass into the alley. It was empty. Glancing back at the door to the room containing the forge, she pulled open the square window and pulled herself through it as quietly as possible.

Edging her way along the dark walls toward the entrance, she listened. Not a sound. Trying the entrance first since it was the most likely possibility for where the spy would be creeping, she peered around the corner. After searching the dark road for any signs of life, she swiftly headed back down the alley. Rounding the corner to the narrow passage behind the forge, she caught the sound of scuffling shoes. A flash of silver in the shadows. The back door stood cracked open.

The figure's head was tilted carefully, as though they were listening. Their head shook and Isolde saw their shoulders stiffen in realization as they leaned toward the door. Pulling herself back around the cobblestone wall so she was hidden, she watched with a grim satisfaction. The realization wasn't that they were being watched. It was that they hadn't heard any sounds from inside for a long while. *Idiot.*

Moonlight spilled into the alley as some clouds passed and the person hastily pulled the door shut. With something akin to panic, they sprinted down the path, thankfully in the direction opposite her. As they turned onto another side street, their profile was caught between the dancing shadows and the moonlight fighting the darkness.

Isolde turned away and started walking. Down every questionable road, dark and stinking, and muddy. Through broad alleys and lengths of packed dirt that could hardly even be called paths. She kept walking. Sweeping through places she would have no memory of later, Isolde breathed like humans did. She didn't feel human though. She felt nothing. She saw the paths in front of her and decided right then that she wanted to see them all. Every last one. Without anyone following her or knowing her whereabouts. Maybe without anyone even knowing she was still alive. True freedom only came in the absence of others. Isolde wanted to be nameless. On and on she went, throwing herself into the night, numb to everything the world had tried to make of her.

Chapter Thirty-One

Isolde

23 Years After the Viridian Phoenix's Rebirth

I solde didn't visit Turia the next morning like she usually did. She was still floating through the city, breathing in the cold morning mist. By the time she did return to the palace, it was past midday, and she still didn't visit the queen. She passed through the kitchens. Ate a meal methodically and mechanically. Paced through the palace, passing couriers with their curious eyes.

Unbidden memories of her grandparents plagued her mind. Every threat juxtaposed with every kind word. The old confusion about love and trust rose again, pressing down on her chest. Her grandmother had been carved into someone who would hurt Isolde for the promise of money. Had it always been that way? There had always been a resentment toward Isolde, certainly. But wasn't that fair? Especially when her family already had had to scrape by to survive before she had crashed into their lives and become their responsibility? She remembered the fear in her grandmother's eyes, often spurred on by her grandfather's displeasure. What room was there for real love, when survival took priority? The words of love existed, but there was scant evidence to support them.

She'd been taught that survival trumped all else, every other relationship and every other feeling. Isolde's wishful thinking, her weakness, had led her astray. She'd forgotten the ruthless lessons she'd learned at the hands of the real world.

Slipping into the armory, she looked carefully through the swords hanging on the walls.

Some were basic practice swords, quickly beaten out by apprentice blacksmiths learning their trade. Most were nicked and worn weapons, the kind that Isolde and Tristan usually practiced with. Isolde trailed her fingers over the fancier jeweled swords, which flashed brilliantly in the dim light of the single torch hoisted in the sconce on the wall. They seemed cold and sleek. But too clean. The kind of swords that Isolde didn't trust because, although they seemed to proclaim wealth and boldness, it was clear to her that they had never seen a day of battle in their lives. Most were gifts from minor princes trying to ply favor from the former high king. Hanging beside them were those Turia had received from sovereigns pledging their loyalty to their new high queen. There were still a handful of provinces who had yet to send a token, despite the threat of the war. One of the many things that worried Isolde.

Sometimes she wondered if Turia really did understand the precarious position she was in. But maybe Isolde was only so set on convincing her of it because of her own role in foisting the throne on the young queen. Perhaps that was the case, but perhaps not. Isolde was always trying to step into the future and was always being dragged, clawing, back into the present.

Caliburnus hung on a wall away from the others, glinting in a fluid way that might have made a casual viewer uneasy. It was clearly not of this world. There was no denying it. It hadn't been put to the test yet, but it still looked as though it had weathered many a war. Just another lie woven into its being.

Isolde turned away from it and to her favorite section, which held the plain, sharp swords of the palace guard. No elaborate wrought-iron workings on the hilt, no engravings, no jewels, no confusing words. The sword hanging at her waist was of this variety. She ran her fingers lovingly over them for a moment, nicking her finger on the point of one. Isolde watched the blood swell on her fingertip carelessly. She pressed her finger to her skirt, then strolled over to the jeweled swords once more. Plucking a sword with an ocean-blue gem on the hilt from the wall, she turned around and strode from the armory, her steps sharp on the stone beneath.

After tucking the sword into her belt, she left the palace grounds, ignoring every single person she passed. She didn't slow down to listen to their conversations. She didn't greet them and offer words of reassurance. She didn't visit the queen.

The sun began to sink below the horizon. Isolde still wore the same clothes from the night before and her eyelids were heavy from lack of sleep, but she kept walking. As she made her way to the cliffs on foot, a lengthy journey, her fingers traced over the vines on the hilt of the jeweled sword almost of their own accord. It was a colder night than the previous one. A cool breeze swept over her face, especially as she neared the ocean. She'd blocked out the phoenix who she hadn't seen for days. Ryth had called to her yesterday, but she hadn't answered.

The sun fell below the horizon in a fiery mess, giving the moon the room it needed to ascend. Once Isolde reached the cliffs, she stuck closer to the trees than she normally would have, keeping her pace slow and steady. She wouldn't want to lose her ghost, who wasn't particularly good at what they were attempting anyway. Good enough though. *Good enough to escape my notice for so long,* she reminded herself.

Finally, she broke from the tree line, making her way to the edge of the most prominent cliff. Isolde withdrew the jeweled sword from her belt and turned to face the gentle darkness.

"Well, are you going to come out?" she shouted, her words clipped and short.

She listened as the wind picked up. There was a bit of low scuffling off to her right.

"You're just going to retreat then? Nothing more than I would expect from a coward I suppose."

The sounds ceased for a moment. It was like she could hear their thoughts racing as they realized they'd been noticed. She half expected them to flee.

"There's no point in pretending you're not there, Tristan." Their name flew high over the rustling grasses, somehow louder than she'd meant it to be.

A shape emerged at the edge of the woods. Even from this distance, she could see the tenseness of their shoulders, though the shadows still hid their face until they quietly left the cover of the trees. They didn't look at her as they picked their way through the grasses, hands in their pockets.

They should have been smarter than that. Isolde could have killed them right there. Attacked while their eyes were focused on the earth, slit their throat, and been finished with the whole ugly business. But she held her position as the wind grew in strength, sending her hair flying. She'd forgotten how much it loved them.

Tristan stopped a few feet away, keeping their head down, refusing to make eye contact.

"I'm sorry. I just wanted to see where you kept going at night," they said, but their voice was too strained.

"We both know better."

They took a deep breath. "Please, Isolde. Let me explain."

Isolde threw the jeweled sword down at their feet disdainfully. The air stilled as they finally looked up and met her gaze.

"Surely not," they said quietly, but there was no surprise in their voice.

"This is a kindness. I suggest you take it."

"What if I refuse?"

"Pick up the sword, Tristan."

"I never wanted this." They took a tentative step toward her, but was brought to a halt as she raised the tip of her own weapon to their chest.

"If that's true, you're a fool. Pick up the sword, or I kill you right here without even giving you the chance to defend yourself. I try to be a woman of honor, but you're testing me." Her words hit the air sharply, tinged with the danger and violence she felt stirring in her chest.

Keeping their eyes fixed on her face, they carefully stooped down to retrieve the sword. She was on them as soon as they were upright once more. They stumbled backward from the force of her first blow. Blow after blow, they were driven backward, dodging or blocking her thrusts weakly. The sound of blood and wind and waves rushed in her ears, shaping the world into a blurred, angry contortion of itself as she watched the fear flare in their moonlit eyes. The wind still played with their hair, even now. The force of each of her blows ripped through her arms. She could feel the heat rising on her cheeks and all she wanted to do was scream, but she held it in.

Again and again, she was almost close enough to feel their breath on her face. Making a half-hearted attempt at a strike, they missed and plunged forward, where she had been a moment before. Isolde seized the wrist on their right hand and they reached out, catching hold of her other wrist. The blood beat out a terrified pulse where her fingers met their warm skin. They held her wrist firmly, but there was still a gentleness to the touch that made her shove them. They only ended up closer, whirling around, locked in a struggle while still holding their swords. Giving them a swift kick in the shin, she caused them to stumble. Unfortunately they held on, dragging her down as they crashed into the moist night earth. Dirt flew into her mouth. But she was quicker than them and soon had her knee in their chest and the edge of her sword glistening at their neck.

The jeweled sword lay out of Tristan's reach, but they weren't reaching for it. They weren't even struggling as they met her eyes in the darkness. There was something resigned in the expression resting on their face. Her white knuckles tightened on her sword hilt as fury coursed through her. Their eyes were much too earnest for the liar she knew them for. Why couldn't anything ever be straightforward and true? Why couldn't people be honest? Why did the life she wanted have to run away from her, always twisting into the opposite of the thing she desired? *Perhaps it is simply the fate of a liar to always be thwarted by the lies of others*, she thought bitterly. Heartrendingly unfair. But she couldn't deny the truth of how that always seemed to play out for her. She knew the Soulless didn't care.

Her throat grew thick as Tristan just stared at her in the moonlight. Dirt streaked their cheek, as if signaling the beginning of their burial. They were a person resigned to death. This image of them was so at odds with their usual liveliness that seeing that suddenly stripped from them caused her to falter. The new hollowness growing in their eyes...she recognized it. It was achingly familiar to her. A neutrality about one's own life. They were ready to suffer the consequences and wasn't that what she wanted? Wasn't that what she had imagined since the pieces first clicked in her mind. She wanted to see them begging. Scared. Ashamed of the lies they'd told her. Here she was having the twisted honor of watching the world crush them, and Isolde found she didn't want any part in it.

Isolde's hand tightened on their arm. She braced herself, pushing the sword just the slightest bit further into their skin.

"Just make it quick," Tristan whispered.

Isolde let out a frustrated noise. In one quick motion, she rolled off them, stood, and yanked them up by their arm. Keeping her sword at their neck, she drew them close so they had no choice but to meet her eyes.

"You must never return."

Cautious realization dawned on their face at her words.

"I won't spare you a second time, Tristan. The Soulless know I should kill you right now with all the harm you've done."

"Isolde…"

"Not a word," she growled. "You're not meant for war. I suggest you find a path that suits you better."

She pushed them away, releasing her grip on their arm, but they just stood there staring at her.

"Are you waiting for some kind of blessing? Go, you idiot."

They turned and, with quaking footsteps, broke into a run, not even bothering to take the sword she'd offered with them.

She watched their retreating form until their shadow had disappeared among the trees. Her jaw was tight as she turned back to the ocean. No tears came. No words. No thoughts. Only the hollowness in her own chest spreading out as she stared out at the waves. But even that hurt.

Swallowing the lump in her throat, Isolde swept up the discarded sword and trekked back to the city with quick, precise steps. Back in her room, she mechanically changed into her nightclothes, only to spot a clump of green flowers embroidered on the hem. Snatching a pair of shears from her bedside table, she cut into the night dress and relieved it of its embellishment, tossing the scrap into the slowly dying fire.

Isolde had no words. So she closed her eyes, hoping that the morning would bring a distraction from the heaviness in her throat. She drew the covers closer to her and tried to banish the queen's face from her mind.

Chapter Thirty-Two

The Sylph Princess Anore

23 Years After the Viridian Phoenix's Rebirth

S he saw them, and she shattered.

What was this breaking blossoming deep within her? How long had it been? The pain sparking caught her off guard—threw her off balance, causing her to spin in the hazy sky. It was almost as if the air reflected the smoke billowing up, up, up from her starved lungs. Was this Feeling? Surely not. It had been so very long since anything had knocked her off her axis. But this human...

They rode the air with their eyes closed, giving themselves completely to the griffin carrying them and the clouds they soared through. They stretched out their arms and a gentle smile caressed their face.

There! There it was again! The...*Feeling*. Feeling in one of the Soulless? Unheard of for generations, but such was the power of this individual. They made her...Feel. She watched them, breathlessly tracing their path with glassy eyes.

With a sudden rush, she knew that she wanted, no *needed*, more of it. She inhaled, greedy for their scent and the Feeling.

She lifted her hand and blew a gentle breeze forth to rustle those lovely brown curls.

Chapter Thirty-Three

Isolde

23 Years After the Viridian Phoenix's Rebirth

It wasn't hard to avoid the queen when she wasn't leaving her chambers. Isolde continued about her business. She attended the council meeting the next day. The insights weren't sensitive, so she sent them to the queen by way of messenger rather than going herself.

Her mind turned through the possibilities spilling out in front of her, irreparably staining her future. Ever practical, Isolde began indexing all the things Tristan would know about their strategies. Everything they would be sure to convey to the Griffin King. They would have to change it all and do the unexpected, which the Griffin King would know if he had any sense at all.

Rage burned the bottom of her feet, reminding her with every step that she should have killed them right there. Should have purged them of their remaining knowledge of the inner workings of their court when she had the chance. Isolde would have to tell the queen and soon. But it had to be on her own terms. She had to have next steps in place. A plan. A way to calm the already suspicious high queen.

Until then, she ate her meals. Talked to the couriers. Slept. A day passed. Then two. Then three. The fourth morning, a knock on her door startled her awake.

"Isolde?" A strained, tired voice called. She froze. The queen.

"Isolde, are you in there? If so, I suggest you let me in."

She didn't respond, trying to quiet her breathing, just in case the queen could detect it from the other side of the door. Who was being paranoid now? Maybe she would leave if Isolde didn't respond. Something delicate rose up in her though. Turia had risked leaving her rooms to find her. Her miscalculations overtook her in a sudden wave crashing down over her head.

"I'm all for young love, Seer, but I suggest you don't lose sight of your duties in service to that apprentice of yours."

Her soft, teasing voice broke something in Isolde that she couldn't identify, no matter how hard she tried to put her finger on it.

The door cracked open cautiously and the queen peered through. Isolde allowed her eyes to flutter groggily as though she was too tired to have an intelligible thought in her head. Turia eyed her with confusion and closed the door behind her. In one arm she carried a glazed pot brimming with the red petals of asclepias flowers. Tears pricked Isolde's eyes at the sight as she watched the queen purposefully place them on the barren windowsill of the seer's sparsely-decorated room, adjusting the pot and stems just so. The bright flowers declared war against the stoic beiges of the rest of the room. With brisk steps the queen swept over to Isolde's bed, holding her hand to the silent seer's head.

"You're not sick, are you?"

"Your majesty. What brings you here at such an early hour?"

"Early? It's nearly lunchtime, you dolt."

"What kind words for your seer," Isolde mumbled, pulling a pillow over her head to hide her expression more than anything.

"Come now. What's the matter with you?" Her voice slipped into its more typical serious tone. "You haven't been to see me in three days."

"Contrary to what you may think, my whole life doesn't revolve around you, your majesty."

"I know you well enough to know when you're lying."

She swallowed. The discomfort soon twisted into a harshly-restrained laugh at the irony of that statement.

Turia yanked the pillow away from the seer's face. "Is it that apprentice? Surely not. For some reason I can't picture you with a broken heart."

Isolde sat up in bed, smoothing down her hair and sewing her jagged edges back together to hide their sharpness. The queen's gaze was trained on her, concern knitting her eyebrows together as she touched Isolde's shoulder.

Abruptly, the seer stood up, pulling a robe over her nightclothes, using the time spent tying it around her waist to plan out her next words. Isolde faced Turia with the same cool expression she'd perfected over many years.

"It is Tristan, but not in the way you think."

Turia's neck tensed as it suddenly twisted to the side.

"They've fled the city. We have good reason to believe they were the Griffin King's source of information."

The queen's expression remained frozen. Slowly she said, "They were the spy?"

"Yes, they were the spy," Isolde stated quietly, admitting it to herself.

"And they fled?"

"Like I said."

"The person you took everywhere," Turia asked quietly. "The one who sat outside our council meetings and in our ballroom and went with you nearly everywhere."

Isolde bit back a curt response, instead simply nodding.

"Is there still a chance to catch them before they make it back to their king?" Turia asked.

"I'm afraid not."

"And none of your visions warned you of any of this?" Exhaustion echoed in the queen's voice as she turned away. "Maybe I made a mistake by depending on you."

Isolde wanted to run after the queen as she walked away without another word, closing the door softly behind her on her way out. She pictured herself catching Turia's arms and apologizing. She saw herself crying into the queen's shoulder. She imagined hearing her gentle voice in her ear. But Isolde stayed where she was, refusing to allow herself movement until she recovered her senses. The seer shook herself from the fantasy, anger barreling up in her stomach at the ridiculousness of it. Her life hung in the balance too, and she couldn't lose sight of that. Not even for the princess. She'd let them go. Idiot was certainly an apt description.

~

After Isolde had collected herself, she headed to the queen's chambers immediately, knowing that she would have returned to the comfort of her own space. She didn't even knock. Perhaps a bold choice for anyone else. The room was empty. Her guards informed Isolde that the queen had left some time ago.

Miscalculated. The word rang through her mind again and again as she headed down the hallway toward the court, trying to contain the panic blossoming in her chest. Flying through room after room, she searched for the queen to no avail. She didn't ask anyone else if they'd seen her though. No need to cause alarm. After all, the only one in danger was the seer. The kitchens were quiet, the gardens were empty, and the court filled with the normal buzz of gossiping nobles. Had her foolishness driven the queen from the palace?

Isolde sank onto a windowsill in an empty hall, exhausted by the search. She pressed her hand against the ragged stone until it started to hurt, then she hit the cold stone until her hand stung, trying to suppress the noises rising in her throat and the hot tears forming in her eyes.

Surely this wasn't cause for her to flee Viridian? Her brain sorted through the practical concerns of the situation even as she begged it to just give her time to breathe. Turia wouldn't harm her. Most likely. No, Isolde wouldn't leave. No matter what. Not unless the queen herself forced her away. Isolde's stomach fell away as she stared at her knees, pulling them up to her chin. The silence of the hall echoed too loudly in her ears, causing her to spring up and make her way out of the palace. She screamed for the phoenix in her mind as she walked to the cliffs. The day was tinged with cold, but she wasn't even wearing a cloak. She found she didn't care about the goosebumps running over her arms. When she reached the cliffs, Isolde called out for Ryth out loud.

The grasses rustled as the phoenix circled overhead for a moment before gently landing in front of her in a fiery blue blaze.

"Why?" she screamed at her, her hands shaking. "Why? Why?"

The phoenix looked half-asleep, her eyes almost drifting shut as she settled in the grass. She didn't respond.

"For soulssake, answer me!"

"You made choices. That's why."

Isolde stalked closer. "No, you don't get to play morally superior. You're the one who ended up suffering divine punishment because of your choices." The creature's eyes flared with spurts of green fire at that comment. "I want to know why this is my lot in life. Why things are so far out of my control. Why was I chosen to be saddled with this curse?"

"Don't try to change things out of your control. It does no good. As you so kindly pointed out, I learned that the hard way," the phoenix stated evenly. "Our choices are already made. Maybe you weren't chosen for any particular reason. Maybe it's just a cruel trick of the universe."

Isolde froze, the breath knocked out of her by the sound of her own thoughts coming from the phoenix's mouth. After a moment, she straightened. "That may be the most true thing you've ever said."

"Regardless, it doesn't make a difference. You are slotted for this role. Your choices have already been made, child, which is why I'm never surprised at your anger or sadness or bitterness."

"You knew," she growled. "You couldn't have told me?"

"When will we stop having this conversation?"

"When you finally choose to be kind to your only friend."

They stared at each other. Isolde refused to break eye contact, letting every bit of vitriol in her heart make its way into her gaze.

"It's sad you think we're friends." Ryth left and Isolde just stood there, staring after her.

"Well, I use the term friend loosely," she muttered under her breath.

Isolde turned toward the woods as the sun set. If ever she needed to spend time with the Soulless, it was now. She had no delusions about them caring. She knew there were no answers. But she needed them to feel her pain anyway.

The silver of the leaves glittered eerily, high crystalline sounds floating through the air as the wind ruffled through the trees. As soon as she entered the sacred copse of trees, the rage seeped from her body. She collapsed on the ground, digging her fingers into the earth as the tears fell, streaking the dirt under her.

"Why?" she sobbed. The temperature dropped and she swore she heard voices on the breeze, but she didn't look up. The Salamanders would do nothing for her. If they were present, it was merely out of curiosity. Her tears watered the soil, her body wracked by sobs that she couldn't seem to stop. Slowly, her throat grew thick and head began to hurt, yet she still had not shed all her tears. Finally, her heart had little left to give.

"Guess we had the same idea," said someone behind her.

Isolde startled, swiping at her tears in panic, keeping her face turned away from a voice she knew all too well.

Once she'd composed herself, she turned stiffly toward Turia.

"It's unsurprising, I suppose. We could all use guidance from the Soulless from time to time," she said, standing and desperately trying to reclaim her dignity. The words rolled off her tongue, an old response from her former life.

"Is that what you were doing?" Turia asked disbelievingly.

"If I had seen less of the world perhaps," she answered after a moment.

Turia studied her, moving closer.

"I'm starting to feel like maybe I've seen too much of the world myself."

"The faithful princess? Surely not," Isolde replied, the words coming out more sharply than she intended.

"Queen." Turia's voice dripped with ice.

"Queen," Isolde conceded, bowing her head.

"If anyone is faithful, it should be you."

"Indeed. And so I am."

"But according to your own words, it's useless to ask the Soulless for guidance," Turia said.

"Not useless, but fate will play out the way it always has regardless of whether they interfere or not. The path is set unchanging." Was the recovery enough? Isolde took deep breaths, remembering to keep her tone distant as she suddenly realized the edge she was teetering on. Her earlier words had been careless. The queen's eyes were fixed on her, likely remembering the conversations they'd had about her fate when they first met in this very grove.

"How hopeless. Especially when the visions they do send don't seem to help us."

"My queen," Isolde pleaded, her voice softening.

"How did they escape?"

"Left their rooms in the middle of the night. Didn't return. All of their belongings were cleared out." The lies fell from her mouth so easily.

"More importantly, why didn't you see it, Isolde? How, exactly, did your foresight fail you so greatly?" Turia asked with quiet suspicion flaring in her eyes.

"It can be...unpredictable. It's harder to see fate's path when it comes to myself and those close to me. I wasn't asking the right questions when requesting prophecies. I wasn't looking in the right direction."

"Seems to me like you were looking at your apprentice an awful lot."

Shame filled Isolde at the insult, even as she tried to make her untruth convincing. What was she to say when there was not a single actual prophecy to be had? The distrust in Turia's eyes terrified her.

"Alright, that's a fair jab. I'll admit it."

"Tristan has so much information about us. We have to change everything about our strategy, and I don't know how quickly we can do that."

"I know."

"Knowing isn't good enough. I don't understand how you didn't sense something was wrong."

"I already explained," Isolde snapped.

Turia's mouth tightened, and she turned away, but Isolde stepped closer. "I apologize, my queen. You have to...you have to know I would do anything for you. This was just an honest mistake."

"How do I know you weren't working with them from the beginning?" she asked tiredly.

Isolde's throat felt thick. She caught Turia's hand, meeting her unwavering eyes. "My queen, I promise you I didn't know."

Turia didn't respond, her eyes just drilling into the seer's soul.

Isolde sank to her knees, brushing her thumb gently over Turia's hand. "I swear my undying loyalty to you, my queen." The air fell silent. It wasn't a lie.

"I thought you only served the Soulless, Seer," Turia said.

Isolde bit her tongue, pushing down all the words she wanted to say. "Things change, your highness." She pulled Turia's hand to her chest with trembling fingers so she could feel her seer's wretched heartbeat. "You have my loyalty, my queen. I swear it on the Soulless and the sea."

Turia's eyes brimmed with confusion. Her hand floated up to Isolde's temple, tucking a stray strand of hair behind her ear before pulling away.

"I guess we'll see if that's true," she said softly.

Chapter Thirty-Four

Isolde

23 Years After the Viridian Phoenix's Rebirth

War drew near as the winter fell away. The armories churned out weapons and a constant flow of messengers swept through the palace bringing news, arguments, and reports from the front. Turia spent long hours in the council room, mediating between the ladies, lords, and generals. They won and lost as the two armies tested each other, but the losses began to outweigh the previous patriotism that had boosted the people's spirits in the first weeks of the war. They had recovered part of Zeuldian but not the ports.

Coffins began to flow into the city from the front. Mourners' banners hung over more and more doorways as the weeks crawled on. Death had a way of creeping closer in the quiet. Their lines were holding for the most part though and Isolde comforted herself with that thought as she stared out of one of the palace windows.

The days following the spy's betrayal had been a flurry of activity as Turia worked with her generals to halt plans in progress that Tristan might have overheard. It was too late to halt one particular ambush, which resulted in steep casualties since the soldiers were expected. Turia couldn't look at her for a week after that. Isolde still sat at her side at council meetings. She talked with her in the evenings. She attended court when Turia made an appearance. But it was different now. The queen spoke to her stiffly and met her eyes with distrust. Their old rapport had dissipated in the wake of Turia's caution, which left Isolde feeling like she had lost something she hadn't even known she'd possessed.

Whenever she tried to bring some levity back into their conversations, Turia would just turn away, leaving an awkward silence in her wake. Isolde soon stopped trying, forcing herself to adapt and conform to her new role as the queen's advisor rather than friend. After all, she'd adjusted to her circumstances a dozen times before, changing to survive, molding herself into something new and acceptable to those around her. And if not something acceptable, something powerful. Something that had to be tolerated. In the grand scheme of things, who cared if one more person disliked the Viridian Seer? The question haunted Isolde because, for some inexplicable reason, she did care.

Anger tightened her jaw and fueled her activities. Isolde's nights grew longer as she slept less, pouring herself into her craft at the forge until dozens of daggers and swords were scattered about her room. Each was different from the last. None of them soft or kind or beautiful. Every one of them was unnecessarily sharp. Isolde made sure of that every time she tore herself from the physical realm and pulled the stars to her soul. They broke a lot at first, especially the daggers. The first time it happened, she brought back a silver-white dagger in three pieces and she fell to the floor screaming. Not from the pain, just the frustration of something within her interfering in the one thing that was supposed to be her own. Forging was no longer just hers, but she couldn't find it in herself to admit that. Not since she'd taught Tristan how to forge and not since she'd created Caliburnus, forever tied to the princess by the stars themselves.

She kept herself busy, her rooms gradually becoming an armory. Daggers clung to her walls, her thighs, her tables, and everything that was hers. Isolde reminded herself that the rooms weren't even hers, they were the queen's. She was merely an occupant. Never once after that, though, did she consider leaving. That thought was somehow even more unbearable than the thought of trudging through life and war with nothing of her soul intact besides her pride and stubbornness. After that first broken dagger, she didn't feel much at all besides a dull anger and a quiet sadness buried so deeply that it put her to sleep whenever she did finally start to feel it.

The toll of the war rose along with the number of broken daggers stored in her room. Isolde listened in the streets, a chill running along her spine every time she heard someone mention the absent queen. The dangers of public opinion were nothing to be scoffed at, as dozens of past high rulers could attest. Turia may have thought she didn't know her history, but Isolde knew the parts that mattered. Even though the queen carried out her responsibilities, no one saw her doing so. She made fewer and fewer public appearances. Which meant she might as well have been doing nothing.

Isolde had taken to looping in other members of the council to press the queen to show her face more, though never deigning to turn to Robin, who might have been the most effective messenger of all. Isolde no longer had the influence she needed to convince Turia to do anything. In fact, very often the queen would do the exact opposite of her seer's advice when it came to what she perceived at small matters. Isolde wondered what was happening behind closed doors. Were Turia's symptoms growing worse? Was that part of the reason she showed her face in public even less than before? The city needed the queen for more than running the war and holding their borders. She desperately hoped Turia understood that.

Isolde knocked on Turia's door waiting patiently for a response. It seemed to take longer and longer these days.

Finally, she heard a faint, "Come in."

Isolde bowed stiffly. "How are you today, my queen?"

"I'm well," Turia said, turning toward one of the trees in her room. Flowers blossomed all over its branches in striking shades of red.

"Glad to hear that since the council has decided the court needs to play a prominent part in the annual festivals this year."

"And by "the court" you mean me."

"You are, indeed, part of the court. The people need to love you and it's difficult for them to do that when they don't see you."

"Not this again."

"More coffins are being carted in every week, and we're at a stalemate. It doesn't take much for people's good opinion to be lost. The longer this drags on, as food shortages grow and more people die, you'll be lucky if you can keep people from turning on you. I, for one, very much don't want to see your head on a stake," Isolde stated calmly.

"I know that, which is why I am working to end the war as quickly as possible and maintain the merchant agreements and make sure taxes aren't too high. All the things a good queen should be doing. If that isn't enough, it isn't enough."

Isolde held in a sigh. "I know you don't care about public perception, but please believe when I say it's most of what matters."

"That's where you and I differ, isn't it seer?" Turia asked as she pruned the tree, carefully setting the clippings to the side.

Isolde froze. The queen wasn't wrong. Why did she have to be so damn frustrating?

"The council is just trying to keep you alive."

"Enough."

"We've already announced that you'll be leading the procession to the spring altars and bestowing gifts there. I'm afraid it's too late to change it."

"What about Robin? Shouldn't she be leading this."

"Robin will be there. She'll follow behind and make the secondary sacrifice. It took a good deal of wrangling on my part, but she has agreed to participate, as is proper."

Turia closed her eyes and sighed. "Get out, Seer."

Isolde turned, keeping her face neutral even as she imagined the satisfaction of punching a wall. Turia could fight her every day for the rest of their lives, but Isolde was going to keep her alive.

~

The day was much too bright. It matched the false brightness on Turia's face. Isolde watched the stiff lines of her neck as she waved to the people lining the streets. Her dress was beautiful, yet modest in terms of extravagance, like everything about this procession. Isolde's dulled in comparison, but she didn't mind. She wasn't trying to stand out as she walked behind the queen as a sign of her deference. Perhaps if anyone still respected the wisdom of the seer, they would be reminded of her endorsement of the queen and respect their sovereign as well. Robin came next in the procession, for once wearing her tight robes properly. They swept around her in a dizzying ombre of reds and oranges that did nothing for her complexion. She may have been doing exactly as she was supposed to, but it was clear from her wrinkled expression that she was peeved about it.

The energy of the crowd was restless as the queen completed the spring ceremonies in every square they passed through and then Robin bestowed a blessing on all present. Hours dragged on and the sun grew warmer until beads of sweat peppered the lines of Turia's face. Members of the court passed out food and coins in celebration of the new season as the phoenixes wheeled overhead. While Turia wasn't happy about this, Isolde didn't regret setting it up.

Normally the procession was led by the high priestess, but to have the queen call on blessings from the Soulless herself demonstrated to the people that she was with them. That she was there with them in the war efforts, in their daily activities, and in their celebrations. In Isolde's opinion, showing modesty and humility was just as important when so much was being asked of the citizens. They didn't need to think of the queen as someone shutting herself into her palace and hosting expensive balls while they died.

When the procession finally made its way back to the castle, Isolde was relieved, ready to eat a meal and then run off to the forge. To her surprise though, Turia didn't immediately make her way back to her room. Instead, she took a seat on the throne and watched as the nobility dispersed around the room.

Turia caught Isolde's eye, then looked away with an airy grace. Isolde had no desire to stay, but Turia knew that. The look meant, "If I have to endure this, then so do you." With a sigh, Isolde climbed the steps and stood behind the throne, her hands clasped behind her back. Isolde couldn't be too irritated at this though. The more she was out in public the better. Isolde's eyelids felt heavy as she stood in silence. It all seemed pointless and frivolous if she thought too hard. So she tried not to think about anything, which was much easier to do when her hands were busy. Turia, on the other hand, didn't seem to be having any trouble staying awake. Her eyes were sharp, watching the people in the way Isolde usually did. Her thumb beat out a rhythm on the arm of the throne on which she was stiffly perched, looking like she might take flight at the slightest sound.

Aeryt and Gahera joined the queen, chatting away with her. Gahera laughed and Aeryt smiled as they reminisced and poked fun at each other with the familiarity that only comes from years of experiences together. Aeryt held her hands clasped stiffly behind her back, braid as neat as always. Not a hair was out of place.

Musicians struck up a song on their strings, as was their routine in the afternoons. Light refreshments were served as men gossiped and ladies schemed. Isolde's mind floated off and images started crossing her mind, blocking out the sight of the throne room. Vines curling around pillars and broken daggers and talk of love—something she wasn't sure she really believed in.

A sudden commotion jerked her from the dreams that had been crowding in. She took a deep breath, blinking and then squinting to try to see what was taking place across the room.

Someone was struggling with a group of palace guards. Not very successfully from the looks of it. People backed away, gasping at the struggle. Her heart stuttered. Their eyes caught hers as they dragged them closer and she couldn't look away. She swore to herself, cursing everything holy and unholy even as it felt like her throat was closing in on itself.

Tristan.

Isolde's eyes shot over to Turia, whose fingers were curled tight on the arms of the throne with her back ramrod straight. Isolde took a step closer to Turia protectively, but stopped herself from placing her hand on the queen's. Tristan stopped struggling once it became clear that the guards were dragging them before the queen herself.

Their knees hit the marble with a loud crack as the guards shoved them down. Their hair was trimmed, earring glinting in the lazy, slanting light from the windows. Clothes clearly marked them as a noble but certainly not one from Viridian.

Isolde assessed them, trying to piece together why on earth they sat before them. They weren't dressed to avoid detection. If anything, the opposite. The Griffin King's crest was emblazoned on their tunic in gold thread. Silence settled over the court. Fury cascaded over Robin's face. It seemed like she was only just holding herself back from throwing a punch at them. Tristan looked up at the queen, something like sorrow in their eyes.

"Decided to show your face again, spy?" Turia asked.

They inclined their head toward her. The guards kept their hands tight on their arms as if they would lunge for her at any moment. Maybe they would. As it had turned out, Isolde didn't know them all that well.

"Queen Turia, my name is Liege Morgan of House Faye. I come as an ambassador from the esteemed King Kyrdis of the griffin court," their tone was unflinchingly formal. None of the turbulent emotions in their expression made their way into their voice. Morgan. So that was their real name.

"If you're expecting a warm welcome, I'm afraid you'll be sorely disappointed."

"I expect nothing, your majesty, but I bring a message of some importance."

Turia nodded her head, granting them permission to continue.

"The Griffin King hopes to offer a truce between our two kingdoms in order to bring an end to these skirmishes between our armies."

Skirmishes. Anger flared in Isolde. War. It was war. To call it anything else dishonored everything that had happened.

Turia rose sharply. "Let us discuss this further in the council chambers."

She led the way from the room. Isolde tried not to look back as she stayed at her side. She heard the guards pull Morgan up as they followed the queen. Isolde kept glancing at Turia, frustration surging in her at this reminder of her failure. The queen didn't return her looks. Her eyes were fixed straight ahead, something cold and detached resting in them.

Turia swept into the empty room. She took her seat at the head of the table while the guards kept Morgan standing.

"So, you were sent as a messenger then?" Turia asked.

Morgan nodded.

"Bold choice."

"You'll find that my king is nothing if not bold."

A chilly silence descended. Turia sat still and tense, looking like a being carved of stone. Dust motes fluttered in the beams of sunlight streaming through the window into the cold room and, for a moment, Isolde wished they could stay suspended in time. Turia permanently set in stone, the sunlight making a dubious promise of warmth, and Tristan still alive. It would be a tomb, but maybe a tomb was better than whatever this was. She didn't want the moment to move forward, dragging her along in its wake. Unfortunately for her, time would not be persuaded and Turia's voice rang out once more, stronger than she'd heard it in weeks.

"A truce you said? I'm curious to hear what terms your king thinks would convince me to overlook the assaults on my people and the dishonorable way he tried to sneak a spy into my court."

Tristan inclined their head politely once more, but didn't acknowledge her words beyond that. *Maybe they were meant to be a diplomat*, Isolde mused. "We wish to bond our two kingdoms through perhaps the oldest rite tying blood to blood."

They meant the oldest way to incapacitate a woman. A chill ran down Isolde's spine. Of course.

"Pretty words. A marriage, I take it?" Turia queried, eyes exhausted and utterly unsurprised. "Very unfortunately for him, I am not seeking suitors to join me on my throne. There's not room in this beautiful chair for anyone besides me and you can tell the Griffin King that."

Lord Percival in the corner looked like he was barely keeping himself from saying something, but Isolde shot him a glare, praying that he would keep his mouth shut. He would surely ask the queen to hear out the offer, but Isolde agreed that even that would be a foolish thing to do. Turia had to be unbudging when it came to her autonomy. Couldn't even be seen to flinch. Isolde thanked the Soulless she had the sense to see that.

Tristan too, seemed unsurprised. "The king would not insult you by suggesting otherwise, your highness. He suggests a different proposal altogether."

At this, Isolde's clutch on her wrist tightened. The fine-brocaded messenger of the king turned their eyes to her with a searing kind of recognition. "As is custom, I request an audience with the Great seer of Viridian to discuss the matter further in private."

Isolde closed her eyes for a brief moment, wishing to block out the whole frightful moment. Turia's eyes fell coldly upon her seer as she realized what the griffin liege was asking. Morgan waited patiently for a response in perfect stillness.

"The audience is granted," Turia replied after a moment. "I must warn you though, Morgan. There will be guards outside the door and, as I'm sure you know, you'd be hopeless in a fight against my seer."

Isolde's throat went dry and she cursed the queen's judgment, but her feet propelled her out the door all the same. In a haze, she led Morgan on and on through the palace until they were outside. One of the guards tripped over himself trying to ask her a quiet question about where they were going, but she waved him away. She didn't have to look back to know that Turia followed at a distance.

The oak door to the guardhouse creaked as she threw it open. This would do for her purposes. The same soldier tried to object but she politely ignored him. With a flourish she entered the weapons room. She ushered Morgan in, letting them spot the fury in her eyes as she pulled the door shut and they heard the clanking of the guards assuming their positions outside. Morgan carefully kept their eyes away from the swords glittering on the walls, trying to appear nonthreatening she guessed.

"If you're just spoiling for a rematch, here's your chance," Isolde remarked coolly.

They ignored her words. Hands clasped behind their back and back straight they offered the words she didn't want to hear. They measured them out carefully, slowly. "Isolde Merlin of Viridian, I am here as a proxy for the Griffin King, who wishes to ask for your hand in marriage. He hopes to bridge the divide between our two kingdoms and put to rest the misunderstandings that have occurred in the past. He…" Morgan stuttered, but quickly recovered. "He has heard much about your intelligence and beauty. The king wishes to forge a blood alliance, while at the same time assuring the queen that he doesn't wish to impede on her rule in any way. If you agree, he will make no further claim on the ashes."

The words reminded Isolde of tasteless wafers. Light and insubstantial. "Beauty, huh? Who told him that?" she asked, raising an eyebrow. Morgan looked just miserable, and Isolde reveled in it.

"I pray that you seriously consider this offer, Seer." They choked out. Tristan rarely called her that. The lack of her name stung somehow.

She took a step toward them. "Is that a threat?"

"It's just the facts of the situation. The king is a good man and he will treat you well. You could do worse."

Isolde's mind whirred through the consequences of those words. Her brain hadn't made it that far. She hadn't considered the practicalities of what Morgan was really suggesting. Isolde gritted her teeth at the thought. It was absurd.

"Being your king's obedient wife is the least of my worries. I have greater concerns, Tristan."

"Morgan. My name is Morgan," they corrected.

He looked up at the ceiling for a moment, as if sending up a prayer. A sickening realization hit Isolde at the familiar gesture. They'd been doing that the entire time they were with her. Praying to the Sylph. No wonder the Soulless rulers of the air loved them.

It should have been a dead giveaway that they were from the Griffin Kingdom. She cursed herself.

They stared at each other for a minute, time stretching out between them in a conversation neither of them were able to have.

"You could stop this war, Isolde. The Griffin Kingdom is a beautiful place to live, I promise you. We could be at peace."

"You and I will never be at peace, Morgan," Isolde spat. "I've seen too many faces cold with death because of your lies."

"You're one to speak of lies," they said quietly.

"I don't know what you're talking about."

"You're always lying, Isolde. Always crafting the perfect turn of phrase. You've become so good at it, I don't think you know what's real anymore."

Her mouth pulled tight with indignation, even while her mind relaxed. They didn't know her biggest lies. Those she had concealed flawlessly.

"Death. Death is real."

"But it's not the only real thing."

"You can't find me anything else as constant or real as death. In the end, there is nothing."

"There you go, lying again."

She took another step closer. "You can't entice me with descriptions of how beautiful your home is or how your king would make a passable husband."

"You would be a queen," they said sadly.

Isolde laughed caustically at that. "So, that's what this is supposed to be? Bribery? I don't want to be a queen. I just want to be in control of my own life."

"And you're in control of your life now?"

"Yes. I am. And you have the audacity to think that you could *pay* me to leave Turia behind like some slimy mercenary you dredged up from the sea."

"That's not what this is."

"Of course that's what this is, Morgan. It's not about my happiness. It's not even just about ending the war. It's a political ploy, but I'm happy to report that it wouldn't do you any good. You think that somehow separating Turia and I would make her weaker and more malleable? That's a miscalculation. She doesn't need me," Isolde said vehemently.

Morgan paused, weighing their next words carefully. Their voice resumed its formal tone. "We aren't trying to weaken your court. I give you my word. We are only offering a peaceful solution to the tragedy of war."

"A bit late for that, don't you think? You don't seem to understand Turia's strength. When I say she doesn't need me, I mean it. You've misunderstood my loyalty to her this whole time. It's not because she's weak, it's because she deserves support. I've given her every last shred of care I could strip from my heart. That's something you wouldn't understand," she bit out.

They reached out and grabbed her hand, something fierce in their eyes. "Of course I understand."

Isolde wrenched her hand from their grasp. "I doubt that."

"Of course I understand it, because that's how I feel about you, Isolde," they hissed.

"What?" she muttered. It was the only word she could think to say. They kept their voice down, glancing at the door and likely thinking of the court assembled outside.

Morgan took her hand once more, their fingers gentle over her palm. "You think I want to be here, proposing your marriage to someone I know would steal your agency?" they asked bitterly. "Isolde, I care for you deeply."

"You're a fool," she responded breathlessly.

"Now that's just a fact. I expected you to have more insight, Isolde." They pressed their forehead to hers and she didn't move, closing her eyes at the contact. "I'm here because this is how you survive."

Isolde pulled away at that, laughing once more. "What kind of idiot do you take me for? Are you trying to convince me that...you're in love with me? You're a good actor, I'll give you that."

"Not in love," they said in frustration. "I told you I don't feel...like that...often. But I do love you, as my friend. I love the way you struggle with the world, fighting for space for yourself. I love your sharp sense of humor. I love how reserved you are and the passion that boils underneath that facade. "

"It's concerning that you think I'm so gullible," Isolde stated calmly, even as her heart was beating much harder in her chest than it should have been.

"I know you're angry with me, but you have to believe that I still care for you," they pleaded.

"I don't have to believe a word you say," she spat. "You are right about one thing. I don't feel anything for you but disdain, Morgan. It's insulting that you thought such a ploy would work."

Morgan swallowed and straightened, clasping their hands behind their back again. "What is your answer to the Griffin King's offer, Lady Isolde?"

"I will consider the matter."

With that, she turned and left the room without looking back. The queen and her court waited outside.

Isolde stopped by one of the guards. "Please lead the ambassador to the guest quarters and keep them company there. The queen and I have matters to discuss."

Chapter Thirty-Five

Isolde

23 Years After the Viridian Phoenix's Rebirth

The queen seized her wrist in a hold rougher than Isolde would have expected from her.

"Did you accept?" she asked tersely, her fingers tightening almost imperceptibly.

Isolde didn't struggle. They were safely back in Turia's rooms, alone once more and Turia was truly looking at her for the first time in weeks. She savored the moment before responding, stepping closer almost without thinking.

"You think I'd just offer a response without talking to you first?" The seer's brow wrinkled with confusion when Turia didn't answer. "How could you think...You know I am bound to you. Carrying out your desires is my duty."

"I asked for your loyalty a long time ago, and I seem to remember your response was abysmally noncommittal."

"Come now, my queen. We've been through too much since then for you to really be clinging to that."

Turia let go of her wrist, turning away to take shelter in her brittle cocoon of suspicion and Isolde instantly missed the weight of her hand. She closed her eyes briefly, her mind reminding her of everything she wished she could let go and the stupidity of those rambling thoughts. Few things made Isolde's feelings spiral out-of-control. She typically had them locked away in a cage deep in her soul, only on occasion letting them out for a little walk around her heart before fretfully locking them away again. Turned out the queen had seized the key, unlocked the cage, and was now playing keep-away with that precious instrument of control. Isolde opened her eyes. But Turia couldn't know that and she wouldn't. Isolde swore at herself. It was a selfish thought and the seer did her best to dismiss it, remaining unnaturally stiff as Turia began pacing.

"I just want to know what transpired, Seer," she said finally.

"Well, I'm sure you can guess. The traitor proposed a marriage between myself and the Griffin King as a truce with the details to be worked out later." Isolde stopped there, conveniently omitting the rest of the conversation.

"That's all? Just a marriage between you two?" Turia asked.

If she had been one to splutter, Isolde would have spluttered right then. The insult was not to be born. "If by that's all, you mean the determination of the circumstances of the rest of my life, yes," she replied quite calmly.

Turia crossed her arms. "Oh, you know what I mean. That's a surprising price. Not asking for anything else? No offense, Seer, but the Griffin King taking you would be more of an insult to us rather than truly being a benefit to him. If he intends for you to be his queen, there has to be more to it than just being an insult."

"I object to the idea of being *taken*." Isolde stated with a prickly purse of her lips.

Turia stopped in her tracks. "You won't do it then?" she asked quietly.

Isolde had known the question was coming since they first shut the door. "I didn't say that, did I? I wouldn't do it for any noble reason. I wouldn't do it to stop the war or to bring an end to the bloodshed. It's as likely to be some kind of trap as anything else anyway. I'm not convinced it would actually bring the fighting to a halt. I wouldn't do it if all the princes and princesses came to me begging on their hands and knees. I'm not that keen to throw away my freedom and live in a foreign land. But I would do it for you. If you thought it was the best option, my queen, I would do it for you."

The queen granted her a half-choked laugh. "Why are you like this?"

"I don't know that you want the answer to that question."

"What if I do?" Turia asked slowly, surprising even Isolde.

"What, you want to suddenly understand my whole life and everything that's brought me to this godsdamn low? Which is saying a lot, by the way."

"Yes. You never talk about yourself. Not really. Don't think I haven't noticed, Isolde. I don't know how to trust you because I'm not entirely sure I know who you are."

"You know me better than anyone on this earth," Isolde admitted.

The queen tilted her head. "Perhaps. I don't believe people blindly, Seer. Especially not when they come in with an arsenal of powerful words like you do."

"Byproduct of being a sacred seer, I guess."

"No, I don't mean that. I don't mean your visions, Isolde. I mean *your* words. The ones you choose to weaponize for your own purposes."

For a moment, Isolde couldn't breathe. The queen's gaze felt like hot coals being shoved into her chest, working to burn away any last shred of composure she was clinging onto and doing an incredibly efficient job of it.

Isolde held her tongue as her mind raced through possible answers. It carried out its constant calculations in the way it always had, running through scenarios to find the one that would most benefit her in the long run, only this time the effort felt somehow more uncertain.

"I'm good at surviving. Surely you wouldn't begrudge me that?"

"You're missing the point, Isolde. Purposefully so, if I had to take a guess. I don't begrudge you anything. Maybe I even admire your skills. But they terrify me."

"You shouldn't be frightened of me," Isolde said softly, trying to assuage the queen's fears.

"I would be stupid to not be scared. Fear has kept me safe this entire time."

"Don't be ridiculous. *I've* been the one keeping you safe."

"I don't need you, Isolde," Turia spat imperiously.

"I know that better than anyone," Isolde said, clenching and unclenching her fists in an effort to reign in her rising frustration. "That's not a question."

"See, you turn around and lie right after you just said I'm safe because of you."

"The Soulless have mercy. Just because I've been trying, at the very least, to keep you safe doesn't mean you need me. I'm just saying, maybe I'm useful. Just let me be useful to you."

Turia squinted. "That doesn't seem like something that would be important to you. Safety—sure. Control—definitely. Ambition—only a fool wouldn't see that. But usefulness?"

Isolde scrubbed a hand over her face. "Well, maybe, like you said, you don't know me." Her pride stopped her from spewing the rest. For explaining just precisely why she felt that way. Maybe she didn't even fully know herself. Isolde tried to start building her wall again, brick by painful brick, to recover some of her dignity.

"What would you have me do, my queen? Don't leave me in suspense."

"Like you said, this feels like a trick. I don't understand their reasoning."

Isolde looked away. She did know the king's reasoning, but she didn't have it in her to tell Turia the Griffin King thought she would be weak without her seer. She had clearly failed to do her job of strengthening the queen's image, instead inadvertently, enhancing an image of her own strength. Months ago, at the beginning of all this, she might have been proud of that. Isolde clenched a fistful of her skirt in one hand. And the queen didn't need to know, because, as had been reinforced time after time that day, the queen didn't need her. If that was the king's only motive in drawing her away and he would truly submit to peace, then let him make that miscalculation.

"I want more information," Turia said.

"Not sure that's a luxury we have at the moment. We can't know what we don't know."

"Tread carefully, Isolde." Turia winced as the words exited her mouth. She knew exactly what she was asking and so did her seer.

So, that was what it was to be then. Isolde would marry the Griffin King and be the unwilling beacon of peace for a nation she'd never cared much for.

She simply inclined her head. "Wouldn't be me if I wasn't careful, now would it?"

"I don't know. I think you have a wildness in you, buried somewhere very deep down. A recklessness."

Isolde almost laughed at that, but she caged in her bitterness before it escaped and flayed open the one relationship she cared about far more than she would dare admit.

"Hope the king is prepared for the mistake that's about to be his queen. Unfortunately, I very much doubt he is my type."

"And what is your type?" Turia asked. Curiosity lit in her eyes.

"Look at us, talking about boys like a couple of young girls scurrying home after lessons," Isolde said merrily. The cheer in her voice was forced. How could it be anything else? But she found she didn't want to leave that room. Didn't want to be alone with the cruel twist of emotion she knew was coming. The future might as well be a wall of gray mist, obscuring everything from her, while leaving her sick and shivering in the hold of its unnavigable maze.

"If only," Turia said.

"What's your type, my queen?"

Unexpectedly, Turia blushed furiously. "I think I'm done with this conversation."

"You're the one who started it," Isolde protested.

"Well, now I'm the one choosing to end it, Seer."

Turia started to turn away, but paused for only a brief moment before her features settled into a new mask and—with a speed that startled the seer— rushed to Isolde to enfold her in a tight embrace. Isolde's hands hung uselessly at her sides for a moment as she collected her thoughts. The warmth of the queen pressed against her made her feel like she was choking and maybe she never wanted to stop. The queen didn't say a word. Neither did her seer. But her fingers trembled against Isolde's back, pulling her even closer. Isolde wondered if maybe the girl was crying— a perilous soft urge to comfort ran through her at that thought— only to realize that it was her own cheeks that were wet with salty water.

Unable to stop herself, she wrapped her arms around Turia, hiding the embarrassing tears by burying her face in the girl's golden hair. This was an easy feat given she had at least three inches on Turia. Her hand trailed slowly down the queen's waist, pulling her closer and holding her tight like their lives depended on it. Turia's breath skittered over Isolde's bare neck, making her stomach drop with a tremulous longing.

She ran her other hand through the queen's hair, taking comfort in its softness and giving in to the brief pleasure of allowing herself to imagine that she would always be by the queen's side—that they had endless days ahead of them filled with picnics by the sea, quiet nights by the fire, sunrises plunging through the skies together on Ryth's back. Then it was gone. She drew away, because she knew that too much hope would break her beyond repair. It would splinter her open. She would be dashed against the rocks with a bleeding kind of yearning, crying out for something to spare her, but—as always—no voice would answer her plea.

~

"You have your answer," Isolde stated, a blinding coldness edging her blue-green eyes. She didn't even bother to step foot in Tristan's elegant guest room. They'd already made themself at home. Clothing and sewing materials were spread across every available surface.

Morgan's face blanched. "I see," they answered carefully.

"We will discuss the details of the truce tomorrow. As for tonight, there is a banquet to celebrate my engagement and the queen expects your attendance as her honored guest. I trust you won't have an issue finding appropriate attire."

They glanced back at their room, red spreading over their cheeks. Morgan inclined their head gently. "As you wish."

"As the queen wishes," she corrected.

"Of course. Always the queen."

Isolde failed to bite.

Despite the multitude of clothing strewn across their quarters, their own garb looked wrinkled and dark circles lurked under their eyes. She wondered fleetingly how much sleep they'd been getting. She searched their tender eyes for a moment, trying to find answers there to her many questions.

Even as she'd said the words that bound her fate to that of the Griffin King, something inside her had whispered caution. She couldn't afford to underestimate Morgan yet again. The queen would never trust her again if the king's motive for marriage turned out to be something beyond what she thought. So she fixed her eyes on them, stubbornly searching, until they shied away from her gaze uncomfortably.

"I look forward to forging a peace between us," she stated formally. "The queen has many allies who will rejoice at this development. Just as they support her in peace, they will defend her if her honor is slighted in any way, by anyone." She leaned in conspiratorially. "Remember this, my friend: You never know who the most powerful players in the game are until it's over."

"I swear upon my honor that this engagement is nothing more than an effort to make peace. The king is tired of waging a hopeless war. It was just a desperate effort to halt the plague in its tracks."

Isolde bit back a smile. *Oh, Morgan, just giving away information like that.*

"I hope for your sake that's true."

"You're going to be a terror at the Griffin court, aren't you?"

"You forget yourself."

They bowed again, their expression smarting with shame.

"As my future queen, I hope you know you will have an ally in me, if you ever need it."

"Let's not get ahead of ourselves. If I have it my way, you will spend the rest of your life far, far away from me. The courier will come fetch you when it's time, ambassador."

Isolde left them standing forlornly in the doorway, their forehead wrinkled in consternation.

Chapter Thirty-Six

Isolde

23 Years After the Viridian Phoenix's Rebirth

I solde shrugged on a demure dark blue gown. It was perhaps slightly fancier than her typical outfits, but still practical. This was to be a celebration for everyone but her, even as she would be the focus. She knew that rumors had already started coursing through the palace corridors and out into the city.

The girl steeled herself for the eyes that would be upon her with a well-practiced sense of bitter pleasure. Already her mind poured through the scenarios she might experience at the Griffin Court from being completely ignored and disregarded to being an active target for assassination. She recalled some half-lit portrait of the aging king she'd seen at some point as a child.

She remembered the emptiness of his eyes in that picture. He already had plenty of children to compete for his throne so hopefully he wouldn't press her in that manner. Isolde winced as she tightened the back of her dress with her own deft fingers. That was a slim hope. She knew better than to expect that he would keep his hands to himself. Part of her couldn't believe she would actually be leaving, so she forced herself to run through the possibilities as a way to acclimate herself to the idea.

With one statement her freedom had slipped from her fingers and, worst of all, she'd simply given it away of her own free will. Her face grew red with an anger that was all her own, caused by and directed at herself. Oh, how far she'd fallen, just as she had escaped her grandparents' controlling hands. Maybe she needed to be controlled. Maybe she didn't know what it was to control her own destiny. Because no matter how hard she tried, she always slipped back into the same cruel patterns. She loved them until she was bleeding out and kept loving them as they stabbed her. So, she tried to let the scars heal and fortify herself against love because it hurt too much.

She didn't want to love. She'd guarded herself against it, knowing the power it could wrench from her grasp because, at the end of the day, Isolde was weak when it came to those she loved. And she knew it. She knew it, and after years of tearing herself away from any love that started to bloom and pushing away any who tried to get too close, it had searched her out. It had taken one look at her, with its vicious jaws frothing, and evaluated her with hard eyes. Love had truly seen her and couldn't resist sinking its teeth into her once more.

When it came down to it, she was the same as every teary-eyed sister and crying husband that made their way to her, pleading for mercy and money for their loved ones. To do so well for so long only to fail at the attempt to maintain her distance now. It was not to be born.

With sharp movements, she twisted her hair into the loose, sweeping style worn by engaged women. She jabbed the pins into her head with a cold precision so that not a single hair was out of place. Well, she had learned her lesson. It would not happen again. Not after Morgan and certainly not after Turia. She had gotten greedy and forgotten she couldn't afford the luxury of love, not if she wanted to live on her own terms.

Plucking a jagged dagger from the wall, she strapped it to her thigh under her dress. She pulled her black sword from her desk and secured the sheath around her waist. Perhaps carrying a sword to an event such as this was somewhat atypical for nobility but, after all, what was typical about the seer's sorry life? At the very least, it was a reminder that she was not to be trifled with.

The setting sun trailed over the warm stone of the palace hallways as Isolde made her way quietly to the Great Hall. She heard the celebration before she saw it. The noise issuing forth from the room was astonishing and with sudden shock she remembered this had once been normal. War had brought a kind of frail quiet with it. People floated about in poor spirits as their lives brimmed with an uncertainty that ate away their joy. But that had changed, for a moment at least, given the news.

Isolde thought with distaste that this was a change that tempted fate. Fighting continued, the war had not ended, yet from the merriment rising raucously into the thin air, the nobility had decided to act as though all was well. Isolde couldn't blame them for their relief, but it still made her wince. She continued her journey though, entering the room through a passage near the throne, where the queen was already seated.

Robin bent low over the throne, whispering into her ear and eliciting a smile from Turia. Isolde quickly looked away.

By the Soulless, how they were all laughing. The nobles were spread across the room in a kaleidoscope of bright colors that looked like an artist with a bad eye had splashed them haphazardly across a canvas. It put the seer in a decidedly dour mood.

As soon as Aeryt spotted her, the congratulations began. Isolde pasted a smile on her face and nodded graciously at the influx of people giving her their most saccharine well-wishes as though the Griffin King had not been their greatest enemy only earlier that day. She thought of the mourning sash she wore under her dress, the only outward consolation she was going to allow herself and it still wasn't one anyone would ever see. After a while, people got tired of her and returned to their drinks as the musicians struck up a lively new melody.

Robin still hovered by the queen because of course she did, studiously avoiding even glancing Isolde's way. Her head was thrown back in that intoxicating, wild laughter that Isolde could never hope to compete with.

A hand touched her shoulder gently and she whipped around, only to find Morgan standing there, dressed in finery she would never have been able to imagine them wearing previously. Certainly not back when they were still her harmless apprentice. She turned away and took a swig of her drink to ease the sting of her foolishness.

"I must congratulate you."

"Enough. We've been through this already."

Their mouth moved like they were about to say something else, but she didn't give them the chance, doggedly making her way to the dais. If her time with the queen was limited, she might as well savor it for all it was worth. Robin had left Turia for a moment to go refill her goblet.

"Quite the uproar," Isolde said, looking out over the crowd from above. It was so much better than being hopelessly lost in the jostling melee of bodies.

"I think they're grateful for your sacrifice," the queen said in a low tone, reaching out to give Isolde's hand a brief squeeze. Isolde granted her a smile. "Now, now. Some sacrifice. I get to be a queen, you know."

The seer couldn't stand the pity in Turia's eyes as she only gave a half-hearted smile in response. Isolde tugged gently on Turia's hand. "You should go dance. Maybe it would help," she said, nodding her head toward Isolde's bouncing knee.

The queen looked up at her forlornly. "But I don't have anyone to dance with."

Isolde looked down, biting back her amusement as she said, "Anyone in this city would absolutely fall over themselves at the chance to awkwardly sway through a single waltz with you."

"Including you?"

Isolde stiffened for a moment before answering quietly. "Including me."

Turia raised an eyebrow. Isolde noticed that her leg had stilled in its perpetual motion, her sheer green skirt cascading around her with the smooth glassiness of water undisturbed.

"So, are you going to ask me to dance, Seer?

The words sent heat flooding through Isolde's chest. She brushed her thumb over Turia's hand, which still rested in hers. "Do I have a choice?"

"I'm afraid not."

Isolde offered the queen a graceful bow of acquiescence. "Well, then. Happy to perform my duty."

Isolde led Turia down from the dais, heart tripping with things she wouldn't let herself name. The pleasant hum of Caliburnus, always present when the queen was near, faded to nothing with the queen's absence from the dais.

The seer tried to shake off the feeling of the court's eyes drilling into them. They crawled over her back and made her want to scream. Something about the lights felt too bright. Couples were already dancing on the floor to a lively tune, sweeping around in a dizzying array of garish color. Turia's hand shook. Isolde snuck a glance at the queen and saw that familiar tension in her neck as she desperately tried to hold in her movements.

With an abrupt pivot, she changed course, steering them away from the dance floor as the music swelled louder and dancers sped up. They passed through throngs of people, past flickering candles, and tables stacked with wedding delicacies, until they had slipped under a burnished archway and out into a side hall. The dancing light from the throne room spilled out into the corridor, sending shadows scattering only for them to regroup moments later in an ebb and flow that reminded Isolde of the sea.

Turia turned to face the seer, a question in her dark gaze as they stood silently in the empty hallway.

"Thought there would be fewer eyes here," Isolde whispered in response, drawing closer until their faces were inches apart. She slipped her hand around Turia's back.

"I would've thought you'd want everyone to see their queen mingling and active among them," Turia said breathlessly.

"Not tonight." Something in her begged for privacy and to be away from prying eyes. She only wanted to be seen when she decided to be seen. This moment, however, was only hers and she wanted no one besides Turia to see her residing in it.

Isolde listened for the muted rise and fall of the stringed instruments and began moving in a dance that both girls knew all too well. They pressed together and apart, their skirts swishing softly as they circled each other. Their eyes locked and Isolde couldn't find it in herself to pull away from Turia's searching iron gaze or the way the light flickered over her bare shoulders.

The dance grew quicker in pace, leaving them both breathless as they spun and the seer wondered what she had done to be blessed with this moment. Light shimmered over Turia's hair, making her look like some kind of goddess. Shadows managed to bring out the depth and brightness of her eyes.

The seer would have abandoned everything to worship her in that moment. She would have forsaken her ties to the Soulless and thrown away her precarious birthright. She would have forgotten the pain of all those years in the indifferent hold of her gods. Hell, she would even have relived every single damn minute, if called upon.

Isolde savored the softness of Turia's hand firm against her own and the cautious pull of a smile on the girl's face. With a flourish, the song drew to an end and Isolde drew the woman she'd staked all of her hope on closer.

They breathed into each other for a moment. With a sure hand, Isolde reached out and traced her fingers down Turia's neck, letting them rest where she could feel the vibrant pulsing of the queen's blood. Isolde's mouth quirked up in a smile. She could feel the queen's heart racing. To tell the truth, so was her seer's.

Turia trembled, biting her lip as she covered Isolde's hand with her own warm one, holding it tightly there with a kind of fragmented desperation, like maybe she thought Isolde was going to leave. Their hearts beat together in a cacophony of rhythms tangled with the new song echoing from the audience chamber. A heated color rose on Turia's cheeks and Isolde thought it might be the most beautiful thing she'd ever seen.

"May you be blessed all your days, my queen," she said lowly, pressing their cheeks together.

"How can I be, without you here to try and spin my curses into blessings?" the queen asked.

"Guess you'll have to learn to spin them yourself."

"I'm too honest for that."

"Maybe that's not such a terrible thing."

"In an ideal world, perhaps."

Isolde raised her head so she could meet the girl's turbulent eyes and study the curve of her lips. In the phantom of a breath, they found themselves braced against the cold roughness of the wall. Turia's body pulsed warmly into her own as Isolde pressed her lightly against the wall, her hand still tangled in Turia's hair. "What strange kindnesses we've offered each other, my queen."

"It's ridiculous for you to always call me that, you know. You could just call me Turia. Arturia if you insist on some kind of formality."

"Why is it ridiculous?" Isolde breathed. "Because I'm the holy seer?"

Turia failed to pluck out the sarcasm dripping from those words. "Not because you're holy to the world…" The queen struggled with the next words, her hands drifting farther down the seer's back. "Not because you've been elevated by the Soulless or blessed with some gift that I can't seem to fully understand, but because you are something holy to me."

Isolde broke away from her then, a panic welling up within her and scattering through her with a surprising violence. She turned away sharply, trying to hide the anger she knew would be written plainly on her face.

"Isolde?" the queen asked timidly.

The question was too much and the vulnerability infusing Turia's voice made a harsh laugh rip from her lungs. The Griffin King thought that by stealing the seer away like she was some princess in a children's story, he would weaken the queen, not realizing that Isolde herself was the queen's weakness. The certain knowledge grew through Isolde, wrapping its outstretched hands around Isolde until she choked.

Turia stood there trusting and innocent, a miraculous feat when she had trusted no one, but in the end all the seer's efforts had done was bring grief. As it turned out, the queen believed in a terribly false thing, and Isolde wasn't sure she could ever be anything but the weighted old gambler's coin. The seer couldn't stand to turn around. She didn't want to see the face behind her or answer the call of that voice.

With quick steps she hurled herself away from the queen and all the mistakes that had led her to this point, only to find something much worse. The revelry back inside the great hall carried on with an astonishing energy, everyone entirely unaware of the happenings of the last few minutes. It was too loud. Her eyes skated around the room over the banners and food and dais. The empty dais. Chills prickled over her skin. Something was wrong with the dais. Isolde blinked slowly, hoping the sight in front of her was some cruel trick of her brain or some trickster god testing her.

The sword hung regally in its place above the throne, where it always rested when the queen was present. The ancient words along the blade were highlighted in the fathomless blue-green of the Otherrealm, casting a deathly pall over the throne. A now-sinister tune hummed below the cheery song plucked out on the musician's instruments, a persistent undercurrent that left Isolde's mind reeling.

The dais was empty. She glanced back at the doorway hopefully, but Turia's solemn countenance was nowhere to be seen. Few people were near the dais at all, since the dancefloor resided in the middle of the hall. The music pervaded her senses until her mind was numb to anything else. It howled a screaming storm inside her head as she neared the platform, her eyes raking over the few people perched near the throne. Only one had never been in the room with the sword without the queen present. With a deadly calm, her gaze came to rest on Morgan who was sitting stiffly at a small table alone, a goblet of wine clasped too tightly in both of their hands.

"You traitor," she hissed, seizing them by their tunic and jerking them to their feet. Their cup crashed to the floor, wine sloshing across the stone in smooth rivulets. Someone nearby gasped. Isolde didn't care.

"What have you done?" she demanded.

Morgan's eyes widened and they held up their hands in defeat. "What are you talking about?"

"Oh, not this innocent act again."

The seer's mind reeled. They had to get away from the courtiers. Above all things, she had to get them away from the sword before people realized it was issuing its song while the queen was absent. Had her own handiwork betrayed her?

"I don't…I don't know what you mean."

Isolde yanked them close. "The sword. Caliburnus is answering you, Morgan. What I want to know is what in the Soulless's name did you do to it?" she whispered dangerously.

Surprise flushed over their features as they shot a glance at the sword. They just shook their head slightly. Nobles stared at them and their unwelcome interruption of violence, the music slowing as people left the dance floor to figure out what the commotion was all about.

Isolde seized their arm and dragged them through the crowd making a beeline for the gold-encrusted arch of the main entrance. Morgan stumbled after her, not fighting at all. Yanking her chin sharply at the two guards posted at the door, they followed her out into the humid hall. The stillness of the air very much called to mind another night in this same passage, back before she'd come to understand just how poor a judge of character she could be.

Isolde cast Morgan onto the ground. The torchlight shrouded them in its faint amber glow. Their face was blank. The guards hesitated behind their seer, shifting their weight anxiously from foot to foot.

"Watch from the doorway," she ordered, waving them away. With grateful steps the two men retreated to the entrance of the throne room, keeping their swords drawn in case she had need of them. The ocean crashed in the distance as Tristan and Isolde faced one another. Morgan. *It's Morgan,* she reminded herself. Tristan had been a figment of her imagination bolstered by an admirable performance.

Morgan got to their feet, slowly and carefully as if worried about startling her.

"I don't know what you're talking about, Seer."

Her mouth tilted up in an unkind smile. "Sure you don't."

"What can I say? Tell me what to say."

"No. Use your own words, coward," she spat.

"I don't understand."

"You have no claim to this throne and you never will. I don't care what magic you've used to mold Caliburnus, the throne will not fall from the queen's hands. Not while I'm alive."

"Claim to the throne? Isolde, I don't know why the sword is responding to me. I swear."

"So that was the plan all along? Lure me away so I couldn't refute the sword's choice or sense how you'd corrupted the magic, then use it to lay hold of the throne."

"What?" they gasped. "You're being ridiculous." Their tone hardened. "I don't know what's happening. This has nothing to do with me, but I would tread carefully threatening the Griffin King's ambassador."

Isolde laughed and drew her sword. "Consider the engagement broken." Hurling herself at them, she didn't hesitate to go straight for their throat this time. Morgan scrambled away, just barely managing to draw their own sword.

"Are you sure?" they managed to get out as they struggled to block the force of her unrelenting blows. "Don't be so quick to throw away peace, Isolde!"

She shoved them, but they managed to block her blows and get in a hit of their own, drawing blood with a shallow nick on her arm. With a smooth movement she'd shown them, no less.

They danced around each other, lunging, only to withdraw as swiftly as possible. With a twist of her sword, she caught their weapon and locked them in her hold so they were unable to disengage.

"Control dearly loves to masquerade as peace. That's a slow, painful way to die and Viridian will have no part in it. You're under arrest, Morgan. Long live the queen," she said, venom lacing her words.

Morgan wrenched themself from her grasp. Isolde called out to the guards and they were at her side in seconds. Backing away with frantic movements, Morgan turned on their heels and fled. Isolde cursed and tore after them with the two guards in tow. They sent up a shout to summon other soldiers. Out through the courtyard, down the streets of Fabricfirst, careening around corners, they ran with the rising wind. Isolde cursed, pushing herself to move faster, trying to keep their black-clothed back in sight as the breeze pushed against her.

A warning bell rang through the square. More guards would be with them soon, but she had the lead on them all and was still the closest to them. Their eyes glittered in the dark as they briefly glanced back at her. On and on they went, through square after square, flying past surprised street vendors and the few people who dotted the streets at this time of the night.

Isolde's feet pounded the ground and she savored the force of the impact, speeding up in her sprint, even though her lungs wanted to give out. The lights of the city began to fade, and she realized where they were going. The cliffs where they had fought the last time. It was a moonless night. The only thing keeping Morgan from fading into the blackness were the torches held by the mob of soldiers hurtling after them, still further away than she would have liked. What was keeping them from catching up?

With another push, she started closing the distance between them. Morgan looked back again as they raced through the knee-high grasses. Wetness glistened on their cheeks. An angry cry ripped from her throat as the wind picked up, pulling hair over her face to obscure her vision.

A rock slammed into her foot and she tripped, flying into the dirt, just barely able to catch herself with her hands. Isolde leapt up, snatching her sword from where it had fallen and shielding her head with the rollicking wind sending dirt ricocheting around her. Her hand tightened on the hilt of her sword. She'd be damned if they got away again. They were almost to the edge of the cliff now. Shouts echoed in the distance along with the faint glow of the lights, but she didn't spare another glance backward, instead lunging toward the figure. There was no way out for them this time. The sea grew louder. It sounded turbulent, slamming into the cliffside below.

Morgan skittered to a halt at the edge of the cliff. Everything about them agile and ready for action, even at rest. They turned as she drew near, not bothering to slow her pace as a warning echoed in her head, a sensation from Ryth.

"Isolde, I swear I didn't know," they called, their voice breaking. Whispers inhabited the breeze, almost obscuring their message as it cocooned them and pushed against her presence. With that, Morgan leapt from the cliff.

Her heart ground to a standstill. Breath didn't exist. All of it had been stolen by the wind. They were there one moment, then vanishing into the darkness of the sea the next.

"You fool," she screamed, tripping and falling to her knees, unable to tear her eyes away from the starless horizon spreading before her. Empty. Filled to the brim with wild noises that had consumed Morgan's body without a second thought. She wanted to get up, to force herself to move to the edge and look over, to see if she could spot any movement in the waves below, but she knew that would be an utterly fruitless endeavor.

Her teeth pressed against each other until her jaw hurt as she tried to contain the feelings coursing through her blood, hot and rabid. At that moment, a sound pierced the sky unlike anything she'd ever heard. It was much lower in pitch than the voice of a phoenix, but it still writhed with the same kind of wildness. A shape shot up over the edge of the cliff, wheeling into the air overhead, wide tawny feathers coating the wings spreading outward. The creature—the griffin—let out another protective cry, even as its rider placed a calming hand over its beak.

Morgan sat there like a ruler, the other hand loosely settled on the beast's neck familiarly and their body completely at ease, shifting easily with the griffin's movements. They flowed together like water coursing through a riverbed. With a start, Isolde realized that she was watching a person at home, the spirits of the Sylph happy to support them in their endeavors because they were blessed. And she pounded her fist against the ground until it was scraped up and bloodied. Isolde heard a voice in the wind, but when she looked up once more, the creature and his liege were almost out of sight, gliding away to the south.

Guards tripped over themselves, speaking to her in frantic tones, trying to pull her up from the ground and checking her for injuries. She didn't hear a word they said. Her eyes were focused on the skies and their echoing emptiness.

Chapter Thirty-Seven

Isolde

23 Years After the Viridian Phoenix's Rebirth

The party still raged on when Isolde reached the palace. The guards surrounding her whispered when they thought she wouldn't notice but were otherwise painfully silent. Turia sat perched on the throne once more, as though she had never left. Isolde leaned against the doorway with her arms crossed, meeting the queen's hurt, questioning eyes but refusing to take a step further in her soiled dress and wild hair, which had long since come undone from its pins.

Some foolish part of her wished none of it had happened, that she didn't have to know the sword responded to Morgan's presence. Questions rendered her speechless as she'd begun to realize that there was a very slim chance they would have been able to compromise the sword's magic. Morgan didn't have the kind of skill needed to alter her magic and, even if they did, the sword was guarded day and night without interruption. Isolde drifted into the shadows, watching the increasingly drunk nobles falling over each other, laughing at jokes that, most certainly, weren't the least bit amusing. Robin floated among them, eyeing the seer's disheveled appearance with a raised brow. Isolde ignored her. No need to alarm people by ending the event early, even if what they were celebrating had just fallen apart in a matter of hours. She haunted the edges of the room, letting the party peter out until one by one people left and servants had begun clearing away signs of the revelry.

Turia remained on her throne, her guards at attention in the empty room, watching the bustle of men clearing away trays and dimming candles. Her eyes trailed Isolde's presence in the shadows, but the seer didn't want to emerge yet, so they were left at a stalemate.

Finally, a servant asked if the queen needed anything else. With a slight smile, she dismissed him and the rest of the palace staff, including the guards. Only a few sconces were still lit, leaving the room dim and quiet. Still the two women didn't move, frozen in a relief, Isolde almost out of sight while Turia sat there, her hand twitching impatiently. She leaned back and closed her eyes.

"It's over, isn't it?" she asked.

"It's just starting, I'm afraid," her seer answered from beside the great pillar where they had spoken at the beginning of all this.

"I assume they're gone. Again."

Isolde looked down in shame. "We confronted them and they had their griffin waiting, ready to flee."

"How did it unravel so fast?"

Isolde finally made her way away from the wall until she was in front of the queen. She knelt there, her pride too tired to allow her to stand a moment longer.

"They had another plan to try to take power, and I realized it tonight."

Turia stood, walking quietly down the steps and sinking to her knees across from her seer.

"No prophecy warned you?"

Isolde shook her head, trying to stop herself from laughing, but only partially succeeding in the effort. The queen brought her hand up to Isolde's face. Isolde leaned into the touch, closing her eyes.

"The sword, Turia. I don't know how, but the sword was responding to them."

The blood drained from Turia's face. She looked back at Caliburnus, its quiet tune humming through the room.

"Is it forsaking me?" she asked uncertainly, her neck twitching.

"No," Isolde said fiercely, "It named you as queen, and I don't believe that's something it can undo."

"But why would it choose another unless I have become unworthy?"

"The council can't know," Isolde said.

"That's what you're concerned about?" Turia asked.

"That's only one of a great many things I'm concerned about, but perhaps the most pressing. They can't doubt that you're divinely-chosen."

Turia met her eyes then. "What if I'm not?"

"What do you mean?" Isolde sputtered.

Turia just looked at her then, dark irises highlighted by a blue striking in its softness. Inviting an admission that Isolde couldn't stomach giving her. Did she suspect?

"Don't start to doubt now," Isolde said.

Turia rose, pacing through the hall, moving from pillar to pillar.

"I had another idea but I'm almost frightened to ask."

"Well, don't let there be any secrets between us now, Seer," Turia replied tartly.

"I've noticed a...resemblance."

Turia's neck jerked sharply and she stopped mid-step.

"Did your father have any other children?" Isolde asked.

"Not as far as I'm aware. The king was loyal to my mother until the end of her life," she stated coldly.

"I didn't say he wasn't," Isolde said, trying to tread carefully. "Morgan...there's something about the shape of their nose and the quirk of their brow. Something that reminds me of your father. Something that reminds me of you. If you share the same blood, maybe the sword would answer them."

Turia shook her head, "But it didn't respond to my uncle or brother."

Isolde struggled to spin out an answer. It would if they had both been born within the space of the same month. She had tied its loyalty to the queen's bloodline and birth month, thinking that would be enough for it to only choose her. But she couldn't explain that. "Maybe they've beguiled it somehow. Whatever the case, it would still only answer to someone of the Pendamon line," she said.

"Are you suggesting Morgan's my sibling?" Turia asked in astonishment.

"I think it's a good possibility and I think they were here to claim the throne for the Griffin King."

"How could I have an entire sibling living in another kingdom that I never heard about? That's insanity. I don't believe it. I suppose my father did go on that diplomatic mission before I was born, but..."

Isolde interrupted. "The important part is that they were going to try to assert their right to rule, Turia. They were going to try and steal the crown. And, much to my shame, they escaped."

"I'm guessing you broke off the engagement?" Turia asked listlessly.

"What other choice did I have? It wasn't a sincere offer."

"I know." Turia paused. "Did anyone else notice Caliburnus responding while I was absent?"

"I don't know. There was...a bit of a scene when we expelled Morgan from the palace."

The queen sighed. "What do we do now?"

Isolde rose herself and made her way to Turia's side as she gazed out one of the arched windows at the impending dawn. "There's nothing to do but fight."

"Will there ever be anything else?"

"I wish I knew."

Chapter Thirty-Eight

Morgan

23 Years After the Viridian Phoenix's Rebirth

The marble under Morgan's knees felt much too hard and cold as they knelt before the Griffin King in his dark hall of heavy stone built into the mountain itself. The king was an aged man with locks of gray hair falling to his shoulders and just the hint of a shake in his pale, once-steady hands. Morgan could not meet his eyes, lest the king sense the lie living there.

For all their attempts, Morgan could not convince themself to turn over the plans for the weapon that could devastate Morya's armies. The idea of that much blood on their hands curdled their stomach. War itself was contrary to their healing nature, but they'd stepped out of their comfort zone as a spy, pulled by their loyalty to home and family. But there was only so far Morgan could force themself to go. The plans for the Firefiend currently sat gathering dust, hidden underneath their floorboards. Not only that, but they'd been uneasily stuffing down the startling revelation about their parentage, which they feared the king would somehow sense.

Morgan sat there, nervously waiting for the king to tell them why they had been summoned to the palace after their many failures as a spy. Their one chance to prove themself and they'd made an utter mess of things. The sky was so much easier. It expected nothing but joy from them and didn't punish them for things outside of their control.

"And here you are, yet again, Morgan. Forgive me if I'm tired of seeing your face. Maybe this time something good will come of it, though. Do you know why you're here?"

"No, your majesty."

A light of wonder shone in the king's eyes. "Hmm, well, nature is offering us a boon."

Morgan's eyebrows furrowed in confusion.

"The gods plan to bestow their favor upon us. When I first sent you to be an informant in Viridian, it was not only because of our limited options, but also because you were born under an extraordinarily prosperous set of stars, according to the Altar Attendants. Some are born under stars that promise wealth or happiness or pain, but rarely prosperity." The king paused, fidgeting in his chair with a barely-concealed excitement.

Morgan took a deep breath, pressing down their frustration. They'd heard this so many times before. Even as Morgan grew to be someone too softly strange for the nobility's liking and untethered to the normal pursuits of people their age, their mother clung to the idea of their prosperous future as someone who fit into the typical mold of respectability. Whenever she rattled off the words of the Altar Attendants, who Morgan believed had less actual insight than any gambler, an old wound ached with new pain. When the king had assigned them the role of informant, Morgan had sworn to do their best and maybe, at last, live up to their mother's expectations.

The king continued. "My lifelong faith has, at last, been rewarded. As it turns out, you have made a striking impression on someone who decided to grant me a visit this morning. I awoke from my slumber to an emissary of the Sylph accompanied by one of their princesses standing in my bedchambers.."

Morgan finally raised their head. "What do you mean? The gods do not… visit us."

"You are correct. Not in a very long time, at least. The prosperity outlined in your stars seems to be coming to fruition at last, Morgan. They came clothed in a glory I can hardly do justice to in words and they only want one thing from us."

A warning echoed in Morgan's mind as they grew more uncomfortable. "What do the gods want from me?"

"A simple proposal may yet help us win this war and save our people. The Sylph have agreed to break their neutrality if you accept the hand of their Princess Anore in marriage. For whatever reason, she is enamored with you. Who knows the inner workings of fate. What I do know is that this is a divinely-bestowed gift we cannot reject."

"I…the Sylph…they haven't spoken directly to us in centuries," Morgan sputtered.

"Well, they've chosen to speak now. We've discussed it in depth. They're willing to help us on the battlefield and help us avoid air scouts to reach Viridian if you marry her. You owe your kingdom this, Morgan. You owe this to me."

Morgan knew better than to ask if they had a choice.

"There's one other thing you must do if our attack on Viridian is to be successful."

Morgan swallowed, their mind reeling with each new sentence.

"The Sylph's one condition for helping us take Morya is that we must lure the Viridian seer out of the city during the initial attack. The Sylph don't wish to anger the Salamanders by destroying someone particularly sacred to them. You must get her out of the city. You have the best chance of doing that."

Breathing became hard, but Morgan fought, trying to keep an even face.

The king stood. "Now come meet your bride."

Morgan followed. Thought after thought reeled through their mind as they tried to figure out what to say. More than anything though, they felt their heart falling.

The king opened the door to a warm antechamber with a fire burning in the hearth. The fire was unnecessary though. A woman stood robed in light, her white hair defying gravity. She was heartachingly lovely, even with her uncanny, large eyes that took in the world with a dangerous curiosity. But she was not peace or joy or their choice.

Morgan's heart broke.

Chapter Thirty-Nine

Isolde

23 Years After the Viridian Phoenix's Rebirth

A t first, the court rippled with bitterness at the news that there would be no wedding to bring peace. A dreary mood curtained the city as Isolde made her way back to the palace from the forge. She hugged the wall on one side of the street as a unit of soldiers marched past in smart formation. A pang of regret tugged at her chest as she tore her eyes away from them, knowing that in just a few months they would be returning with the light snuffed out of their eyes or not returning at all.

Just weeks before, the court had seen off a squadron led by Sir Gahera. She'd marched off with pride and solemnity, swearing she knew what she was getting into and ensuring the queen that commoners needed to see the nobility risking their blood as well. Their armies had suffered a number of small defeats at the front lines. Their borders shrunk even as they spent their days bent over tables full of maps and missives from generals. Robin now held group blessings at the temple daily, no longer able to keep up with the demand of individual blessings being requested by those about to go to war and their families. While Robin certainly deviated from the script, she did seem to take her role of comfort seriously, acting more soberly than Isolde had come to expect from her.

The night air fluttered softly past her cheek and she recoiled from the breeze, pulling her hood tighter around her head. She had nothing to show for her efforts at the blacksmith's hovel. The Blue seemed to be rejecting her, casting her from its cool, long-suffering certainty every time she tried to lose herself within it. After hours of attempting to reach far enough into the ether to create something, anything, the seer finally had to admit defeat. Perhaps she should have been concerned about the consequences of such a rejection, pondering upon its meaning with a solemn brow and pious supplication. *Should* meant very little to her anymore.

Isolde didn't question it, instead letting a numbness creep inside her veins, misting up her thoughts until she was barely herself anymore. She didn't have it in her to be anything but tired and accepting of her bad luck. She told herself it would pass because, after all, all things do and that was one of the few things The Great seer believed in.

So she floated on through the streets until a sharp shrill brought her to a halt, rising over the silence, pouring over its surface with a relentless metallic voice. It felt like the mourning bells never ceased these days, but this was an altogether different sound. The palace bell issued forth its keening notes unconcerned with the late hour or sleeping court.

Isolde only stayed frozen for a moment before springing into action and tearing down the road to the palace as fast as her feet could take her. A member of the court was deceased. Panic flooded through her mind, churning up murky thoughts and images of Turia dead in a dozen different ways. But she pushed those thoughts aside, focusing on the street ahead of her instead.

People stirred in their homes. Lamps flared to life as people left their dwellings to see what all the fuss was about. The courtyard was still mostly empty when Isolde arrived. Clouds chased their shadows across the damp cobblestones and grass. Besides the tolling bell, a deceptive silence blanketed the palace, even as nobles and commoners began lining the walls, craning their necks to locate the reason for the great sound filling the air. On and on, it tolled, unrelenting. Isolde scrambled up the steps to the first archway, pushing through those gathered there, forgoing any attempt as grace in surrender to the panic pounding in her chest. With a start, she collided with another figure emerging from the corridor beyond the entrance. They almost fell to the ground together, but Isolde caught the girl's arms and they managed to steady each other.

Isolde's breath caught in her throat at the sight of Turia's very-much-still-alive frown. "What's all this?" she asked.

"Gahera," the queen replied tightly.

"Gahera?" Looking out over the courtyard, Isolde noticed a lone figure standing stiffly in the center of the glittering wet grass. She faced the palace gates, still as death, offered a wide berth by those moving in quiet streams nearby. The seer recognized Aeryt's tight braid, her hands clasped precisely behind her back in the way she'd seen a dozen times before. But this time, it looked like maybe she was using her hands to hold herself together. On and on, the bell cried. Aeryt waited.

A procession slowly came into view. Soldiers in burnished armor walked in step with each other, helmets removed and upturned faces solemn in the flickering torches. They guided a wooden cart between them, taking care to not look at what rested within. Horses laden with equipment and other bruised and battered people followed behind, but Isolde hardly noticed them. A disheveled Robin, who looked as though she'd just clamored out of bed, brought up the tail of the entourage. As if in a dream, all Isolde could see was the cart rattling awkwardly and the faint shape outlined by the blue sheet draped over it.

Aeryt didn't move, even as the pallbearers came to a halt in front of her, lowering their heads in deference as they pulled back the covering. Isolde looked away. Turia didn't.

As much as they had tried, there was no disguising the extent of the damage to Gahera's lifeless body, but as was tradition, Aeryt had to look upon her and see her in all her death in order to honor her in all her life. One by one everyone witnessing the scene sank to their knees, lowering their heads in deference to the twisted sacrifice laid out before them. Finally, the bell stopped and Turia made her way to join Gahera's silent sister, resting a gentle hand on her arm. Isolde remained where she was, having no desire to look upon the knight's broken corpse up close. She didn't want to see a face so energetic and vivid in life, transformed into an empty void by the absence of a soul.

Sometimes she wondered where her own soul had taken off to, the numbness settling in her chest offering the simple comfort of dullness. The sight of Aeryt barely breathing but not having yet broken over the sight of her dead sister almost pierced through it. Isolde kept the surging grief and guilt at bay. After all, it was the Griffin King who had brought this about. War was war, and the blame didn't rest on her shoulders. Isolde stood as frozen as Aeryt tried to fight off a flood of feelings she didn't want to deal with. She was so deeply occupied by her mind that it took her a moment to process the sudden broken silence of the courtyard.

At first, Isolde wondered if the sound was human. It reminded her of the tales of the unearthly screams of the Soulless issued whenever someone was about to die on a battlefield. Hesitantly, she too made her way to Aeryt's side as she yelled, the sound filled with a depth of rage and grief that even Isolde with all of her struggles could hardly fathom. The young knight's face contorted with the ugly pain of the thing, still standing but unable to tear her eyes away from Gahera's face.

"People are watching," Isolde whispered.

Turia shot her a cutting look, pressing an arm around Aeryt's shoulders.

"What do you want them to know?" she continued gently.

Aeryt's broken cry trembled as her tortured eyes turned out to take in those witnessing her grief.

"Let not my sister's death be in vain," she declared. "Let none of our sacrifices be in vain. In blood and fire, I swear we will make the bastards responsible for this pay."

Chapter Forty

Morgan

23 Years After the Viridian Phoenix's Rebirth

It wasn't raining. Morgan couldn't remember the last time it hadn't been raining. They couldn't remember the last time the sky was this blue or the air this fretfully fragrant with the scent of blooming flowers. So, when they dragged Morgan's brother's body back from the battlefield, no mud was tracked into the villa. The smell of decay entwined itself with the smell of the blossoms and Morgan swore they would never touch a flower again.

Their father wailed. Their mother cried. Their sister laid a rose on his chest to symbolize a life lived to passion. Morgan did none of those things, instead backing away, barely able to see the body anyway past the fog of thoughts crowding their vision.

A lord had died. Workers stripped the estate's flags from their poles while servants tied white sashes about the waists of the remaining members of that small, broken family. Morgan left them behind after saying the appropriate prayer to the Sylph in the sky and climbing onto their griffin's back, desperate to soothe the guilt burning through the palms of their hands. Ebrian leapt silently from the turret, sensing his rider's all-encompassing grief.

What a fool they'd been. What an utter fool. Every day more people fell to the sickness and still more fell on the battlefield. Morgan lambasted themself relentlessly until no thoughts were left in their brain, only an urgency like nothing they'd felt before. It all seemed very real now. And what loyalty did they have to that queen and her lovely puppet master after all?

The truth was Morgan had already granted the pair some measure of dedication. A deadly mistake. But no longer. Someone needed to atone for the soul of their brother, lost through a war spurred on by their own lack of resolve. Unfortunately, the information to do just that rested in their burning hands, clutched in the feathers of their fiercest friend.

Chapter Forty-One

Isolde

23 Years After the Viridian Phoenix's Rebirth

P aper crumpled under the angry weight of her fingers. Yet another page wrinkled beyond repair, filled with strange words that sounded nothing like her. Words of explanation, words of apology. Sincere, ugly, uncalculated words spinning out beyond her. Stupid of her to even try it. It was a vain exercise, in truth. Some measure of safety hedged her in. The queen would never see these words.

Isolde could trick herself, pretend that maybe someday she would hand her a plain letter during a calm evening. The queen would look up at her with those quiet eyes, trying to parse through the meaning of such a gesture, her brows furrowed.

A lump rose in Isolde's throat and she shook her head briskly, rising from her chair and tearing the paper from her desk. It met the fire without any hesitation. She watched it fall and burn, purging the brief indulgence from her mind. Especially the lingering feeling that maybe, someday it would be possible to see forgiveness grace the queen's face. Forgiveness for the lie she'd told at the very beginning to secure the throne for her queen. A simple emotion twisting in her gut had made her foolish, an instinct she struggled against. It lurked like a predator she could just barely sense in her peripheral vision.

Just as she was about to storm forth from her room and pretend the whole sorry business had never happened, a sliver of paper caught her eye just by her door. Not one of her own. Someone must have slipped it under.

Snatching it up, she examined the envelope with a detached caution at the oddity of a missive so subtly making its way to her. No messenger had announced its presence. It had not been left inside the letter tray just inside her chambers.

The writing though. She broke the seal, slipping the note from inside its unobtrusive gray casing.

"One time. Just one last time on the cliffs. There's something I need to tell you. I know that won't convince you in the slightest. I don't dare overestimate my own pull, though I still consider us friends in the deepest sense of the word. I think I would still care for you if you stole the breath from my lungs. Please deign me this one last explanation. If not for me, then for the one person on this earth that I know you do care about. The queen is in grave danger."

Isolde scoffed. Now there was a trap if she'd ever seen one. She tossed the note in the fire, letting it follow in the destructive footsteps of her half-baked attempts to set her world right. What were they trying to do? Capture her? Hold her for ransom? She wished she could say Turia would throw her away without a second thought, that she would keep her kingdom and rule safe above all else. But Turia didn't have that in her and once again the certainty pulsed through Isolde that she was the worst thing that had ever happened to the unsuspecting young queen. Turia would not let her be taken. She would shed tears and send avenging armies and for who? A girl she thought could be trusted. A person she considered a friend. A woman who had held her even as she spoke gentle violence into her ears.

Why did she always have to be the weakness and the danger? The seer couldn't tear those two qualities away from herself. They were wrapped into her being, poisoning every lying word she spouted.

Isolde closed her eyes. What did Morgan know? What if it wasn't a bluff? Damn it, they knew exactly the right strings to pull. She could show up with a battalion, storm out to the cliffs to confront his ambush. She could leave it be and pretend she'd never seen that cursed missive. She could have done either of those things, but unfortunately her feet moved quicker than her mind and before she knew it they were treading that same old path out from the palace to the edge of Viridian.

The fountains were lit for the dead, as they were every night as of late. They cast their shadows over cobblestones like the ghosts they were supposed to guide home. Everyone spoke of hauntings these days, which simply reminded Isolde of the creeping unease she'd been battling her entire life. She watched the shadows with keen eyes, unwilling to dismiss such stories, no matter how likely they were born from grieving minds. The seer didn't take grief's power to create lightly. Besides, if anyone was likely to be the target of some raging wraith, it was her and her lying tongue.

Isolde used no light to guide her, making her way in the scattered moonlight by memory. Best not to let them see her coming. Drawing her sword, she felt the daggers strapped to her thigh as well, which gave her some reassurance. It was her turn to haunt the edge of the woods, slipping among the silver-laced trees like a shadow until she could see them there, outlined as they stared out at the ocean.

Morgan wasn't even watching the tree line or the fields extending to the city road. The fool. Leaving their back unprotected. Unless there were others though, also hidden among the trees. Isolde stiffened, straining her ears for any other sounds, but she didn't pick up anything besides the humming of the bugs and the usual sounds of the leaves rustling with the wind.

Ryth stirred in her mind, but she dismissed the feeling, unwilling to let the creature judge her decision.

Finally, Morgan turned to look at the city, glowing faintly against the sky thanks to its pyres for those no longer able to return home.

Morgan's forlorn voice carried as they turned to a large mound nearby. "She's not coming. It wasn't enough to convince her."

Isolde startled as the mound shifted among the grasses, stretching its wings out to shake them and give a low grunt of assent.

"Of course it wasn't enough," they spat, their voice so much harsher than she'd ever heard it. "I had to try though, you know I did."

The seer steeled herself as they turned away to mount their griffin and leave her to her fate.

Chapter Forty-Two

Isolde

23 Years After the Viridian Phoenix's Rebirth

Morgan heard her voice first, its angry timbre reaching their ears and causing their heart to fall just as it had ever since the first time they'd encountered her on that busy street. And they saw her then, emerging from the forest. Even with the pale light of the moon and the eerie sounds of the ocean below, no one could have ever mistaken her for a ghost. There was something too real about her, too solid.

Her back straight, her steps precise, a gait that they were convinced could send even the Soulless running. She wore no smile this time, but that was for the better. They'd seen too many of her cunningly kind smiles to believe them and much preferred when she let her anger seep through, wreathing her face in the untempered fury of a powerful woman who knew that, at the end of the day, she had very few choices.

"You don't belong here," they called in answer to her curses.

Her eyes took on that cynical hue Morgan had become fascinated with as they forged swords together, and they tried to teach her the intricacies of healing alchemy. "Oh?"

"You're not meant for this city where they try to tell you the sea is to be shunned."

Isolde paused before them. "I don't know what kind of ambush this is, but the Phoenix Guard is already on the way." Her stance was tense, she looked ready to fight them at the drop of a pin, but gods she was here. She'd come.

"You stand here at the height of your power but not the height of your potential."

Isolde drew her sword. "I'm quite happy with exactly how things are. Did you summon me here just to criticize me with idiotic riddles?"

Morgan quickly shook their head, reaching out to her but stopping short.

"No, no, I'm not saying it right. Isolde, you're not happy."

"And happiness is all we're supposed to strive for, I suppose?"

"While you live in Viridian, you can never truly heal, Isolde. I don't believe you can find lasting contentment in these circumstances where you're always at the queen's beck and call, running around to try and save her from her own foolish mistakes. You'll always be trapped if you stay here."

"I've never been prouder of anything in my life than my dedication to being at my queen's 'beck and call,'" she hissed.

Morgan shook their head again. "No, Isolde, you're not understanding."

"Then get to the point before I relieve you of your tongue. Why did you call me here?"

Bowing their head, they moved closer to the end of her outstretched sword. "Leave Viridian. While you still can, please." Tentatively they reached for her hand and she didn't pull away, frozen as she listened. "Come away with me, if you'd like. I never wanted to be your enemy, quite the opposite in fact, which you know deep down somewhere. I know you don't trust me, but by all things holy and unholy I don't…I want…I can't stand to see you rot there for your entire life."

"I'm afraid the rottenness springs from within me, dear traitor. I just take it wherever I go, so it wouldn't be much use to leave. Haven't you figured out yet that *I'm* the poison," she responded in a measured tone, choosing her words slowly and carefully. The truth of it washed over her as she finally faced the mirror in her mind. There was only so much tragedy she could blame on fate and circumstance. Especially when she had claimed the power of fate with her false prophecy about Turia's destiny to be queen.

"Well, I'll gladly drink your poison. Come away with me or if not with me, then go off on your own and find a new name and a place where you don't have to be the seer. There's something in you, Isolde. I see it in flashes in your eyes. You long to be free. Seize the chance to live a life where not so much rests on your shoulders, and you can meet people you trust because they aren't trying to get anything from you."

"Spoken by someone who did just that."

Morgan threw back their head with frustration and began pacing in front of her.

"It…pains me to see you here. Especially when I picture what could be. I see…how can I explain what I see in my dreams."

She watched with careful eyes as their movements became more erratic with every word.

"I don't see why you would have any interest in my life and, even if this entire outburst were genuine, I fear you're seeing things in me that aren't there. I am free, Morgan. Perhaps more than I ever have been in my life." It was an admission. They saw her wince at that slip of the tongue. They drew closer to her, placing their hand slowly on her face to see if she would allow the gesture.

"In my dreams, I see you able to speak and move without having to always change yourself for those around you. I see you flying away from this accursed place. I see you at peace."

Isolde looked up at them. With surprise, they saw that her unrelenting blue eyes glistened. They'd never seen her cry. Not once. She pressed their hand to her face.

"Don't you see, I will always be the poison."

"Isolde, don't…"

"It's a lovely thought, but there will never be peace for me. And if I can't have peace, I will have control."

"Oh, you and your control, Isolde." They choked out a bitter laugh. "Just come away with me while you still can."

"I don't understand why you're asking," she said, her eyes searching theirs. Morgan knew the look, the questioning, and they couldn't take the guilt.

"What do I have to do to convince you that I care about you? That our friendship means something?" they asked.

Glancing behind her head, they began to panic as the need for urgency collided with fear. Why did people always demand proof of a certain kind of love, as though it was somehow the strongest bond and the only feeling that could explain the way their heart yearned to see her soar.

Morgan leaned forward, uncertainly pressing their lips to Isolde's in a desperate attempt to convey their care for her in a way she would understand. Her tears dampened their face as she returned the kiss. There was a hunger in Isolde, but a hesitance in the way her mouth moved against theirs. They immediately broke away, the wrongness of the kiss washing over Morgan and leaving a sick feeling in the pit of their stomach.

Isolde fixed them with that tired, all-knowing look.

"No, why are you doing this, Morgan? I'm not a fool."

"I am, though. That's exactly what I am," Morgan declared.

With an exhausted countenance, Isolde raised the sword once more. "Answer me."

"It's not safe for you there anymore. I'm sorry. I'm so sorry. This is my offering to you."

Chapter Forty-Three

Isolde

23 Years After the Viridian Phoenix's Rebirth

S udden dread rose in Isolde's stomach, spreading through her body like a wildfire as she became aware of a distant roar. The sound had been growing in strength in the back of her mind. At first, she'd simply marked it as the song of the sea winds, always strong and brisk this time of the year.

Their face. She could see Morgan's face more clearly now. The sharp swoop of their nose and the soft shape of their cheeks. Why was there more light? A slightly reddish light too.

Isolde couldn't make herself turn around, already knowing what she would see when her eyes settled over the city that she had loved and hated and wrestled with her entire life.

Instead, in the wake of the perilous reflection of light in those falsely kind eyes, she met Morgan's gaze and thrust her sword into their stomach with a cold precision.

They buckled with only a quiet gasp and she left them there, finally turning to face Viridian with dry eyes. The flames licked ever higher, reaching up towards the darkest regions of the sky like a burnt offering. But the Soulless had long ago forsaken Isolde, and she didn't care what trajectory of fate they had decided on. She would steal their offering for herself. Smoke billowed out toward her, thick and quiet in the wind. The seer plunged toward it, only one thought in her head, even as she heard the weak sound of her name from behind her.

Isolde would not allow her princess to perish as a sacrifice on some onerous altar.

Chapter Forty-Four

Isolde

23 Years After the Viridian Phoenix's Rebirth

The city was ablaze with light, heat, and unholy noise. Heartrending screams joined with the falling of brick, creating a chorus to serenade the ethereal flickering of the red and white flames.

Isolde raced, her heavy heartbeat adding rhythm to an array of horrible sounds she barely had the capacity to process through her clouded thoughts. The smoke made it difficult to see more than a few paces ahead of her. But she knew this path to the palace by heart.

Ryth felt her calling despair as images filled her mind of the palace consumed, the princess caught unaware, only realizing the danger when her floor and doors were too hot to touch and the vial of phoenix blood usually hanging around her neck had been left in another room.

The creature swept down in front of her, and she didn't even give her the chance to land before flinging herself on her back.

"The palace. We have to get to the palace. Where did it start? Where did the fire start, Ryth?"

"They dropped the weapons throughout the city. Isolde, do you really want to go to the palace?" The creature ventured in a way much too demure.

Isolde's grip tightened on her feathers as they careened over the flames, the heat spilling over her in searing bursts. "What do you know, you fiend?"

"Now is not the time for your insolence, child."

"I haven't been a child in quite some time."

"You're all children to me."

"I'll let you know when you've earned the right to that kind of smugness and, I assure you, today is not that day. I ask you again, what do you know?"

Isolde, you're not going to find what you're hoping to find. The voice came softly, whispered straight into her mind this time.

Her scalp tightened with a prickling feeling as her eyes blurred briefly.

"Take me to the palace."

"I will. But I'm warning you."

"What good is a warning if it's already too late?" she said shortly.

"They dropped a weapon directly on the palace. It was all ablaze within minutes."

"How is it alight? It was recoated with fire resin just this past spring."

"I expect your spy had something to do with it. This fire burnt white at first, hot enough to sever the magical bonds of the resin. If I recall, weren't there plans for some such hot-burning weapon that were discussed by the council and perhaps hidden in the Palace Archives?"

Isolde swallowed, her mouth filling with a bitter taste. The plans for the Firefiend. But everything has been accounted for, nothing was missing...Her stomach dropped. Morgan must have copied them on some night. But that was ages ago, how long had they had the plans in their possession?

"Did you see it, Ryth?" she demanded.

The creatures hesitated just enough.

"Did you try to find her? Try to fly her away?" she asked steadily, coldly.

"That's not my role. I went to find you."

"You will be held accountable for this sin."

"Don't frighten me with such words, oh holy seer. To sin and be punished is surely my greatest fear." Ryth mocked. "I think you forget who you're talking to, Isolde."

The seer squinted, the palace emerging from the smoke and she finally screamed, letting out a cry from the depths of her gut before she even realized what she was doing. All that remained of the palace was a smoking skeleton. Patches of fire burned in the courtyard. In the end, the stone that should have been impervious to the touch of fire gave in to its demands in the same way as the old wooden huts of the fishermen. People ran back and forth, some cowering, some half-heartedly trying to douse the flames with wooden buckets of water from the nearest fountain. One woman looked up at the sound of her scream, but she didn't care, too distraught to be embarrassed or concerned about the woman's perception of her.

"Land!" she yelled.

"No, Isolde. It's time to move on. Trust me."

"When have you ever earned my trust?"

"I'm tired of this conversation, Isolde. Let us speak candidly for once. I care for you as my Bonded. We have always protected each other and always will."

"I differ on the nature of our relationship. Just land."

"You must listen to me."

"Land or I will jump."

"Don't be a fool, Isolde."

"Don't try me right now."

"I don't know why you insist on incinerating yourself."

"That's not what this is."

"Are you sure?"

"I'll only ask once more," she stated, desperation starting to claw its way out of her throat.

"So be it." Ryth plunged into a sharp dive, shaking her hold loose and sending her rolling into the courtyard. She scrambled to her feet as quickly as she was able after getting the wind knocked out of her, the phoenix already soaring away. Isolde didn't spare her a second thought. The sickly sweet smell of smoking flesh forced her to throw her arm over her face. Her eyes remained fixed on the arch at the top of the steps. It still stood, though the walls around it had crumbled into oblivion. Bodies littered the steps, but nothing could convince her to try to look at their faces. No human-made sounds met her ears once she'd raced through the arch into the halls.

The princess couldn't still be here. Surely her advisors would have rushed her out as soon as they realized what was happening. A torn flag fluttered in a sudden breeze, and she resisted the urge to curse. It would do no good to anger the Soulless, even if the Sylph had betrayed her by blessing Morgan. She erased the image of their curled-up form lying on the ground. Her feet echoed too loudly, only magnifying the cacophony of panic in her mind.

"Turia!" she called, over and over again, especially as she turned the corner toward where the queen's chambers had formerly existed. "Turia, are you here?" She stepped over a fallen beam, climbing and crawling through the rubble to reach the queen's bedroom where she surely would have been. A prayer left her lips. "Let all things be weighed and tempered but never let my queen be diminished. Don't let me be here to hear her dying cries. Don't let me find her lifeless body. Don't let me find her forever silent."

A sound. She slipped, scraping her forearm on a brick.

Part of her wished to see the queen and part of her dreaded that if she was indeed here, her life would surely be near its end.

"Turia, is that you?"

Isolde slipped through a space in the caved-in door to the queen's bedroom.

"I'm here," came the voice weakly from a corner.

The blood surrounding Turia's huddled up form almost stopped Isolde in her tracks.

A beam rested over her abdomen.

"You're alive," she gasped, rushing to her and brushing the queen's matted, dirty hair away from her face. Everything about that moment reminded her of a bitter old pain, a fear that she could never be close to anyone without inevitably bringing them ruin and horror. That kind of softness, that kind of love, would never be hers. In moments, perhaps, she could grasp its fleeting shadow, but as the bloody cut on Turia's face proclaimed, it would never be hers to keep.

"Open your eyes," she commanded.

"Would a please hurt you?"

"Please."

"It must be bad if you're actually listening to me," the queen muttered, her green eyes fluttering open.

"Have you been paying any attention at all, my queen," Isolde retorted.

She examined the scene, the blood loss that would happen if she risked moving the beam. If the blood already spreading across the wooden floor was any indication, it was a risk she'd have to take. Isolde clasped Turia's hand and received a weak squeeze in return. Pushing up her sleeves, she took a deep breath and heaved the wood away. It crashed into the floor, the sound mixing with Turia's strangled cries.

The seer examined the queen's pale face, keeping the extent of her concern locked away inside, and gently knelt to place her hand on Turia's bloodied stomach. Perhaps Tristan would be good for something after all. An image flashed through her mind of blood spilling from their abdomen as they curled into themself. The cascade of anger coursing through her washed away any hint of regret. Instead, she focused on the sticky liquid coating her hand, on the queen's breathy moans, and the utter calm she felt coiling inside her. It was the remnant of something deeper and much more ancient than her body.

Isolde called to the wind and the ocean and the earth, in tandem with the ancient thing accompanying her soul. They were made of the same star stuff and the ocean answered first, filling her with a heavy power. Her vision blurred and she plunged into the Blue, powerless in its hold. She wrangled with it at first, fighting, demanding the wind and earth join her. She demanded the sea meet her requests, that it channel its power into the queen to knit her body back together. But the sea laughed at her. The wind hissed as it darted about, doing nothing but mock her. The earth sang with a strangely aching and disconcerting song, indifferent to her plight.

You will obey. She willed it, only for a soft voice from her memory to chime in. It took everything in her, every ounce of effort and strength, but she stopped fighting. Uncurling her fingers, she loosened her body, giving in to the waves tossing her soul about and in response the ocean and earth and wind calmed as well. They mirrored her. Awkwardly, she tried to remember healing Tristan, tried to remember the feeling of drawing power from the green-blue life buzzing around her. She didn't have it in her to seduce them, as they would have said, but she could plead.

The seer mustered every bit of gentleness buried deep in her bones. It was a stilted, unfamiliar gentleness that was far from comfortable for the likes of Isolde, but for her queen she would do this. The vulnerability nearly washed her away, but with a soft sentiment she whispered life and healing. She channeled it through her soul and into her hands. With a gasp she was thrust back into her body. Blinking, she realized that Turia's breathing had evened out. Isolde examined her bloody hands. The evidence was there, but not a scratch or bruise remained on Turia's skin.

"You're going to be alright," Isolde stated quietly. She had no room left in her for emotion or tears or surprise.

"I thought forging was your alchemir speciality?"

"I could be an expert in anything for you, Princess," she said with just the smallest hint of a smile.

"You flirt. Why don't you give a dying woman some peace," she said, even as she sat up.

"I'm afraid peace continually eludes me. It always goes running the moment I appear."

"Maybe you need to learn how to sit with it then."

"You really think peace is something that can be learned? Believe me, I would have acquired it long ago if it were possible."

Turia just smiled, seizing the seer's hand and pulling her into a bloody embrace.

"I've never been more glad to see your face, my friend."

"No doubt."

Turia refused to let go, even as the silence lengthened. It took that long for Isolde to realize that the queen was crying warm tears into her shoulder.

"How many are dead? It's all over, isn't it? Wait…" A faltering horror crashed through her voice. "Edrune. Edrune!" she exclaimed, trying to pull back, but Isolde kept a tight hold on her.

"Isolde, he has to have escaped, right? Please tell me he escaped, was evacuated, something."

The seer looked to the ground, pleading for strength. "My queen…I don't think…when I came to find you, that entire section of the floor over the dungeons had caved in. It's doubtful he survived."

Sobs ripped through Turia's body. "My brother…my brother…" Isolde held her close, rocking with her. "He can't just be gone. He can't…" They stayed like that for some time until Turia had no more tears to give.

"It's all over. They've won," Turia muttered.

Finally, Isolde pried herself back so she could hold Turia's shoulders and force her to meet her eyes.

"Don't you dare give up this easily."

"Easily? How did this even happen? How did our security fail this greatly? I'm assuming they got the plans for the Firefiend. And we never even noticed."

Isolde winced.

"My brother is dead. Everyone is dead."

"Not everyone, my queen. This is when it counts." Isolde stood up, searching the ground for something until she spotted it, relief washing over her. Sweeping up the silver vial of phoenix's blood, which had been torn from the queen's neck in the explosion, she held it out to Turia. "Now is when you fight for your people. Let that hellbent king know that the high queen of the Fire Folk has been blessed as such for a reason."

It broke her heart to say the words. She wanted to entice Turia away, tell her that she wasn't strong enough or there was nothing she could do. The seer wanted to paint a picture for her, a vision of a life where they both had peace in each other's arms. But as she'd established, peace was not one of the many fraught threads that made up her own fate. Something in her knew that Turia would never stop resenting her if she didn't encourage her to rise and meet this moment. She'd already committed too many sins against Turia's desires over the course of her life. So, she told one more lie in the service of her queen, knowing how much she valued her people and the life she wanted for all she ruled.

"You are, indeed, blessed, my queen. This is a battle you will not regret fighting. I have seen victory for you."

Turia eyed the vial solemnly before her gaze floated back up to her seer, carefully considering the uneven gray shore surrounding the pupils of Isolde's blue eyes.

"Do I trust you?" she asked.

It nearly broke Isolde's heart. Perhaps one of the few questions that could do so.

"Only you can decide that, but know that I care for you. You can trust me to be your friend to the very end."

"Is this the end?" Turia asked.

"I don't know that you will ever truly end. I think that you will exist, in some form, for ages. I imagine your name being whispered around campfires and traced out in fine poems. I think that you will be endless."

Turia's mouth quirked up. "Who is going to write me fine poems?"

"So many questions. I said fine poems, I didn't say they won't be supercilious works used by teachers to bore children to tears for centuries."

"Well, then." Turia's fingers slipped around the vial, quickly fastening it around her neck. "Here's to boring people for centuries to come."

Chapter Forty-Five

The Sylph Princess Anore

23 Years After the Viridian Phoenix's Rebirth

She saw them and she shattered.

Isn't this what she had wanted, Feeling? Well, she had a Feeling now. It tore through her, and she screamed at the viscerality of the thing. The princess swiped at her face, which was, to her surprise, raining.

That bitch had stolen her lips. Morgan's lips were hers and hers alone. What right did this so-called seer have to press her face against theirs?

She yelled and glared and roughened the air. Morgan would pay for their unfaithfulness. They would pay. But not yet.

Anore would lie in wait, let them think they'd won and gotten away with that stolen kiss. She would wait and then she would strike. She reveled in her cleverness. The Feeling stripped all compassion from her and left her spinning in vicious circles.

Chapter Forty-Six

Isolde

23 Years After the Viridian Phoenix's Rebirth

The city still burned, but in the crackling, nearly-silent way of dying flames. Every courtyard was a battlefield, full of fallen soldiers. The queen gathered her remaining troops. They found the living. The living flocked to them as soon as word started to spread. Only a handful of advisors and knights had escaped the flames, but it was enough simply because it had to be. The opening wave had only been that. Isolde had no doubt that the Griffin King's forces were mounting and moving towards them, even as they clamored to pull themselves together.

They found messengers and sent them though the skies on their phoenixes, declaring war was upon them and any who wished could join the queen to fight to maintain Viridian's autonomy. In a blur, Isolde helped Turia into the glistening virgin armor waiting for her in the armory as generals barked at each other. They yelled about how Camlann would be their last real strategic chance at making a successful stand against the forces of the Griffin army while Isolde brushed Turia's hair aside to fasten her breastplate with numb, fumbling hands.

For once, Turia seemed more in the moment than her seer. Taking a deep breath, Isolde tried to force away the fear rising within her. Forces massed in the courtyard and out through the streets of Fabricfirst, some in their issued armor, some simply in homemade wear. Finally, the generals filtered out of the armory to finish final preparations for the army to start moving and to send messengers out to the forces stationed across the kingdom, requesting immediate aid. Everyone knew that there was a good chance those forces wouldn't arrive until it was much too late if the Fire Folk didn't quickly gain the upper hand in the battle.

Only Turia and Isolde were left as Isolde pulled Caliburnus from its place on the wall and presented it to Turia with careful hands.

"I don't know what I'm doing," Turia answered, strapping the weapon awkwardly to her waist.

Isolde placed her hands on the queen's shoulders. "You'll be fine. Remember, your main goal is to encourage the troops. Like always, they just need to see you. Stay far behind the front lines. Your generals will protect you and you'll stay alive."

"That's not what I'm worried about."

Isolde touched her cheek with a sigh. "That's not what I want to hear. When will you start valuing your own life?"

"When it means something," Turia spat.

Isolde nearly shook her then, but refrained, instead just brushing her thumb over the downy skin of the queen's cheek. "You already mean something just by existing."

"Oh, you know better than that, Seer."

"No, listen. You must value your life. Value it for me, but more so, value it for yourself. Stay alive." Her voice grew more desperate as the realization of just exactly what she'd done sending

Turia—her Turia—into a horrific battlefield. Sweet Turia who had never hurt an animal or said a cruel word. The queen who valued her own life so little compared to everyone else's. Turia's neck jerked. "No, listen to me. You must stay alive. Promise me."

"I can't make that promise. Like I said, not what I'm worried about. There's going to be bloodshed, I know, but what if all the horrors are for nothing. That's what concerns me, Seer."

Isolde didn't say then what she was thinking, that horrors are always for nothing in the very end.

"You can't think like that. Trust yourself, trust in us, and trust in the word of the Soulless. You will have victory."

They both took a deep breath, simply gazing at each other for a moment bursting with so many things unsaid. Isolde fingered the vial around Turia's neck, opening the cap with reverence.

"Let all things be weighed and tempered," the seer whispered, dipping her fingers in the burning blood before meeting the queen's eyes and brushing it across her forehead. She sent down a prayer for her queen that in addition to being impervious to fire, she would be impervious to harm of any kind.

"Let all things be weighed and tempered," the queen echoed back.

They left the armory. Their phoenixes were already waiting for them. Ryth vibrated with disapproval, but Isolde ignored it, knowing that at the end of the day the creature had shown up and had committed to this effort since she was going no matter what. Her blue-green flames stood out amongst the army of silver soldiers and blazing red creatures.

As Turia mounted her phoenix, her crown glittering in the rising sun, Isolde wanted more than anything to climb on the creature behind her to make sure she was protected. She reminded herself that was what the queen's guards were for, but where had they been when she was crushed under a beam? She reminded herself that the Viridian Phoenix would do nearly as much for boosting the army's morale as the queen herself and that would also keep her safe. They set out, rising into the fresh air with an army of creatures soaring around them and the sound of ground troops marching serenading them.

Isolde wished they were greater in number, but still appreciated how many had answered the call. She was even glad to see Robin, who had immediately evaluated the queen with concerned eyes and kind words. What was left of the city marched and flew forward with them.

The seer flew nearly beside Turia but gave her the lead in a show of deference. Even battered, with purple under her eyes and traces of blood still in her dirty hair pulled behind her, the queen was perfectly beautiful.

Chapter Forty-Seven

Isolde

23 Years After the Viridian Phoenix's Rebirth

They left the ruins of the city behind, flying over the cliffs and the bronze forest until a large plain came into sight just over a hill. A tumbling, dirty-green river called Camlann ran through it, watering the earth so that drooping red flowers filled the dew-drenched fields around it. That's when Isolde's breath caught in her throat because she saw them, and they were greater in number than she'd feared, even with her generous approximation.

Ranks of leather-clad soldiers spread across the valley on the other side of the river, extending into the distance as far as they could see. Griffins with sharp claws issued terrifying screeches as they circled the air above the stationary legions. The message rang clear. Without a doubt, they meant to wipe out Viridian's government for good and replace it with their own.

Turia looked back at her, fear written clearly across her face. Isolde hadn't let her fear get that far. Instead, she held her head high and nodded at Turia with a reassuring smile. The queen's shoulders relaxed, and her face calmed as she realized what she had to do.

Isolde motioned to her neck briefly, reminding Turia to keep hold of the vial so she could reapply the phoenix blood before its effects wore off. The queen nodded before calling a halt. Joined by Isolde and her advisors, she landed and rode ahead to meet a small delegation of griffins moving toward them.

Isolde scanned their war-worn faces, most of them older emissaries whose fighting days should have been long behind them. Unsurprisingly, she didn't recognize any of them. Only one wore a royal crest. Presumably one of the Griffin King's sons. Then her eyes landed on a face at the very back of the retinue, and she had to turn away. Surely Morgan was merely haunting her. A ghost on the battlefield. It was bound to happen as the first life she had ever taken with her own hands.

Isolde risked another look, expecting a different face, but instead being met with those endless brown eyes that were all too alive. Her mouth hardened. Their own features settled into a tired mask. She saw a fear in them that she'd never seen there before and realized all of a sudden that fear and something else too—resentment perhaps—were because of her.

"You attack my city and dare to meet me in my own lands. What excuse does your party have to give for yourselves?" Turia demanded, bringing Isolde's eyes back to her once more.

"These lands are being claimed on behalf of the Griffin King," the prince said in a soothing, snake-like voice. Isolde recognized the tone well, seeing how it had often spilled from her own throat.

"For what reason does he think he has this right?" Turia demanded.

"By right of strength and blessing by the Soulless. To save our people," the emissary responded.

"This insult and the deaths of my people will not go unaddressed. What did you think? We would accept your rule without questions or resistance?"

"You must admit, you stand no chance," the prince answered, shaking his head.

"Don't speak of blessings when you know nothing of such things," Isolde said, speaking up.

The prince's face fell for only a half-second as he realized her identity. They could not get rid of her that quickly, and they should have really thought twice about sending Morgan to complete the task. Then he smiled slowly.

"I could say the same thing to you."

"Let us address the matter at hand. We will not allow you to pass further into our lands."

"Then you must accept a war. We refuse to truce."

"Even if we were to offer you the ashes of phoenixes who have already lived their two lives?" It was a desperate plea for peace.

"It wouldn't be enough to save everyone." The man's voice cracked.

Turia let the words hang in the air. "So be it."

"I'll give you one last chance to surrender," the prince said.

Morgan had eyes only for Isolde. They must have gotten to a healer who fixed some of the damage she'd done. They hunched over, their side wrapped in dark bandages, but she still saw no hatred in their eyes. Only a resentful pain. "Please," they mouthed. And yet they tried to save her still. She turned away.

"Tell me, how would you rule our people? How would you run this land if you had the chance?" Turia asked.

"That's for men of no action to decide once you've been conquered."

"I regret to tell you that's not exactly a satisfactory answer to anyone with half a brain."

"Enough. Will you accept our offer?"

"What do you think?" she asked, anger pulling her mouth into a thin line.

"You leave us no choice, then."

Isolde watched Turia's face then, her eyes alight with a terrible fire Isolde had never seen, something that made a chill run down the seer's spine. It bordered on a murderous glint she would expect to see in her own eyes, perhaps, but never Turia's. And, once more, she asked herself what she had done by dragging her into a war.

Queenly as ever, Turia turned her phoenix without another word and rode away, leaving her entourage to silently follow. They left the griffin representatives behind, regrouping some ways off, both her Bonded advisors on their phoenixes and Unbonded nobility who had met up with the group on their horses.

Isolde could see that the rise and fall of Turia's chest had sped up. She faced her advisors. Her breath came in panicked gasps as she struggled to hold back tears. Robin reached out to rest a steady hand on her shoulder. Isolde prickled. The fool. The griffin retinue remained in sight, and they certainly didn't need to see the queen receiving comfort. That was the only reason it sent a burst of irritation through her chest. Surely. Then again, Robin always had that effect on her.

"What now?" Turia asked, closing her eyes in an effort to take deep breaths.

"You know what now, my queen. We are yours until the end," Aeryt stated from her seat on a gray horse, bowing her head in a moment of silent reverence. Isolde followed suit, but as every other advisor and knight bowed their heads and closed their eyes, she maintained eye contact with her queen. A muttering chorus rose into the air as each person chanted their individual sacred oaths.

Turia's eyes watered as she looked at her seer and remembered everything they'd been through together.

Isolde raised her hand to her heart and mouthed, "I am forever yours, my Turia."

Turia held out her hand, and Isolde clasped it in a moment of helpless fragility, savoring the familiar feeling of her skin. She would have stayed in that moment forever if possible, refusing to move on to whatever future they had on the other side of this pointless war.

~

The drums echoed up from the ground, cheering them along with ancient songs of the sacred sea and the betrayal that had birthed the Viridian Phoenix in all of her fruitless glory. Trumpets called out an opposing song, resulting in an incongruous clash of sound in the air, which was devoid of wind to an eerie degree. It was to be expected though, given the refusal of the Soulless to participate in human squabbles. Despite Isolde's cautions, Turia soared forward at the head of the army. Soldiers marched steadily along below her, heading toward the river, which the enemy hit first. They splashed through it with a terrifying abandon that reminded Isolde of the old stories of rock monsters decimating villages along the coast.

A flock of phoenixes charged along behind their queen. Riding at the front of the winged division of the griffin army was the prince, a gaggle of seasoned mercenaries, and Morgan. Their hair was free, their head foolishly unprotected by any sort of helmet like the ones worn by the ground troops, but they were laced up in leather fittings that made them look so much older than they were.

The clash nearly deafened Isolde. All the sudden the air became a flurry of wings and sound and yelling. One of the griffin soldiers quickly identified and pursued her. She fell into sync with Ryth, diving and dodging as the soldier slashed viciously at them with a sword. Isolde drew her dagger, slicing at the joint of their armor, drawing blood and causing them to lose track of her. She scanned the sky for Turia, her brain flying almost as fast as Ryth as the clash of steel pulled her attention in numerous directions at once.

The unearthly screams of the Sylph rang out as people began to die. Each cry foretold a death. While the Sylph kept to themselves, they gladly observed the blood spilled in their domain. She strained her neck, searching desperately for Turia. Isolde didn't have to wait long, but before she could warn her, the queen hurtled straight at Morgan. In a fearsome flurry, she hit at them again and again, fury playing across her features.

"Traitor!" she screamed.

"No, my queen," Isolde called, hand outstretched, but she wasn't fast enough. The breeze threw her around, right into the path of Morgan's sword, which gouged a deep cut in her arm with a maneuver Isolde had taught them. Where were her guards when she needed them? Panic welled up in Isolde's chest. The queen had no chance at successfully challenging Morgan, as deft and in sync with the air as they were.

"I never betrayed you. I only betrayed my family by waiting this long to give them the key to your downfall," they stated.

The queen winced at the pain of her new wound, her fingers coming away from the cut sticky with new blood. A peculiarly sharp, metallic smell filled the air. Isolde urged Ryth on, her hands buried in her warm feathers, only to hear a yell that caused her head to whip around. An impact hit her, almost breaking her Bonded seat. She only just managed to hang on, her stomach plummeting as she considered just how far the fall would be. Isolde had no choice but to turn and face the wizened man coming at her. The queen would have to survive on her own.

Chapter Forty-Eight

Turia

23 Years After the Viridian Phoenix's Rebirth

The flames kept Turia warm and seated, but the warmth combined with the scent of blood and sweat seeping from her skin overwhelmed her senses. Brushing the beak of Aneal, her phoenix, she indicated an upward direction and the creature agreed. She'd quickly found the fight with Morgan too much. She knew she had no chance if they stayed there, swinging around each other midair, so instead with a sudden thrust they soared upwards at a steep angle. The phoenix spread its wings in a display of fiery brilliance.

"You think it'll be that easy?" Morgan called from below, soon following their trajectory up, up, up. The clouds grew thicker until the ground was no longer visible. Their moisture brought Turia some sense of coolness but also of suffocation. Her head grew heavy with the height, and she found her fingers tightening on Aneal's feathers unintentionally. They finally banked sharply, trying to lose Morgan among the fog. Only a small part of her felt ashamed of fleeing. Isolde's words rang in her ears. She would try to stay alive, if only for her seer.

She could hear the swoosh of wings and the traitor's voice. "The sword says we're family."

Turia wished she could block her ears.

"Don't you want to know why?" They were trying to get her to respond so they could find her. The wind cascaded over her, thinning the clouds. Turia's heart dropped, and she found her sense of bravery weaker than she'd anticipated.

Like a ghost, they appeared then, the sun playing in rivulets across the hard line of their mouth. The pair floated face-to-face, Morgan's eyes just as soft as she'd remembered. For the first time, Turia searched their face for signs of her father. Sure enough, the tilt of their mouth and brown of their eyes looked all too familiar.

"You won't kill me," she stated, voice ringing with false confidence, even as she hefted her sword once more.

"Pray tell why not."

"I don't think you have it in you," Turia said. "Especially if you are my father's child."

"That just begs the question, do you take after him?"

"My father possessed a peaceful heart, but I'm made of something different."

"You're not very good at bluffing," Morgan replied.

She suddenly urged her phoenix forward, swiping at them viciously with her sword and causing their griffin to fall back to avoid the heat of Aneal's flames. The point of her weapon, unfortunately, caused no damage.

"Too many people underestimate me," she muttered, as much to herself as to them. Before she knew it, they were at it again. The sounds of clanging and fire and wind filled her with an indescribable dread as she tried to just breathe through each moment and keep her arm from throwing away her sword of its own will. Morgan darted through the sky with an air of majesty she would never be able to project. They looked like a high ruler.

Out of nowhere, another rider crashed into Morgan causing both creatures to scream.

Isolde.

As the clouds cleared, it became apparent that more soldiers surrounded them each fighting their individual battles. Turia sat frozen, as Isolde took on Morgan, until another Griffin soldier decided to try to unseat her, and she was caught up in another scuffle.

Chapter Forty-Nine

Isolde

23 Years After the Viridian Phoenix's Rebirth

The noise rang in Isolde's ears as Morgan darted around, smoothly looping over her head and nicking her cheek, even as she managed to avoid the full impact of the blow. With the way they soared circles around her, she knew very well they could have done so much more damage.

A grim smile lit their face. The wind picked up, buffeting her as Morgan danced around Ryth and Isolde. Their body and Bonded griffin were one in a way that the Viridian Phoenix and Isolde had never been, which gave them the advantage. Through the sky they chased each other, limited in range and motion. Ryth had already sustained several injuries, deep oozing cuts on her body. She watched them, realizing that for as much as they were fighting and for as much as the wind seemed to be helping them, neither person was trying to deal a fatal blow.

Isolde listened to the wind. Her mind raced with a growing panic as something settled in her brain. The wind. There shouldn't have been wind. The Sylph were supposed to be neutral. The prince's comment about being blessed. With horror, it dawned on her as she took in the injured phoenixes and riders around them. The Sylph were in league with the griffin army.

The queen looked back, her face bloodied, terror written clearly across it. She soon got pulled into a duel with a general. There was no time to deal with the new information. Soon they were both pulled in opposite directions. Never in her life had Isolde been so entirely disoriented. The ranks thinned out as the air soldiers chased each other further away and as more fell. Every time the cries of the Sylph echoed around her, Isolde started, her heart falling as she tried to see if Turia or Morgan had finally succumbed to death's call.

The seer couldn't tell if it had been minutes or hours, all she knew was the taste of blood in her mouth, the slash of metal, and the way that her heart threatened to give out every time she lost track of the queen. Amidst the chaos, it was impossible to tell which side possessed a blessing by the Soulless. Soldiers tired and the ranks grew thinner as sword arms grew slower. They would need to regroup soon. The sun began its descent and the wind picked up, seeming to only interfere with the courses of phoenixes and their riders. But then, the howling suddenly died down, the sounds of the Sylph's cries growing fewer and farther between.

An uneasy stillness coated the air in the fading light, causing Isolde to pause, looking around since she was momentarily without an assailant. All at once, a pair of eerie eyes appeared in the sky and a voice issued forth from nothing, saying something Isolde couldn't quite make out. The vitriol in the speaker's tone, however, was unmistakable. Her eyes landed on Morgan, who floated frozen like her, their face slowly draining of color as they heard the words. With a sudden roar, the wind turned on them, attacking.

Isolde watched with a blistering confusion. They fought it, but this was the kingdom of the Sylph and if they revoked Morgan's privilege to fly in their domain, there was nothing they could do. It sent Morgan reeling, their griffin trying to stay upright. They held tightly to their creature, leaning low over his neck, their Bond just barely keeping them on the griffin's back. Morgan fought with everything in them, every muscle trained to navigate the sky. Sweat fell into their eyes, mixing with tears as they recognized their end and as the breeze whispered their fatal mistake in their ear.

Isolde rushed toward them, but it was too late. Previously so smooth and in control with the movements of their griffin, they were now thrown from its back by the furious winds. As they fell through the sky, an Otherrealmly scream echoed. Morgan flailed, trying to catch hold of anything. She plunged after them, arm outstretched, but the Sylph's scream sent pain shooting through her heart because she knew at that moment from the acceptance on their face that she could do nothing to save them.

Isolde heard the crack of their body landing on the rocks by the river, but she refused to look down. Silent tears poured from her eyes, the small flame of relief that had sprouted when she'd spotted their face among the Griffin King's emissaries died. For all that had passed between the two of them, Morgan occupied a precious place in her heart, coaxing alive a gentleness entirely new to her battered soul. But now they were truly gone. She turned away, a comforting sound issuing from Ryth.

"It was always going to be this way."

"Shut your mouth."

~

No time. Before she knew it, another griffin rider was coming at her. She struck out over and over with her sword, sweat dripping into her eyes and her body barely registering a new cut on her leg. Ryth did her best, but the Griffin army flew in a way she never had. They spun and fell and climbed like it was second nature. None had flown as smoothly as Morgan though. Morgan. Isolde hit her assailant harder. The man cried out as Ryth's flames caught his leg.

When she was free once more. She desperately searched for Turia amidst the orange skies.

The griffin army renewed their efforts, a wave of fresher soldiers descending on the tiring ranks of the Fire Folk. Isolde spotted Turia, bloodied and bruised, sending her sword through the stomach of an enemy soldier.

The queen sat there for a moment, panting, looking at her sword as though she didn't recognize it. Moisture covered her face. Her crown had long ago fallen and her breastplate rested askew, exposing too much of her neck. Isolde flew toward her, only to realize that something else was missing.

Turia's neck glistened with sweat, bare in the sunlight, the vial of phoenix blood gone. Only then did Isolde notice the flames spreading over the queen's dress.

"Turia! You're on fire!" she screamed at the top of her lungs. The queen looked up, meeting Isolde's gaze with disconnected confusion as the fire blossomed forth, swallowing her whole. Time slowed as the seer watched the flickering red light surround Turia's face, climbing upward with the same kind of hunger that had always boiled in the pit of Isolde's stomach.

The seer threw herself at the queen, pulling her onto Ryth, flames and all, screaming at Ryth to plunge into the water below them. As she drew the queen close, the heat crawled onto her skin, bringing with it the sickening scent of her own burning flesh. Isolde hissed as her own arm caught fire.

In a panicked rush, she wrenched Turia with her off of Ryth's back as soon as they were close enough and they fell through the air together into the river's freezing hold. The water enveloped the queen and her seer, pulling them down with the added heaviness of their soaked clothes as Isolde clung to Turia. She fought through the disorientating blue, her eyes burning and her lungs about to give out.

Isolde broke the surface of the water after only a few moments, holding Turia to her chest. She couldn't bring herself to look at the queen. Isolde already felt the new wrinkles and stickiness of Turia's skin. Drenched from head to toe, the seer heaved her queen out of the water, carefully laying her down on a tuft of grass and finally forcing herself to look. Her hand floated to her mouth involuntarily as she tried to unsuccessfully stifle a tortured gasp of a sound.

Very little was left of Turia's face. No hair remained on her scalp and the rest of her body lay a fire-mangled thing. Isolde pulled her into her lap, the tears finally breaking through as she rocked back and forth, running her bloody fingers gently over Turia's bare head. The queen fought to draw stuttering breaths and Isolde knew that nothing could save her now.

"I'm sorry. I'm so sorry."

Panic coursed through her. Maybe it wasn't too late. As much of a mess as she felt, Isolde closed her eyes and tried to fall into the Otherrealm. She pulled at the river Camlan next to them, begging and pleading, holding her hand to Turia's abdomen. Violent, crimson colors assaulted her vision, so unlike the usual cool tones of the Blue. She screamed once more, her hands trembling at the river's anger and rejection of her call. Death overwhelmed the river and thus it denied her plea. A Sylph's cry pierced her ears.

"No. No. You have to help me." But the river refused. Instead she struggled, floating around, searching for the greens and yellow of the lush plant life, but they were cold to the touch of her mind. They apologized, but they would not help her.

Turia was too far gone and this time Isolde was not strong enough to heal her. Someone like Morgan might have been able to, but the seer with her lying tongue and broken heart had no idea how to heal wounds this deep.

Through her tears, Isolde caught a glint of silver on the ground a few feet away. The vial rested broken in the grass and the seer cursed the Soulless with every thread of her being.

"Damn you and your heartless ways!" she roared. "I will never serve you again. Never! Do you hear me? This is not something that can be tempered. Damn you!" With the cold falling of her heart, she finally understood Aeryt's pain.

Sobs overtook her body, cutting off her ability to utter anything else. Turia's burnt eyes fluttered open, still the same perilous green.

With great difficulty, her mouth shaped four words, "You...lied...to me."

At last the queen saw the ugly truth. Isolde couldn't breathe. A whimper escaped Turia's mouth, as her eyelids fluttered shut.

"Don't leave me, Turia," Isolde cried. "Please. Please don't leave me."

"No!" The yell caused Isolde to whip around.

Robin stumbled forward, a long gash covering her leg. "That can't be her. Tell me it's not her, Seer," she spat, her voice a razor.

Isolde simply shook her head, clutching the queen's body to herself even as Turia's ragged breathing slowed down. Robin fell to her knees beside them, desperately reaching out to grasp her hand. But it was already too late. Arturia's chest stilled.

Robin didn't cry. She leaned back on her heels in shock, staring off into the distance as she released the dead queen's hands. She slowly turned to face Isolde.

"What do you have to say for yourself?"

Isolde ignored her, the tears finally slowing down. Turia's limp body rested in her arms, and she couldn't find it in herself to let go.

"This is your fault, false seer." That caught her attention. Isolde's head shot up, but, for the third time that day, too late. Pain cascaded through her and Robin's face glared at her from inches away, her sword buried deep in Isolde's chest. The priestesses' fine hair lay matted with blood on her forehead, her mouth forming a harsh line. The shock hit the seer first, then the cold fury in the priestesses' amber eyes. With a sickening sound, Robin pulled the weapon out and stood.

She stared down at her with a perceptive disdain. "You've committed a grave crime, Seer. I want you to know that for as long as there is marrow in my bones, I will hate you and you will pay for her life. She was a precious thing and you destroyed her."

The seer gasped, falling onto the ground as the world spun and pain enveloped her whole being. She realized the warmth pooling over her hand was her own blood as Robin walked off, picking her way through fallen soldiers. Isolde spotted Morgan's long-dead body and closed her eyes. Ryth landed, collapsing beside her as her life faded.

This was to be the end, but something in her screamed in defiance as the weight of it crashed down upon her. Turia. Isolde would always be the poison, the thing that corrupted everyone good and right in the world. In the end, that belief turned out to be true. Turia. Her Turia. Grief crashed through her with a pain equaling the gash in her chest. Here, finally, Isolde knew what she truly wanted just as it was stolen from her. She wished violently for the living connection she'd been offered and for the love she'd failed to enjoy while it lasted. The terrifying weight of a future that, in her hubris, she thought she might be able to control had distracted her from what she already possessed. Maybe the phoenix was right. No, this couldn't be it. With a splintering desperation, she let out a cry, begging the universe for a second chance.

Isolde would rise again if luck prevailed, but the queen wouldn't. Morgan wouldn't. They were only Unbonded humans after all. A tremulous idea spiraled through her half-dead brain, and she hauled herself up onto her knees, trying to spit out some of the blood in her mouth. She whispered to Ryth, but she didn't respond. The viridian flames rose, growing and blurring her form in a burst of terrible heat, leaving behind a pile of gray ashes that sparkled with a greenish-blue hue.

Everything in Isolde's stomach bubbled up, and she heaved it all onto the ground in front of her at the sight. Half of her already lay dead. Ryth's soul had returned to the Blue and hers would soon do the same. Isolde clawed at the ground, pulling herself along, driven by the harrowing depths of heartbreak. She scooped up two handfuls of the ashes, her hands shaking and cold. She could feel the life seeping away from her. Too quickly.

Black closed in around the corners of her vision, causing her to pause, but she shook her head, trying to push through it. *Not yet.* She made it to Turia's corpse. With clumsy, numb fingers she pried open her jaw and poured one fistful of ashes into her mouth. The black closed in again, but she raged against it, dragging herself over Turia, their blood mingling in the dirt below.

One second at a time the seer told herself, her mind bursting with colors she'd never seen in this lifetime. Isolde collapsed, chest heaving as she coughed up dark clots of blood. The failure surged through her. Her grandmother's voice met her delirious ears, telling her what a useless thing she was to the world. How right she'd turned out to be. But…no. Turia needed her. With a strangled cry, Isolde hauled herself up once more. This one last thing still remained in her control. She'd brought her queen to ruin, so she owed her this. She owed them both this as penance for her lies.

Seeing Morgan's dead body sent a wave of intense nausea hurtling through her. To see them so at odds with the living world reminded Isolde of herself. With angry fingers, she repeated the gruesome process, dropping her second handful of ashes into their cold mouth. Isolde hissed as she swiped her hand over her own bloody wound and then rubbed it into the blood spilled into the earth below their neck.

In a last effort that took everything in her dizzy brain, the seer pulled herself up to her knees and turned her head to the sky as she buried her fingers in the ground. There was no guarantee it would work. It had never been done with three people and Ryth's ashes would most likely be lost to the winds anyway, but she had to try. They both deserved more time. The altered ancient chant bubbled up with her as red streamed from her mouth.

"Let all things be weighed and tempered,
Including my soul as the Soulless see fit.
This I give, in my final hour.
This I give, in my final minute.
Let my life be split between us three.
Let our souls know life again.
When I rise and a new era begins,
Let us breathe in this realm and all its humble offerings,
Like the mingled blood,
The bodies and ashes,
I've given as an offering to the Soulless today.
I freely split my second life between us three,
Even though shorter it will be."

The seer let herself fall to the earth then, comforting herself with one last false prophecy that saw Morgan and Turia full of spirit once more in some far off time. Relinquishing control, she slipped from the battlefield of her life alone, same as she had always been.

Epilogue

Robin

23 Years After the Viridian Phoenix's Rebirth

The battle finally over, Robin forced her footsteps back towards where she knew the queen's body rested. Unlike the seer, she took a moment to truly take in the horror of Turia's burnt corpse. It was the respectful thing to do, to not turn away just because what you saw made you despair. Just because it might break you beyond repair. Robin had always believed in seeing and honoring the suffering. Healing wasn't possible without acknowledging the evil.

After a moment, she turned, searching for Isolde only to find her collapsed a few feet away near Morgan. Of course she would be by them, Robin reflected bitterly. Even after she'd seen Turia eviscerated, she'd still found her way to the person who had brought about her death.

The priestess searched the ground around them. A ways away she spotted it—a pile of ashes shimmering with the greenish-blue of the Otherrealm. Robin sighed, thankful for its unique hue that differentiated it from all the other ashes scattered across the plans. Making her way over to it, she roughly scooped them into a bag that she secured to her belt. While most of the Fire Folk who were on their first life would perish for good, locked out of a second life by the wind breaking up and scattering their ashes across the fields of war, the seer didn't get to escape that easily. Robin raised her face to the climbing sun and closed her eyes, cursing the seer and remembering her queen's sweet face.

Acknowledgements

I deeply, deeply appreciate everyone who helped bring this book into the world. Thank you to my friends and family for their enduring support, despite having to listen to me ramble on and on and on about this project over the years. To the cover designer, all beta readers, and all ARC readers: thank you so much for your time and energy! Hopefully it will take me less than five years to get the next book released.

About the Author

Quinn Elmsworth believes in the power of stories. She holds a BA in English and History from Emory University. Currently a resident of Georgia, she enjoys frequenting bookstores to pick up the latest queer book, crocheting lopsided blankets, and diving into fascinating conversations.